THE SLAVE SHIP

The Slave Ship

By MARY JOHNSTON

AUTHOR OF

"Croatan," etc.

A. L. BURT COMPANY

Publishers   New York

Published by arrangement with Little, Brown and Company

Printed in U. S. A.

THE SLAVE SHIP

CHAPTER I

IT was after Culloden. Though I, David Scott, was an unimportant person yet I lay in the Tolbooth, in Edinburgh, with my betters. I was a young man — twenty-two. I had fought for the Stuarts at Prestonpans, Falkirk and Culloden, without the least question that I can remember arising in my mind, that being the politics of my chief and my family and nearer acquaintance. Now I made as little question that I would not lie there in irons if I could help it. No, nor be shipped to Barbados or Virginia if I missed hanging!

I loosened a clamped bit of iron from the wall and turned it into a file.

It was dark night, a week later, when I got free. Dark and stormy and chill — in June, I guessed. I lifted the stanchels from the window and laid them all quietly upon the floor. Then I got through, and it was narrow indeed, that window, but I was thin enough from little fare and much misery. Got through and held by my hands for a moment, and dropped, and I knew that there was deep depth and I might break my legs.

I did not so, but I was sair bruised and shaken, and I thought I heard all around me whistles and calls, "He's out! After him!" I crawled across the narrow, narrow lane to a buttress of Saint Giles and lay there shivering until I made out that it was only wind and rain and my own heart pumping in my ears and that my bones were not broken. A bell struck the middle night. I started up and began to weave around that church, close to the abutments, skirting the shops built against the wall. Every half-minute I looked toward Tolbooth. It was a wild night, with gusts of wind and rain and strange sulphurous lights racing through the clouds and at moments raising into an eerie quarter-light Giles above me and that black mass I was leaving, and other tall, grim houses of Auld Reekie. "A witches' night!" I thought and wished I had a broomstick to fly over the Luckenbooths and away. I was ragged and cold and dizzied with hunger.

A fancied sound made me stand, scarce breathing, against the wall. The sound proved nothing, but while I stood there I had a vision. Gone was Edinburgh, gone the witches' night. I saw and I breathed and I knew, and yet could give no name nor circumstance, a blue salt sea that rolled its long waves against a shore of dazzling sand. The surf was high and strong and white; on the burning sand lay a row of sharp-prowed, narrow boats; the sand stretched

on and was met by palm trees, I that had never
seen palm trees knowing them well enough.
Stretched on and met palm trees, and a great
mass of white masonry, wall and gateway and
turret, and a strange kind of keep rising behind,
and over all drooping an English banner. And
I knew it and I didn't know it, and in a moment
it was gone, and this was Edinburgh on a wild
night, and young David Scott, an escaping prisoner, with o'ermuch of practical matters before
him to spend time with visions. Scots folk are
liable to vision. Scots folk are baith the salt
of the earth and the dung of the earth. Scots
know the hills of heaven and the pits of hell.
And there is a Debatable Land, but no Scots, I
think, stay there long. Young David Scott was
already, I know, on his way across, to the side
of the dark.

This night in the material dark, in the material town, I had a goal that was no more nor
less than Sandy Scott's small house on the out-
skirts. If I could win there Sandy would hide
me. I did it, stealing and stopping and now and
then running, through the witches' night.
Crossing High Street, all the tall houses seemed
to flare lights and shout at me. Later, two men
did rise to question me. But, "What are ye doing out at sic an hour, on sic a night? I've an
honest airrand, but I misdoubt yours — an' I
think I hear the Watch!" With that, they
turned quick their heads to listen, and I dived

into Willy's Wynd, and worked through that into Auld Man's Wynd, and so pursued my journey.

An hour before the dawn I was at Sandy Scott's and threw a clod against his window. He was a cautious man, but at last he let me in.

"What good will it do you if two are hangit?"

"It isn't a question of hanging but of slaving in Virginia. I've seen it where I'm put down 'Young and misguided.' Let me lie in your barn, Sandy, and if I'm tracked you can swear you didn't know it."

"If my name were Campbell that would pass. But it's Scott."

"Aye, I came on that. Let me in, man, let me in!"

For the better part of a week I lay in his small, small loft amid old hay, and at night the cow munching and sighing below. Sandy brought me food, and each morn a drop of rum, and at night the news. "They're speiring for you!" — "Jock Andrew at the Cannongate tauld me he saw ten soldiers had seized a laddie, thinkin' 'twas you." — "Now they're saying a Dutch ship left Leith and you may ha' swam out to her — and it seems to me a ship's the best you can hope — and I wad gae at once!"

But I was not determined. I did not want to go to sea, nor to a foreign land — not yet! There was a glen that I wanted.

It was dull lying there upon the hay with a little light streaking through a handsbreadth opening. On the second day I twisted around at a noise and there, coming up the ladder, was Sandy's wife, a pale young woman with a kirk look. "I hae brought you," she said, "the Book. It maun be sair lying with naught tae do but picturing gibbets!" With that she gave me a brown volume and shook her head and descended the ladder.

Well, I had the Book, and there's no denying that reading made the time pass. And that is all it did for me then — made the time pass. I was turning from the light even then, David Scott at twenty-two, foregathering with ancient, ancient cronies of the cave!

So I lay there and read about King David from the time he watched the sheep and slew the giant until he died in Jerusalem. There was Jonathan and the cave of Adullam, and the water that his men brought him, and Michal, Saul's daughter, and Abigail and Ahinoam, and Bathsheba the wife of Uriah, and at the last Abishag the Shunnamite. And then I read of King Solomon. And I read Ruth and Esther, and Haman's gibbet made me see the hugeous gallows in the Grasmarket built for them who had fought for a Stuart, and the head on the spike atop the Tolbooth, and the legs and arms of "traitors" nailed above the Leith Port. It darkened while I saw all that until I could no longer read, and I lay there cold in the straw and ached for vengeance. Off and on during the night, which was wakeful, I saw these things, and when I started from dreams I knew that I had been killing. Hawley first, and then all Hanoverians. They were against me and thought they were victors; they were making me and mine suffer, suffer terribly; they were altogether hateful and unworthy to live! I killed them. Lying awake, panting a little, I still killed. And as for the Stuart Cause, it was Ours and therefore exquisitely right.

I slept and when again I waked was rid of that frenzy, but felt hard and dour. Dawn came in coldly, viewed from that strain between boards, in Sandy Scott's barn.

Mysie Johnston — that was why I wanted to go west from Edinburgh, not east to any boat upon the salt, sair sea. Mysie Johnston — Mysie Johnston.

Saying and feeling that brought me away from the evil anger and the caked and frozen mood. Mysie, Mysie, Mysie, Mysie, Mysie!

The glen would be green now, and all the birds singing. We would walk there, and our arms would be about each other. Mysie, Mysie, Mysie, Mysie, Mysie! *And I will be a better man. And I will be a better man!*

So I thought, and maybe so I would. But I never saw Mysie Johnston again — not in the outer world, not in the outer!

For the fourth morning they took me. That very night to come I was to leave the barn and Sandy, for we thought, poor fools! that the search was given o'er. A neighbor — and I mistrust that neighbor! — had told him that a sergeant of Cope's had told Phemie Nicholson that they had tracked me to the waterside at Leith. — Sandy had a decent suit for me, and I would foot it to a laird I knew beyond Melrose, who might give me a horse and an errand west. For my name now, it was Will Anderson, a good Whig name. Once in that glen that I kenned I might blithely hide the summer through. After that it was just possible that the ill wind that was blowing so fiercely might quiet down. In other words the *wrong side* might tire of hanging and drawing and quartering and sending over seas in irons. So many " mights " and so many " ifs ", and it all came to naught, and I had Mysie only in dreams, and after a time the dreams died away.

Well, there I lay in the loft, quiet enough, and to wile the time read of Daniel in the lions' den, and about King Belshazzar and the hand that wrote on the wall — when suddenly there was Sandy's wife with a white, white face and world's end in her voice. " They're hauding him — they're hauding Sandy by the aik tree! Five soldiers — they're coming! "

With that she slipped down the ladder, and the next minute I heard her singing at her work, for all as if there was never but one party in the world and that God's party.

> "O God, do thou raise up thyself,
>   The earth to judgment call;
> For thou, as thine inheritance,
>   Shall take the nations all."

I made a burrow deep in the hay and covered myself and the Book and lay there stifling with a drumming heart. I remember — I remember! I clasped that Book, and I cried, *but not aloud,* "O I was reading Ye! If Ye are, save me now, save me and Mysie! And Ye will not let Sandy suffer that's doing a friend's part. Save! Save!"

But they came into the barn. I heard them below, and one mounted the ladder. "It's dusk as sin up here!" Below him said another, "Look out that he doesn't dirk you through the hay!" The first, at that, contented himself with a small trampling that did not bring him where I lay under the eaves. Presently he spoke. "Time lost to toss all this stuff aside! Easiest to fire it, and that's what we'll do. If he's here he'll come out, and if he isn't it won't be Holyrood that's burnt!"

He went down the ladder. Presently I smelled the brand. I came out. They had taken away the ladder, so I held by my hands and dropped from the loft, flame singing now in my ears. The lower room was filled with smoke; through it I could just see them without

the door, waiting for the tod smoked out. I had
no weapon. Out I came, helpless as the tod.
I was big and strong — " Big David Scott " —
But what was that against five armed men? If
I turned wolf from tod and sprang at their
throats, then more surely still Hawley's gallows
in the Grasmarket! I walked out of the barn,
hands up.

Oh, waly, waly, waly, Mysie Johnston!

The Tolbooth opened once more and swallowed me. I lay there two months expecting
hanging. To this day I do not know the truth
of my escaping that death. Some influence
somewhere, but whose it was I do not know.
Mysie had not the strength. Maybe after all
it was God. But lying there in the dungeon
that was for folk like me, for big, strong
young men who broke gaol, I cursed God and
was glad his book was burned in that burning
barn.

In August I was taken from prison and
marched with five Jacobites, young and middle-
aged men, to Leith and set aboard the brig,
King William, bound for Virginia and carrying
thither a great parcel of poor men signed for
servants to planters, and we six who had not
signed but who natheless went.

CHAPTER II

IF you've been for what seems a lifetime in a black and narrow place, sky and sea, salt air and sunshine make you drunk and childish happy and childish sad. Even if you're leaving your land forever — even if you're leaving a loved lass. Just for a time it turns you a bairn — just for a time!

There was a man upon the *King William* who bulks in my memory. Morrison was his name, Gervase Morrison; he had a lank but stately figure and a face too early withered, was from London or thereabouts and ten years my senior.

The *King William* was no Scotch ship but an English one from Hull, owned by merchants of that place. Captain and crew were King George men, and King George men the three score and upward who for reasons of wretchedness had signed papers to go and be sold in Virginia for five years, receiving after that time freedom and certain perquisites and opportunities. We six Scots were upon this ship the only willy-nilly men, transported and sold without any " by your leave ", or a set term of years. We alone wore outward shackles.

We wore them for ten days until England and France were behind us. Then said the master of the ship, "Pass me your word that you'll make no trouble and you may go like the others!" We passed it, the six of us, and we were named Alan McGregor, James MacLeod, Alan MacLean, Fergus Ross, Alexander Gordon and David Scott. That captain comes to me across the years as a decent man, short and red and bluff and well-spoken.

The mates and the crew were not so bad either. But those English merchants had sair crowded the brig and had laid in for their merchandise but scant and wretched food. Most of their bondsmen were very young, youths of the poorest condition, scraped from field and village. Four or five had taken a loaf or a coat or a guinea, and might have been hanged but had mercy shown them after this manner. The rest seemed honest enough, but some were dull and few had any learning. Yet there might be found those who had been to school and were born to better estate, but had come down in the world. Such an one was that stately man, Gervase Morrison.

Even before we were free of our shackles he had marked us out for talk. At last, I know not why, he settled upon me. The weather held good, else we had had a horrid time, packed like herrings below. But the master said, "For health, stay in the air!" and morning, noon and night we lay like fruit upon the decks. Morrison came and sat beside me.

" So I suppose you drink 'to one over the
water, and Jamie and Chairlie are your favorite
names! "

I said, " There's not a drop of drink aboard,
and that's a sair loss! "

" It is," he answered and politely cursed those
merchants of Hull who treated human beings as
though they were casks of tobacco.

" I know how I got here," I said. " But how
did you? "

He told me. He was younger son of a good
family, had gone to Oxford and worshipped
knowledge. But it was that very drink that
killed him — drink and the cards. Three years
ago he had reformed. Only in a sty like this
would he really look at a bottle of port or a
puncheon of rum — only there was none here to
look at! As for gaming he touched it no more,
only looked on over others' shoulders. But the
devil was that he had no means and was about
to starve. No one gave and no one lent, and
as for earning, " I wrote for a bookseller. It
was then that I grew so lank, and this suit is my
only one." The end was that he met a man who
was gathering poor youths to go to Virginia.
" I was not a youth but I was damned poor. I
would be a rare figure in a tobacco field, and so
I told him, but then he pulled out a letter from
a rich planter who wanted sent him a man with
education to be clerk or what not. Five
years' service, well fed and lodged and ap-

parelled, and at the end a start in life, and a determined man might do anything and mount fast in the New World! I was tired of my bookseller and the Old World. Here is my Indenture." And he tapped a paper in his breast pocket.

"You're luckier than me," I said. "I'll be at the tobacco, and for all I ken for the rest of my life."

He turned a little — he was seated upon a coil of rope — and studied me. "You'll run away," he said and took snuff. He had a very good snuffbox, and in a bundle a number of small belongings that marked him off from the rustics around. Among them were a dozen small books, poets and Latin authors. In large part I read the first, borrowing from him from week to week of that weary while upon the *King William*. But now he said, "You'll run away," and helped himself to snuff.

For David Scott, he looked at the green seas thrust from the bow of the ship, and at the piled canvas and the blue sky above. "Where to?" I asked.

He did not say and what came to me did not wait upon him. What came was again that vision of the black night between Saint Giles and Tolbooth. It came like the levin, unearthly clear. Ocean bluer than this ocean, white sand, strange, narrow boats, palm trees, and a pile of whitened building, wall and keep. What it was and where it was I had no idea at all, *but I saw it*. It departed like the levin.

" Where to? " I repeated, without well knowing what I said.

" God knows! " answered Gervase Morrison. " I am not well acquainted with the geographical *minutiæ* of our country to be! "

In truth, however, he had a great fund of knowledge and he liked to give it to any listening ear, prisoner of war, Hodge from the plough, or Tyburn Tom, as the case might be. Or all three together. He was out of the bonds of gentry but into those of the learned man, given to philosophizing and to relating as he saw it the history of the world. He saw it somewhat darkly, with an acid interest that never went so far as to interfere. I listened to him fitfully, staring between times at the sea and my own unhappiness.

I remember another day. A red sun was burning down to the sea, setting a path of fire and blood. There was a listening ten of us and he discoursed on Poverty and the heavy hand of old Law. He had a dry, didactic way that took the edge off his startling things. It was November wind in dry leaves, accomplishing little. Now he said " Slavery ", but the word did not groan.

" Slavery! And isn't there sufficient slavery in Europe? We don't precisely have to seek it out in America, in red and black folk, though I won't deny a certain exaggeration of it in those colors."

A weaver began to curse and swear. "No, we don't have to seek it here!"

Morrison went on. "Greece and Rome knew all about slavery, and all times and countries since. Before and since. It's only the foolish who don't see that men are slaves in England! The four winds blow over slaves and have always blown up and down time. What does it matter what they are called? I've heard of Russia and I've been in Italy and Spain and the Low Countries and France, to say nothing of the British Isles. Always the same. Slaver and enslaved, however they trim the name! 'I want to ride — it's right that *I* should ride — let me ride on you!' Through time. They change places. Now the slave is master and the master slave. But the precious model remains!" He laughed. "That's the jib and cut of the good ship, Society!"

A young boy who was listening said, "It's so and not so."

"You can't make that out. It's so!"

As he spoke he stared round, and I followed him and saw two-score examplars and instances. Again David Scott blasphemed. "It's the Nature of Life. *His* doing, if *He's* up there!"

"Oh, I don't think *He's* up there! *He's* gone out — like a candle!"

That pleased me. "Yes! Like a candle!"

It never occurred to me to dispute what he said about the Ship that Man had built and was sailing. I saw it and I hardened. If it was so, then let it be so! *But it was pleasanter to ride than to be ridden.*

He considered the sun and then said further, " It is true that it is bottom as well as top. The bottom man will have his woman and his dog, and if ever he creeps to the top thinks of no other course for the ship! "

The sun went down so red! The path over the sea stretched so sinister, so red. It faded and there came velvet blackness and the sorrowful stars.

CHAPTER III

AFTER seven weeks of tossing sea we saw
the capes of Virginia, Cape Henry and
Cape Charles, and the *King William* passed between into that vast bay called Chesapeake.
And now the agent of the Hull owners aboard,
Mr. Ransom, grew mighty busy. All of his
cargo must be freshened and heartened and per-
suaded with honied words, or drubbed with hard
ones, into looking healthy and smiling. It had
been easier work if his merchants had fed us
and if there had not been so much sickness from
spoiled food and from the laithly crowding.
Alas, David Scott, and it taught you little!

But the land looked good after the salt foam,
for few of the merchandise were seamen. And
they were young, and change is change. And
they understood, so many of them being parish
poor, that it was better go meet a master with a
smile.

As for us six Scots, we had consulted. We
meant devil-may-care! So we laughed at the
others and cracked our jokes. But it came with
a shock when, Fergus Ross having remarked to
Mr. Ransom that he trusted some rich planter
meant to buy the whole of us, the agent, a cold
man, stopped in his going to and fro. " That's
not to be! Orders are, one to one master.

You're plotters and we'll have in Virginia no plots! You're rebels and we'll scatter you! Moreover, back on you go the irons till you're sold."

Angus Ross lengthened, then shortened, his face. "And not that shall make me look sick and sorry, though your Whig world is the Devil's pleasant seat!"

"And what, may it please you," asked the agent, "would have been your Tory world? And I'll tell you that. The Devil himself!"

So they had it. And we six wore irons again, wearing them already of Party, as did the agent and others.

The land showed low and in part covered with forest, much of it being pine. It was the autumn, and oaks and other drop-leaves stood in flames of red and gold. We saw marshes turning tawny, and above them and above the water flashed endlessly the sea birds. On the northern side the great passage, sprang a jut of land with a fort. Morrison spoke behind me. "Point Comfort, the Captain saith, where they landed first in sixteen hundred and seven."

Angus Ross asked, "Were there any kindly Scots?"

"I think not. They came on the next ship."

"There are plenty now!" That was Billings the mate, passing us.

But we six, Highland and Lowland, young men, and our chains galling us and our company

soon to be parted, felt Loneliness and Exile.
They rose, gigantic dark shadows, from this low,
strange country, where we saw no mountain nor
even a goodly hill, where there grew, they said,
neither gorse nor heather. When the ship came
to Point Comfort and dropped anchor before the
fort, and the Captain went ashore in a boat with
his papers for clearance, we crowded with the
others to mark that place and the no great life
about it, but Point Comfort gave our hearts little
comfort.

David Scott felt a kind of dread upon him.
Twenty-two, and an overseer and a tobacco field
for one who loved the high glen and Mysie
Johnston!

Back came the Captain. Weighing anchor,
the *King William* stood into the River James
that measured seven miles from shore to shore.
The cargo had never seen such a river. Presently we passed a rude town named Norfolk
with no little shipping lying in the roads before it.

By sunset we were a score of miles up stream,
into the land. The land was always low, and
here stretched forest and here showed clearings
and brown fields and solitary good-sized houses
with clusters of small houses a-near, and running
far into the stream thin, gray " landings " like
skeleton fingers. So broad was the river, we
keeping in midstream, that we missed the life of
fields and road and wharf. All to us had a

melancholy spareness, — vast distances and the much forest and the yellow, enormous river. The clearings were chiefly upon the northern shore. There were a few ships upon the river or anchored about the landings, and we saw cockle boats with gray handsbreadths of sail and oared craft. But taken all together, to us, bondsmen and from an ancient country, for all the beauty of the air and beauty of the colored trees, loneliness and a melancholy spareness! The sun went down behind long, long bars of purple cloud. The *King William* came to anchor for the night, and the ship's lanterns made other lanterns in the water, and the slow-marching stars, for all they kept the old formation, seemed an alien host from them at home.

With sunrise rose another mood. Sick, sick, we were heartily sick of the ship! Any land that we might come to still was earth, and adventures might be predicated. In short, as the sails were made, as the sailors with their chantey raised the anchor, as the river turned red-gold, as the fresh wind filled our nostrils and the gulls screamed about the ship, as the cook served us a far better breakfast than usual, and the Captain sent forward with his compliments a small measure of rum for each man, we became the courageous soldiers of Novelty. When a canoe with Indians passed us we crowded to the side and exclaimed at the raree show.

Now a good wind took us farther up that wide

river, and still in the early, gay morning, we
sighted Jamestown that was our destination.

We six Jacobites stood together.

Our lot seemed the hardest upon that ship.
The others had determined periods. Five years,
even seven years, pass! But for all we knew we
might never be our own men again, opposite us
standing an infuriated Monarch and Party that
might reign, if not forever, still until earth covered us. We wore irons, were marked " dangerous " as though we were powder flasks beside a fire. The comfort of company, alikes together, was going from us. Those around us
seemed better off.

But David Scott, looking at those youths
peaked and early wizened, or dull, sodden,
branded by ceaseless, hopeless labor, or fever-
bitten, restless and weakly turbulent, felt a sudden pride and glory in " big David Scott." So
perhaps did Angus Ross in Angus Ross and
MacLean in MacLean and MacLeod in Mac-
Leod. Pride and glory of the body!

That Jamestown enlarged before us, and it
seemed but three or four brick houses and a bit
tower as of a church, and a landing, and around
this sloops and small boats. It seemed, at tide at
least, an island, and it was shady with great
trees, green and yellow and crimson. Morrison
stood beside me.

" Here beginneth a new chapter. Rather a
pretty place! Well, English made it and here

come English to it — English and Scots. As to indentures and seven years' service and so forth, we've known all that since Father Jacob served Laban. Earlier still, I make no doubt! It's venerable — can be defended. As to you six, mercy has been shown you. Mercy is venerable too."

"There's something in a book I once read about ' the tender mercies of the wicked.' — The wicked! Well, I'm that and will be that too!"

"Is that what you Scots name second sight?"

"I dinna ken ——"

"It's a pity," said Morrison. "I have ' kenned ' it as you say, also. Kenned wickedness. It doesn't pay. It's never paid. — But I'm no preacher. I'm only a ' sair ' piece of shipwreck that says, ' Look out! ' "

As though he were echoed, the mate cried "Look out!" and the anchor, rattling down, clutched the bed of the River James. The bare masts and spars and rigging of the *King William* gently rose and fell against a bluebell sky. We were riding close to the landing that was crowded with folk, and boats were putting off to us.

"Those are gentlemen of the country," explained Mr. Ransom, " coming off to buy you lusty fellows! Range yourselves, and remember that the worst thing that can happen to you is not to be liked! Look at yourselves when five and seven years are over and be smiling and brisk!"

A good big boat was speeding toward us. Negroes rowed her and the cargo of the *King William* who had never seen such before stared as at a dark miracle. "Negroes! Why did God make them black? Have they got souls?"

"Black men and red men and yellow men and white men, that's the way they mount in importance ——"

"The saints and the angels are white. All the ruling people in heaven are white. There couldn't be yellow or red or brown or black angels ——"

"Maybe they have half-souls. Dogs and horses have quarter-souls. Look at that big one laughing!"

The boat came closer and there were three white men seated in the stern. One, the tallest and biggest, had a gold-braided hat and a fine coat.

"That's one of the first gentry," quoth Mr. Ransom, "and probably a heavy purchaser. That's Colonel Amory."

"Indeed!" said Morrison. "Then I'm to keep his books. Well, he looks polite enough! Hardly an ogre."

So far from that was he that one and all preferred to be bought by him. Even when other boats arrived and other planters, most of them well enough looking, much like English squires and Scots lairds. But he bought only three men beside Morrison who was already his consignment, — that quite young boy who had said that the world was both so and not so, a ditcher and woodchopper named Dick Merry, and that Culloden man, David Scott.

CHAPTER IV

HE had a handsome, cheerful countenance —
Colonel Amory — and a genial voice. He
talked a deal and talked well, was a three-bottle
man and gallant with women, a hunter, a dead
shot, admirable with a horse and a dog and an
obedient Negro, an out-of-doors man, yet with a
taste for politics, a vestryman, a member of the
Governor's Council, and a possessor of books
which sometimes he read and sometimes only
talked of reading. A part of all this David
Scott had opportunities for observing, and another part was told him by others.

Axeman during the winter, clearing land for
tobacco; man of the tobacco fields so soon as
spring set in; in the fields the hot, hot summer
long, roused at dawn, worked till eve, dead with
sleep before the evening star had sunk — as little
as any laborer at home did I have touch around
the circle of Colonel Amory's life. But since
I had had some knowledge of laird's life,
squire's life, lord of the manor's life, across the
sea, I reckoned well enough how this southern,
new land, life of easy business, ran straight or
meandered through the year. It had a fairness
and ease and a good nature, and the good nature

was for all so long as all swung to the commanded music; and the ease was the hunter's
ease with good dogs around; and as for the fairness, in small matters it tripped forward, but in
large it always curtseyed to the heathenish law.
But almost every one thought him — and he
thought himself — a kind master, not seeing that
to be master at all was the trouble.

Big David Scott cut down trees for Colonel
Amory, to clear Colonel Amory's land, to plant
Colonel Amory's tobacco that would freight the
King William and other ships to England, that
would be sold, that would buy more young men
to clear more land for Colonel Amory. The
years pass slow when one is young.

Up the river, a few miles from Williamsburg, lay Amory Hall. Land and land, some
thousands of acres, the " great house ", the various " quarters " — Pine Tree quarter, Big
Spring quarter, Indian quarter, Old Mill quarter — the barns and tobacco houses and offices of
kinds, the two overseers' houses, the mill and
smithy and other workshops, the store, the creek
landing, the river landing — that was Amory
Hall. The fields were tobacco and maize and a
small amount of wheat and other grains, but tobacco, tobacco, tobacco overtopped and over-
spread. The great house stood two miles from
my quarter, Old Mill quarter. I rarely saw it
close at hand — a good-sized brick house, like
many in England, with trees and shrubs and

flowers about it. All day, all those blazing summer days in shadeless fields, the trees looked so
good!

At Old Mill were twenty men. Much the
smallest quarter and remotest from the great
house, it touched on one side a forest uncut since
time began, and on the other tobacco. In the
winter we felled the first, in the summer we
worked that tobacco.

The twenty men were not always the same.
They were changed, drafted in and drafted out.
Nineteen of the twenty. But David Scott, who
was " political ", rested at Old Mill for three
long years. They seemed to have said that they
would never change him.

Five of the men were white, the rest black.
It was the penal quarter for refractory or erring white servants or for any who for reasons
were not to be indulged. They came and stayed
and stayed and went, but I stayed. Small cabins, two or
three men to a cabin, and one larger building
where we ate, the white at one end, the black at
the other, a black man cooking for all. And
at a little distance the house of Barget — Mr.
Barget — who oversaw us. A ragged, dreamy
place — Old Mill quarter.

We had enough to eat, though of a coarse and
monotonous sort. We slept on pallets stuffed
with corn husks. In winter there was covering
enough, and at any time we might have a roaring fire. In summer we dragged our beds out

of the stifling cabin. Our clothing was poor
enough, but a Negro woman washed our shirts
and drawers and stockings and kept us fairly
clean. In all this we were no worse off than
the laboring poor across the ocean. Better off!
Barget was a decent man. When the general
overseer, Williams, came around as he did every
three or four days, still there were decent words
and decent treatment. When Colonel Amory
rode a splendid horse our way he was cheer itself and almost fatherly and all that. There were
even holidays, and we did not work on the Sab-
bath, and some leisure could be stolen out of
most week days. Not much, but a little to gloat
over. When it was exceedingly hot weather, we
lay under a pine tree in the middle day for an
hour or two. On great occasions we had a little
rum to drink. The white servants were expected
to go to church, there being one within two
miles. The preacher often preached for a quarter of an hour directly to us, seated on the hard
benches at the back, behind all the others. Our
happy lot, to change hopelessness at home in
England for hope here in America! There were
men sitting near me, with serious, rugged faces,
who tasted that hope. I saw it in their eyes. At
last, after hard service, they would lay hands
upon their own fortune, and she would be good.
I saw it, I saw it! We heard stories of men,
now highly prosperous, planters and burgesses,
who had come out as some other man's servants.

The preacher said it lay in our own hands, and in a measure what he said was true.

There were those white men who chose a sturdy patience, and those who never chose at all, but stayed or went in apathy. And others were always reckoning how much longer or how little longer they had to serve. In the meantime, in some ways, it was worse here in Virginia than at home in England, and in some ways it was better. A good many ways, said some of them. It was not just heaven in Merry England for poor men! But while all that was true, and while this especial plantation had a name for an almost foolish kindness, and while the Law, without wink or blink, doubled the caught runaway's original term of service, and while almost to a man runaways were caught and returned — yet men ran away, men black and white ran away.

In much, with many, it was the very ease of the first step, the first dozen steps. You were hewing, two and two together, at the edge of the step-by-step retreating forest, on the one side stumps and fallen trees and the broad light and the sound of axes and the ever-present sense of masters and overseers and Monotony that had begun to gibber at you — on the other the deep, deep forest, right beside you, whispering, beckoning, "Come with me! I stretch afar, so far, away from all this!" Or you transplanted or weeded or wormed or suckered or cut tobacco at

the edge of a huge swamp, and the reeds whis-
pered, " Here is the little path — you know it.
Put down the hoe, slip in here! I will meet
over you and hide you. Tom and Dick will not
tell. To-night you may make the river *and find
a boat.* You know there is deep forest on the
other side and a trail or something into Carolina."

Men black or white sometimes went without
forethought, without intending to go, just because Freedom suddenly sang to them, or
Monotony lifted and clanked her chains. The
first time David Scott went he did that, and afterwards cursed himself for his improvidence.

Days, weeks, months. The first year. Into
the second year.

Once, in the first six months, I was sent with
a message from Barget to Williams the head
overseer, and not finding him, made bold to go
on to the great house where they said he was.
There was a front door and a back door, just as
it is in Europe, so I went to the back and asked
a negro wench for news, and I was heard from
a room to the right, and a voice called to me to
come in. Here, in his place of business and a
great armchair, sat Colonel Amory, and on a
much lesser chair the overseer, and at the back
of the room, on a high stool before a desk and
a huge ledger, Gervase Morrison. I gave my
message — three drunken Indians had come
across from their town and were making trouble

— and the overseer said that he would ride down
and get them laid by the heels, " If your honor
has finished ——? "

" Aye, go ahead, Williams."

Williams departed, and David Scott made to
follow him out of the room, but was halted ere
he got to the door.

" You're the Jacobite. Would you like a mor-
sel of news from home, man? The *Sally* has
just brought London letters."

Naturally I would, and he spread a letter
and read me of how great and good was King
George and England, and the French were
beaten and London bells were ringing, while in
Scotland the wild Highlanders were being dis-
armed and forbidden to wear their ancient cos-
tume, and Stuart Scotland generally was in
course of " pacification." " And that's the best
thing that could happen to you, as you'll be
agreeing before you die! What turned you the
wrong way? "

" What turned you the ' right ' way? " I asked.
" Family and bringing up? Perhaps neither
way is just the path to glory."

" You've got a dour way with you," he answered. " But you're pithy." His good nature
was enormous. " Now that you're here, would
you like to see the house? " So he condescended
to show it to me, and I've known Scots lairds
do the same for a cotter.

It was a good, big house, fairly furnished,

with silver in the dining room, and some portraits and a spinet and books in a spacious parlor. He gave me a single glass of wine in the dining room, and in the hall he showed me a drawing of what on earth but a Scotch glen with beck and mountain, and in the parlor a young woman in a flowered print gown with her hair richly done was playing the spinet. She looked over her shoulder and made a mouth and went on making music, and what should she be playing but an auld Scots air named "The Four Maries"?

She did not speak to me, and when the master was done with me I went away out of that house, and I cursed the Stuarts and the ways that men are fooled in an ill world.

As I was walking a voice behind me called, and there was Gervase Morrison, overtaking me. "I've got an hour and I'll go with you a bit. Rather a handsome place! Not much beside some English lords of the land, but very creditable for a new country."

I said, "He showed me over, and thought I would take the purest pleasure in all that was his and not mine. The pleasure of contemplating God and Heaven. — Skulls are so thick!"

"Granted. However, he's not a bad sort."

"No. Only stupid."

"Oh, we're mostly stupid when we get on top!"

We went on by locust trees in bloom and

cedar trees. "Who put him on top? Not himself, I'm thinking! If it's the system of things, then it's a damned system!"

"You wanted to put James Stuart on top."

"I don't know if *I* wanted to or not! I got caught. We all get caught in a net. And something or somebody eats us."

A small, black, land turtle lay on his back in our path, some urchin having turned him over and left him there. Morrison stooped and turned him correctly, and he put forth feet and a head and crept away. "The system now. Systems interest me. I'm not blindly plunging against the thing that hurts me, as you are. For one thing, I'm older. Then perhaps I am slow-going like that tortoise and haven't your consciousness of pain. — The system. We must have — or we think we must — tobacco to smoke and snuff. Or if it was not tobacco, it would be wheat or maize. Farther south, sugar and rum. We must have them, or others like them. We must eat and drink and be clothed and have desires fulfilled, like the fireflies here for number. Well, there might be two ways. Everybody might work, no man holding more acres than he and his family could till. I work — my name for instance, being Robert Amory — and master my son and my fine daughters. Everywhere workers. No exceptions. Helping one another as is fit — combining to make work easier — taking counsel to make it intelligent, to find bet-

ter methods, save waste and so forth — sifting
the mind man into the mind place, and the hand
man into the hand place, but keeping neither
there longer than he himself showed it was his
own. Probably a deal of our toil to-day would
be thrown overboard. When we had to make
our own fantastic luxuries, probably we'd begin
to crack up the Stoics! We'd teach our pleasures to hang on other boughs. No bad thing
either! The whole's worth trying, sometimes I
think, just from that point of view. What good
there was would be accessible to all. Nothing
artificial in between. Not Law and Custom
shrieking, 'You can't', when Common Sense is
thundering that you should. There would be
no slaves nor servants. In short, it would be
Scriptural, ' Be ye servants of one another, in
honor preferring one another.' Something like
that. All gaining by whatever each did. All
rising together. It's a dream! Of course it pre-
supposes that all would try — even if not in
quite the same degree. But each according to
his light. And those with most light would be
very patient and sunny kind with those who had
less."

"That's a religious Society."

"Yes. A religious Society."

"What's the other? "

"The other is what we've got."

"Ha, yes! "

"The few with much, the many with little.

The few doing about as Colonel Amory is doing with the much. The many doing about as we do with the little. And the few may go down into the many, and a corresponding number of the many come up into the few — and there's no change that counts. So we spin around the sun."

David Scott cursed the plantation and Virginia and the spinning earth. "It isn't worth the while," said Morrison. "I am coming to the conclusion that there's a bare possibility that it's in oneself. If it's not there, it's nowhere."

"What is?"

"Oh, God or salvation or wisdom, or whatever you call it!"

"I call it a Jack o' Lantern," said David Scott and thought of his next runaway, and also of a quartern of rum that he had enticed out of the hands of those Indians.

CHAPTER V

A QUARTERN of rum, and if I got into trouble with Barget I got into trouble, that was all! David Scott told himself a day of forgetting was worth the price, but what he truly wanted was the rum. His body wanted it, having learned to love the taste of it and the thrill of it in the brain two years before. Wanted it headstrong and hot like a colt, — but colts may be broken. David Scott did not break his soon enough, and it turned to the deil's side, miscalling it Nature and a man's right. A big, gaunt, red carle!

I hid the rum and drank it all in two days. I was working with Tom Tripper at the Narrow Patch. The sun was not yet up, the river mist heavy, the rows of huge-leaved plants ghostly gray at no distance, thin as the pipe smoke they would eventually pass into.

" Where did you get it? " he asked and leaned on his hoe.

" That's telling."

" If I had a bottle, and I was in London, down by Paul's, tell you what I'd do! I'd drink it, little by little, all day, and then when it was empty and night, down I'd go to river and drop it and myself in together."

" It's empty for you now, and there's the river, and night will come."

He had a laugh like a kelpie's. "No! Thames is your only river to drown in."

I worked dull and heavy-headed, but the work got done. I could work. I could run and fight and read. I lusted to know life and the world, but I liked not the part of it I was knowing. Months went by, and I did not get any more rum that gave me gorgeous visions and expanded me to thinking I had the world to turn and twist and toss and catch!

There dwelled a kind of beauty in Virginia. I was not insensible of it. They said that under the setting sun it had green hills and mountains like great walls and small, swift, bright streams. Here was naught of that. But yet was beauty. I must see it and grant it, though palely and grudgingly to what Great Nature should have! Morning was the divine time, though evening, at sunset, and when the moon rose, or when it was soft, deep blue around huge stars, and against the lower world played ten thousand thousand fireflies, ran it close. For all the English clearings of a hundred and twenty-five years, and for all the tiny Indian clearings of unknown centuries, the forest yet cried, " Mine! Mine! " It was a strange forest, beautiful in the spring and the summer and the autumn and the winter, but with a sad beauty. The marshes had the same, and the still creeks that wound among them, and the monstrously wide, deeply moving tidal rivers. Mist from the fat land and broad waters hung in the air and made all colors sheen-like and melting.

I leaned against the tree I was hewing down, or I straightened from the earth where I was setting, plant after plant, to the thousands, the wee tobacco plants, and I saw that there was beauty though it would not stay, though my heart went hot and sick again. But I had the gleam; from my cradle I had that gleam.

And David Scott, servant for he could not guess how long on a Virginia plantation, could not utterly forswear mirth, though the limmer and he made great spaces between their meetings. But about once in so often she came to me with the deil's own slant about her!

When I ran away the second time and after two days and nights was taken in a marsh twenty miles nearer the sea, Williams and his helpers carried me before a justice of the peace and I was lashed. To serve fourteen years and have twenty-nine lashes well laid on the bare back — I sent for mirth that time, and she came with skirls of laughter.

I was twenty-four. I heard Barget tell two fine guests of Colonel Amory, riding past Old Mill quarter, that I worked well, but needed watching. "Runaway. And has spells of darkness."

So I had! Spells of darkness.

All this time, at Old Mill quarter, the few white men came and went, but the score of black men stayed. Mingo, Barbadoes Tom, Pickaninny, Great Joe, Cæsar, Dominick, Bob and Dick and Frank and others. From time to time Mingo or Great Joe or Pickaninny ran away, were found — Mingo got as far as Baltimore — returned, and were severely whipped. You see there is no way a Negro *can* pay but with his skin. The white bondservant's time may be doubled, but Negroes are already slaves for life. Elsewhere man may be put to forced labor, but servant and slave already labor from red morn to purple night. To give them any more would be quite to break down and irremediably injure — property. Again men may be fined; but from what should servant-without-wage and slave pay a fine? Culprits may be put in prison, but if you put servant or slave in prison, it is the master that is punished, losing the delinquent's service. The only way out — since it was nonsense to say that Negroes and white servants did not transgress — was to make them remember it by bodily pain. Hence the whip everywhere, ancient Egypt or Chaldea or some antiquity having found out, for the use and benefit of every country since, that this was the simplest, easiest, cheapest, everywhere handiest instrument with which to inflict pain that should warn and deter (and revenge) and yet not necessarily cripple even for a day. Nothing else could be so nicely graduated from little to much. If an example were to be made, it *could* cripple for any length of time. Pushed far enough, it might even slay.

One could see the human reason in it — at cool seasons. The lawgiver might point at vice enough and folly enough among slaves and servants. Murderous rages, obstinacy against orders and against work, lying, stealing, wantonness, jealousy, laziness and tale-bearing, I've seen them all, in Guinea Negro and white bondsmen. Not in all Guinea Negroes nor in all white bondsmen, but in many. The planters may well have said, " What can we do? It is law and custom and perfectly right that we own these Negroes, and in a sense and for a time these white men. We don't particularly love — no, nor our overseers don't particularly love — the whip. But what, for instance, would you do? "

Pickaninny — called so because he was so big a fellow — and Old Hannibal began to sing, breaking the clods with their hoes. They were born in Virginia, and Pickaninny's parents before him.

> " When hab I done wid de trouble ob de world,
>   O-hhh! when hab I done?
>   Trouble ob de world!
> I ask de Lord how long I hold 'em,
>   Trouble ob de world!
> I ask de Lord how long I hold 'em?
> I ask de Lord how long I hold 'em?
>   Hold 'em to de end.
> My sins so heavy I can't get along.
> Aahh!
> Ah, trouble ob de world! "

Eboe Sam differed from these two. Bought naked out of the *Albatross,* straight from Bangalang the same year that I was bought clothed from the *King William,* we apparently experienced the same trouble in settling down. I had to face the "seasoning." He missed that, his native climate being many degrees hotter and ranker than Virginia. He had run away. So had I. But he had gone, madly and desperately, over and over again, chance or no chance. I had not. I was Scotch and sought straw for my bricks, though bricks in the end I meant to have, bricks and my fortress and palace! He was, I should reckon, four or five years older than me. He said he was a chief's son. "Son of Mongo — same as him!" He flung his hand toward Colonel Amory who had just paced by, on his bay mare Cherry.

"African chief!" I said. "I'm the cousin of a Scots chief. Mickle difference does it make!"

He had little English, and he came under Barget's wrath continually. A proud and haughty one! used, that was the trouble, to slaves of his own.

"Ah! Trouble ob de world.
When hab I done wid de trouble ob de world?"

I asked Eboe Sam many questions about Africa. He took a fancy to me, perhaps because I was at pains to learn a little of his language, perhaps because I was big of frame and cousin to a chief, perhaps because I once did him a small kindness. He had as much sense as many a white man, and there, while we tended tobacco in a blazing July, I gathered a notion of the things and ways of his country. To him it was the finest country in the world. Like Scotland. It was totally a mistake, he said, *his* being taken and sold.

I had from him my first notion of how, from ancient, ancient time, African men were the gowden guineas of Africa, aye, and the silver coin and the note of hand. They did not use metal money; they bought with men and women and children. How did they get them? It spread as big as forever, that land; he ran over names of tribes and peoples, and it was worse than the Old Testament! All warred with one another for that very money, just like us. Money was money, whether it walked itself or was carried. Also they battled because of bitter feud and family quarrel — again similarities! — and they lifted each other's cattle and in foray strove always to take prisoners, for prisoners were money. It was gleeful so to drain the foeman clan's purse! If there were dead peace and no good wars going and chiefs were waxing poor, then was the time *to make one's own village smaller.* There were always men and women who could be spared. And children. Plenty people did wrong. Sell them to the white men! But here he fell into a fit of rage so

sorrowful and righteous indignant that it made
one quake. He — Jarroo — had done no wrong.
He was not liable in any way. He was chief's
son, Great Jarroo's son. All he could say was
that Satan had been at work. He had slept on
his mat after a feast. When he waked he was
out of the village and a rope was round his neck,
and so many men pushed him along whom, when
it was light, he found to be Mandingoes. He
killed one, but they dragged him to the coast.

"Kidnapping or Spiriting!" I said. "Don't
you know everything about that too?"

Yes, he did. But he was chief's son, Jarroo!
It shouldn't have befallen *him*.

Another time I asked him what folk in his
part of Africa bought with their money. His
eyes gleamed, his tongue moistened his lips, he
looked around the bare cabin — it was at night
— with disdain, and began to describe. Muskets
— I made out those at once — knives, cutlasses,
powder, rum, red cloth, blue and white and
figured cottons, looking-glasses, shining ewers
and basins, fine coats, bells, trumpets, beads to
give women — all that he craved he told of in
a kind of triumph. He had had them; nothing
could take that away from him. England had
given them to him for black and brown, walking
ingots. But he liked it not when the thimble
fell in his own lap.

Though he was still a young man he had

because there must be slaves for sale. So when there wasn't quarrel, pick quarrel. The white men at the castles on the coast, the factories, helped the chiefs pick them.

The fire on the cabin hearth glared. They were dancing before the long cabin — Mingo and Great Joe and Pickaninny and others, and Mingo's wife and two or three women from Big Field quarter. They had a fiddle; Barnabas played it. The music screamed and laughed and lilted. All their voices and their shuffling feet and the flame.

CHAPTER VI

BARGET had a shrew of a wife, and a daughter, a slim girl of eighteen, not beautiful, but with a kind, freckled face and bright blue eyes. Ten years ago this overseer had been an indentured servant like the many others around. His own man at last, he then worked for wages, and saved and bought a little and sold a little and saved again until he had saved enough to bring over from England his wife and child. Now he was overseer under Williams at Amory Hall, living in a decent log house two hundred yards from Old Mill quarter cabins. With him lived a young fellow, his assistant, whom he was training for his successor when Williams should have retired and he himself have stepped into Williams' shoes. For his successor and his son-in-law.

My eyes began to seek this girl. It was three years since I had walked with Mysie Johnston in the glen. I was twenty-five and unhappy. Nelly Barget! She had not been at Old Mill at first.

All this time in Virginia I had seen young white women afar, at church, on the road to the landing or at the landing itself, or in boats that passed, or in coaches that came a-visiting to

Amory Hall. I had seen young Mistress Maria
Amory, seated at the spinet, playing " The Four
Maries." I had seen, nay, I had touched hands
with six young slips of the ruling order.

And how on earth did that come about? I
will tell about that.

It was the day before the ball at the great
house. Not even Old Mill quarter was without
talk of that ball and the fine folk who would be
there. They would come by boat, they would
come by coach, they would come on horseback,
arriving from other great houses up and down
the river and from Williamsburg. A dozen fine
young men and women, Amory kindred and in-
timates, were already at Amory Hall. Colonel
Amory had three daughters. The ball was for
the birthday of the oldest, my young Mistress
Maria of the spinet.

This day before came Barget to David Scott.
Did I know Scots reels and strathspeys and
maybe the Sword Dance? Without taking
thought, I said I did. Then I was to make myself clean and go at once to the house. Dances
of surprise were being arranged for the coming
ball and instruction in the Scotch was wanted.

I said I would not go. Barget whistled.
" What d'ye think the Colonel will say to that? "
I did not care what the Colonel said for I was
in a rage. Then all of a sudden that changed
and a great wave came over me of I know not
what, save that it might be just youth and long-

ing and " Mak' what ye can of it! " and I said I
would go.

We had two suits of clothes each, we white
servants. Work clothes and church clothes. So
I put on my church clothes — shoes and stockings and a coarse white shirt, and breeches and
coat of indifferent cloth. It was a tingling, gray,
winter day, and Dick Merry and I had been
cutting an oak nine feet in girth. When I came
to the great house fires glowed through the windows and out of an opened door poured laughter. I entered the hall, and when a mulatto boy
appeared, told him to say that the Scot was here.
He grinned and I followed him. They were
dancing in the great parlor, and large enough
was the room and all polished the floor. They
had two Negro fiddlers and everything was in
practise for a great affair with masks and dress-
ings-up. They lived, these Virginia planters,
with no little jollity.

Well, here I was, regarding as from an
enormous distance a dozen or more young men
and women and two or three elders. The
Colonel saw me and exclaiming, " Ha, Scott, are
you there? " signed me to a place by the fiddlers.
So at last they came to the reel and called on me
to state if this were right or that was wrong.

They were good-natured and flushed and free
with the dance. They wanted one step and then
another. David Scott was there to answer them,
and he answered.

In the auld historic movement upon which we were engaged, there is a good deal of handling and clasping and flying together. And of all there there wasn't any who danced with the spirit that showed the Colonel's second daughter, who was named Judith. She had dark ringlets and dark flashing eyes, and a rosebud cheek and a laughing mouth. "Is this the way — what's your name — David Scott?" She gave me her hand. I showed her and swung her, and presently in the wheel she came to me again. Up and down and around and across went the auld Scots dance, and I was dancing both in the glen at home and here in Virginia, with the cold and the hot alike in my heart and my head. I danced like the deil.

A girl they named Catherine — we were dancing so fast, the feet were so twinkling — came plump into my arms, screamed and laughed and skimmed away. Judith again took my hand. "It's right now, isn't it? We're doing finely!" Up and down and around and across, and the great room and the fiddles and the blazing fire, and we were all one being and that in a mad dance.

The fiddlers ceased for a moment. We stood panting a little, at rest before the final and intricate square and wheel. Across, from the group of elders by the fire, pointed and keen as a poniard, came the thin voice of a yellow and wrinkled woman in a satin gown. "Well, for

a bought servant, I must say he has his boldness
with him!"

Instantly the fiddlers were fiddling again and
we were all dancing. But "Catherine!" called
a voice from the fireside and called twice, and
Catherine, so imperiously bidden, left our company. The next step brought me facing Mr.
Warwick Beaufort, who had, I had already observed, an interest in Mistress Judith. I divine
that lightning and thunder had been gathering
there for some minutes. At any rate his brows
now were as black as Erebus. We danced, and
down the line came Judith again, and she
laughed at him and laughed at me, and her eyes
sent their own dazzling lightnings. Her slim
white hand was in mine that the ax had hardened. We danced, and every Scott and Stuart
and all Jacobite Scotland, and David Scott himself and all his wrongs, and men and women
everywhere, just their essential selves, were dancing on an oaken floor to the music of eternity. —
Then it all broke, the figure was confused. Mr.
Warwick Beaufort had said something offensive,
and I struck him.

Well, the end of all that was that I went back
to the tree-cutting and never entered that house
again.

Nelly Barget!

When first we talked together the blackbirds
were chattering in the March trees and the
bloodroot whitening the forest floor. I was hew-

ing by myself, Dick Merry having cut his foot
and gone away to quarter. She had been on an
errand to parsonage a mile up river, and instead
of using the high road for her return chose the
forest path. The spring, I reckon, was in her
blood, and a maid as well as a man may like
wild flowering. Now Dick's foot had bled beside the pine tree we had been chopping. She
saw it and turned aside and came to me — just
showing I must have been, through the trees, and
my ax not ringing at the moment.

"Yours?" She knew my name. "Have you
hurt yourself, David Scott?"

"No. It was Dick Merry. He cut his foot
badly, but we bandaged it up and he's gone to
quarter."

"Well, I'm glad nobody's killed!" A patch
of little purple and white flowers growing beside
her own foot she stooped and plucked them.
"It's a lovely day."

"Aye. 'Tis spring."

"Don't you get tired chopping? Chopping
trees and tending tobacco?"

"No, of course not."

"That's a lie!" said Nelly Barget. She
moved to gather violets from a sunny place.
"How do you like Virginia?"

"If I were not a slave I might like it well
enough."

"You aren't a slave. Not like Pickaninny.
Not like Eboe Sam."

"There are differences. But still I am a slave."

With that I began to cut the tree, and having gathered the violets, she moved away.

Two days afterwards she came again this way, and still Dick Merry was crippled and could not work.

"Tell me about Scotland. When I was a little girl I lived in England. I remember mountains and a city ten times as big as Williamsburg."

I rested my ax and sat upon a log and told of Edinburgh and that glen and loch I best knew. She sat near me with her hands over her knee, but all the time she kept a sharp watch. "There's somebody coming!" she said at last, and starting up walked sedately away upon the wood path that wound between Barget's house and the parsonage and one or two other small dwellings. That morning as I worked I constantly saw her face among the branches — kind and freckled with wide mouth and bright blue eyes.

Sunday I saw her at church. She sat between her father and mother and looked straight through the window behind the parson, and sang in a lilting, sweet voice:

"*I was glad when they said unto me,*
Let us go into the House of the Lord ——"

On Wednesday I saw her again on the path.

But Dick was with me, and she went by without a sign or look.

But now I meant to see her and talk to her. By this time Dick Merry followed me in what I did or said, and had the staunchness of a good dog. I told him, "I want to talk to Barget's daughter. She will talk with me, but not when you are by. They don't care how we cut, so that we get this tract done. To-morrow about this time you take those trees in the hollow."

"All right!" answered Dick. "I've seen her look at you in church, when she thought everybody else was marking the other way. Lord! If there happens a snatched kiss, who's the worse for it?"

And nothing ever happened more than the snatched kiss — the snatched kiss and the pressed hands, and the arm around her one day when it was all so sunny gold and fine, the small flowers blooming around and one rich bird singing, singing, in the beech tree overhead. And that was the last, as it was the best, for a child, going through the wood, told her mother.

Barget stormed at me. "She's gone to Williamsburg to my sister. And either the Colonel will sell you from this place, or he and Williams may find another helper than me!"

"I did her no harm, man!" I said. "She's nothing but frank and young and kind, and it's the springtime — even in Virginia! I kissed her, yes. It's a fearful crime!"

But still he shook his stick. "You're going from here or I go!"

"Shall I weep and howl if I go?" I answered. "I think not!"

For that and other things. I was sold at the courthouse, and Eboe Sam, who likewise was unruly and a runaway, was sold at the same time.

The Colonel on Cherry parted with us that morning before Old Mill quarter. "Scott, you've piled up trouble for yourself steadily since you've been here. I'm not a hard master — I've got a name for just the other thing. You might have accepted the lot you brought on yourself and made something of it, and in the end been a happy enough man. But you didn't choose that way, and now I'm thinking you'll fall into hands less easy than mine!"

He told the truth there. — Well, I look back over years and see that he was a spirit caught in his own toils, as I was caught in mine, and Eboe Sam in his, and Barget in his.

Gervase Morrison also came down to Old Mill quarter. "I told the Colonel I wished to say good-by to you."

"Yes. Well, good-by!"

"David Scott, you could do more with yourself than you're doing."

I laughed. "Likely enough I might become a saint like old Walter who smiles and talks with the Universe while he makes shoes for the Colonel's servants!"

"You've arrived at the man named Bitter. After that comes Vengeful and then Cruel."

"Well?"

"I don't mean to preach," said Morrison. "I can't. I'm no preacher. I'm a wastrel. I don't like preachers, either. But don't go running and sliding and leaping down Perdition's slope! There's something in you — I saw it on the *King William* — that looked like a soul."

"It's hard for souls to flourish in slavery," I said, and bade him good-by with an aridity that I like not now to remember.

In the morning at dawn we went to the courthouse. Before noon I had been bought by Mr. Daniel Askew, a man of little education and less feeling, living twenty miles nearer to nowhere than the Amory plantation, and in bad odor with all the better kind of Virginians.

CHAPTER VII

I WALKED into two years of pelting wretchedness. It is quite true that Amory Hall and Colonel Amory and Williams and Barget and Old Mill quarter took on by comparison an angelic hue. I had been bought by a man who in any land or time would have been a kind of devil.

I suppose many Virginians knew that he was an "unkind" master. But he kept just within the law, that to be sure allowed impatient or exacting masters leeway enough. And there was the greatest feeling of sanctity of property and of the individual rights of owners. So no one interfered. They would have said that they "could" not, that he was within his "rights." It is true that there was a social displeasure, at times coming within sight of ostracism. Virginians are no unkindlier than Englishmen and Scots, whom in truth they are. Domestic tyranny occurs in England too, and now and then arises there or anywhere some misbegotten son of darkness who works havoc. But slavery may place many in the power of a demon.

David Scott did not philosophize those two years. He suffered in a black and dumb rage, and he hardened and grew more evil than he

was. Eboe Sam was with me, but Askew broke
Eboe Sam's spirit. He became an apathetic or
timidly smiling poor Negro. My spirit was not
broken, but I arrived at the man named Vengeful.

I ran away, was taken and maltreated; ran
away again and was taken and maltreated. I
began to think of murder.

It would have come to that, but the third time
I tried *I got away.*

It was September. I left at night, and it was
hot and very still with tension in the air. I
sweated as I ran through the forest. Askew had
great dogs, and I knew he would follow with
them. What I aimed at was a stream running
through the forest. If I could reach it, I might
throw them off the scent. It was some distance
away and a question if I could gain it before
dawn, gain it and wade down it and across and
begin again with a faint, a temporary security.
As I ran the stars went out above me, group by
group. " Storm! " I thought. " Well, it might
help."

The forest leaped into a pale gold, instant
light, then died again into blackness. Thunder
followed. " You're coming up quickly at the
last," I thought, " but you've been on the way
for a day and night." A hot puff of wind struck
my cheek, the forest began to talk. There came
a dazzling glare, a Judgment crack. In a moment the forest was shouting, then rushed a

downpour like the crest of Noah's forty days. I could not run, but crouched beside an uprooted tree and exulted in the deluge that would wash my tracks away.

At dawn still was howling and havoc. I knew now that it was no ordinary storm, but one of those gales, edges or effects of the more southerly hurricanes, that at long intervals struck Virginia. While it lasted I might make hay. It lasted two days, and the land ran with water like a sluice. The stream I sought for had become a dozen, great trees were overthrown and doubtless chimneys fell. None but a runagate with Askew to fear would have liked that being abroad! But I liked it. I liked that great fight with wind and water that were yet my helpers and might be exulted in and with. I was fey. And, ah, God, I liked the loneliness, I liked my freedom!

I went west for a time and then I bent south to the River James that was running high and strong and yellow. I wished to cross it and make for North Carolina, yet how I did not know. It might not be swam as it was, and no boats were forth to-day, and if they were how would they receive me who had not a groat, and " man in trouble " written all over him? Askew's ragged, grim plantation lay considerably to the west and the wilderness from the Amory Hall neighborhood. Hereabouts stretched ancient forest, and any dwellings, few and small, stood far apart. A road ran near the river, bottomless now with mud and pools of water. I stood there in the storm that still raved, though with a sunken fury, and saw no life upon its long stretches to one hand or the other.

I was wet through and torn by the forest; the bread and meat I had abstracted from the plantation I was leaving was long ago eaten; I had had little sleep and no shelter, I was half naked, burned and gaunt as a wolf. As I stood there, back flashed to me Tolbooth Lane, Saint Giles and the high roofs of the Luckenbooths. That, too, was witches' weather, and Sandy Scott's barn had proved no long shelter. Five years ago, five lang, lang years ago! Suddenly night thicker than a knife could cut descended on my soul. Through it I heard the river there below me, swollen and hoarse, flinging itself to the sea. I said, " Drowning's short. Let's be over with it! " and put myself into motion toward the yellow flood that was already carrying logs and broken trees enough.

A bank of earth and a row of huge, ghostly sycamores hid from me the stream's edge. As I came down, my head dizzy now and singing, I heard bagpipes, and knew that I must be dead already and back in Scotland.

It was not the pipes but a man with a flute, seated before a kind of cabin built up from a flatboat laden with skins and other matters, and fastened to a sycamore in a backwater under the bank. I saw him and checked myself and would have vanished among hazel and alder, but his eye was keen or he heard the loosened stone and earth. He took the flute from his lips and laid his hand upon a musket on the deck beside him. "You there in the bushes! Better come out — but in case you mean any harm, I'll just state that I'm a dead shot!"

I left the alders and he saw that I was un-armed. It was the middle of the day, the rain had halted and a cold and lurid light wrapped the world. He stared at me.

"Well, I know what you are! You're a runaway! Isn't Daniel Askew's land over that-a-way?"

"You're in the right," I answered, and came to the water's edge, a strip of flood being yet between him and me. "If you've got a bite of anything, remember that we are both men!"

"Why did you come racing down as though to a meeting?"

"I meant to plunge in and have life over that I was tired of. But life has an awful amount of life in it. My mind's changing."

"If you think you can take my boat, you're mistook."

"I don't, man!" I said. "You've got a gun. And I'm nigh dead, and you look fresh and limber as a Maytime buck. What I'm asking you for is just mercy."

"I'm not putting across to the other side. As

soon as the sky clears and the old river stops her
tossing a mite, I'm dropping on down to Norfolk."

As he spoke there rose before the inner eye
a ship with heaped canvas. If I could get to a
ship, if a ship would take me aboard! Ships
forever wanted seamen and were never too
cautious whence they came. It was like thread-
ing a needle in the dark, but I threaded it, and
willed Norfolk port, not Carolina. *O what
guided ye, David Scott?*

I said, "Take me to Norfolk, man! By any
chance, are you knowing Daniel Askew?"

He spat. "Yes, I know him."

"Then you know why I'm running. If you
hate him, you'll not be anxious to gratify him.
If you love him, you'll be serving him, for if
I'm taken I mean to murder him."

"You may scalp him for all I care!" and he
spat again. "I suppose you'd make yourself
useful? Jim Halfman that was my partner got
drowned at the falls."

"Try me and see," I said. "And in the name
of all that's good, man, haven't you anything to
eat?"

He looked at me hard again, then rising
brought a plank and with it made a bridge from
boat to shore. I came across, and ah, that flatboat and its stinking skins seemed to me as fair
as a palace! And when he gave me venison and
maize cakes to eat and poured for me half a

pint of rum and water, I felt that he was a kind of woodland god.

Christian Todd, that was his name, a man of forty and trader to the Indians for half those years. He had an old hunting shirt and leggings and an otter-skin cap, a long knife and a short knife, a musket and powderhorn and bag of shot, and his flute. His hair and beard were long and tawny yellow, and his gray eyes looked vague and never were so in the least. His tongue lay silent nine-tenths of the time in the cavern of his jaws. The other tenth, if there were no other need, he slowly talked of Indians and their ways or of forest beasts and theirs.

The blue sky shone, the light played, the air grew balm. We loosed the boat from the shore. There were two great oars and also a short mast and small patched sail the color of a dead leaf. The hutch of a cabin, the jut of his heaps of skins and other truck furnished cover for me when boats passed us or we were hailed from the shore. Neither happened often, for this is a hugeous river and country and the human life is not numerous. Moreover, Christian Todd seemed to be known and his ways respected. When he shouted, " Going down the river and I'm late!" none overpersuaded or tried to prevent. The first night, the river still rough and high, we laid to beside an ancient, broken landing, but the second the moon was bright and the water wide and we went on with the flood, one sleeping while the other waked. No one pursued, no one summoned us in the name of the law.

" My luck has turned! " said David Scott, and was no more thankful or in-seeing than that.

But I liked Christian Todd who never asked a question as to my past or my future, who could keep a colorful silence, and who lived with the great forest, not chopped it down. It is true he traded in the lives of the beasts; there were heaped about us skins and fur of fox and bear and marten and squirrel, doe and fawn and beaver. But David Scott thought of that no otherwise than as a matter of course. David Scott and Christian Todd. David Scott, twenty-seven years old, going down James River on a flatboat, good meat and bread to eat and rum to drink, and before him day and night a dream ship, tall and white as the moon, that might even take him back to Scotland.

Now and then Christian Todd took up his flute. He played strange airs, Indian maybe. By now I knew well the melodies of the Negroes. It was not these, nor was it English or Scots. He may have taken them from the Indians or from himself. He was a strange, Panlike creature.

So I went, so safely and securely, down to Norfolk. It was as though, suddenly, a warlock had taken me up.

The river grew enormously broad, the sea was

felt, the sun glistened against gull wings and the sails of tall ships. Now I saw, though still afar, that small, rude, port town that I had not seen since the *King William* bore me by it. And not a hitch; as smoothly had we gone as though Heaven had said, Let it be so! Christian Todd pointed. "That black mark's my landing. The merchant there in the brick house takes my skins."

"It'll be dusk before we get there. Am I at all like Jim Halfman?"

"Not the least bit. And there's always a power of people around."

I shook myself and woke up and tried to plan. The sun was setting, fiery red. Flood and our small sail carrying us on, Christian Todd picked up his flute and began to play an air sweet as the throat of the mocking bird and melancholy as the whippoorwill. In his boat, in the forest, he was a wise man, but I knew without being told that in a white man's town with white man's law around, his magic would depart.

And yet I could not plan. I was in a dream and yet not so. And what it might be I did not know, but I never truly doubted that now at last I was quitting Virginia who had dreamed so often of quitting it. I say I do not know, and yet maybe I do.

The sun went down. There flared a great, red, autumnal afterglow. We were over toward the southern shore, and now the landing, the brick houses of the merchants and the town beyond increased in size, and the anchored ships in number. I had reached the point that I might easily stay upon the flatboat through the night, leaving my wits to work at dawn, and just as I rested upon that and looked again at the sky that flamed as though the earth beneath were on fire, and at the wide water and smelled the sea, the lanterns were lighted upon a large ship swinging at anchor close before us.

"I don't know her," said Christian Todd. "But then I forget ships, being gone so long in the land of canoes."

It was not so dark but that much of her might be seen, lying there under bare masts, and now we drew nearer and nearer. She had a collected and tidy look, her boats were in, her men aboard. We heard the bo'sn's pipe. "She's a creature ready for the sea," said David Scott, and his voice had to himself a fatal and resonant sound.

"Aye, at dawn the stag will be gone."

We were moving past her, we saw her name. The great lantern showed it. *Janet.* The *Janet* of Bristol.

David Scott stood up. "Bring her to a bit." He hailed the ship. "*Janet,* ahoy!"

A man leaning over the rail answered. "Ye crazed wee boatie, what d' ye want?"

I shouted back, "I wad gae tae sea. Tak me and ye'll find me useful!"

Two more heads appeared. There seemed a colloquy, then the first man called out, " Come aboard then if your health's na cracked!"

"This is my ship, Christian Todd," I said, and we lowered sail and took up oars. When we got to her side I thanked him. " If there's Fate or Necessity or something of that kind, then these three days have been just at its beck! Maybe all days are. You've been a spirit of deliverance to me, sent out of the wood, and I'm thanking you, man!"

" I was lying under a tree smoking oncet," said Christian Todd, " and all of a sudden I sat up and said as loud as ever I spoke in my life, ' By Jiminy! there's very few things that aren't meant!' Well, there's my hand, and think of Virginia kindly!"

So we parted, and I climbed the side of the ship, using the rope they dropped for me. When I stood on the deck and looked back, Christian Todd had pushed off; up went his dead-leaf sail, he swung toward Norfolk. The red of the sky had grown purple and a huge, round moon was coming up from the east.

"Are ye a mariner?" said the voice that, I now perceived, belonged to the first mate.

" I was one summer, for fun, on a brig that went from Berwick to Glasgow by the Hebrides."

"' For fun.' D'ye hear that, Michaelson? I'm always telling ye that the sea and the ship

and the trade have got their glints. All right,
my billie, my name's Mr. McNaughton. And
now I'll be taking you to cabin and the auld
man."

By the lantern I saw that he was red Scot, red
as a fox, lean and dry, and six feet two. Of the
sailors with him, one, Michaelson, had been
born in Stirling; the other, Dory, was an Eng-
lishman. I gazed around me, but little could
be seen now save by moonlight. It seemed, however, a tidy, fine ship, and I heard men laughing
in the forecastle.

So we went to the great cabin. "Come in,
Mr. McNaughton, and whom have you got
there?" said a full, reasonable voice. And to
cap the strangeness of a strange day, it seemed
to David Scott that he had heard that voice before.

CHAPTER VIII

THE man to whom it belonged sat at the table with a bottle of wine and a chart before him. He was rather tall and full of figure, with a reddish-brown beard, a big nose and dark, hawk eyes, and might be just this side of fifty. "What have you got here, Mr. McNaughton?" He had a full, deep, slow, rumbling voice. "Who are you?" He stared at me, standing in the yellow light, ragged and gaunt and unshorn. "You're a runaway, that's what you are! What are you doing in this galley, may I ask, Mr. McNaughton?"

The mate explained. "Maybe there ought to have been inquiries, sir. But I was leaning on the rail, and he came by, and it was as though a fish takes your line, and you've drawn him up and in before you can think or wink! A bell inside just rang, 'We're short a couple of men, since Ralph Daughter died and the Dutch lad left the ship.' And anyhow, what's the care, considering we're leaving, not coming, and 'twas all in the dark and none seeing?"

"You're an immoral man, Mr. McNaughton, with your no care at all for civilized laws!" He addressed me. "It'll be some trouble setting you ashore, but I can take it!"

" I hope you won't, sir," I said. " I can serve you as a sailor, and I'm sair wanting to see Scotland again."

" So that's where it lies? " he answered. "And when did you leave that poor, cold, barren land, and for what? "

" I left it five years ago, and for being at Culloden."

He jerked back from the table. " They were fools at Culloden! Some kin of my ain were involved, but none the less they were fools at Culloden. — What's your name? "

" David Scott."

" Scott! There are a mort of Scotts. Scott of Where? "

I gave the name of our old house. He looked at me thoughtfully. As for me, I turned two dice around in my mind, and then cast one, seeing I must choose quickly. " You are Captain William Bartram. I remember you. You came to my father's house when I was fourteen and I rowed you across the loch. I called you Cousin Bartram, and you gave me a Spanish gold piece."

He stared. " Why, so I did! Well, this is the strangest world! " He drank the red wine. " And what is it you think you'll be doing? "

" What I said, sir. Mr. McNaughton has just stated that the *Janet* needs seamen. I'll work for my passage."

" Your passage where? "

" To Scotland." When I saw him that time,
years and years ago, he was captain of an East
Indiaman. His ship, I remembered, was then
the *Margaret*. " To Scotland," I said again, and
Edinburgh rose before me, and a mountain, a
loch and a glen.

" Scotland? " he repeated. " And what
should a Culloden man on the wrong side, that
has been deported for life or the better part of
it, do in Scotland? I'm thinking you might explain your disappearance for five years, but not
your reappearance! As I sit here, I'm remembering the case, for I was told of it when I happened to be in Carlisle. You broke gaol and
were taken in a barn. Aye, there are plenty of
informers in Scotland who sit by the roadside
and mark such as you! — You're noticeable,
too," he said, and again drank wine.

David Scott stood in silence. A window was
open; he heard the light washing of the river
down which he had come. In the desperate ache
and urge to escape and find a life that was not
this life, Desire had made a picture and had
declined to shadow it. I had thought somehow
of easy hiding, and men having forgotten, and
safety, and old, sweet life. But now I saw the
shadows and that they hid an iron, inimical
power that might well toss me back across the
ocean, a marked ball, precisely into Daniel
Askew's hands. Then I would do murder and
be hanged for it. But likelier than all that, they

would hang me first in Scotland. There was no refuge; home was home no longer. I may have known it all along, but never realized it. Dark, dark, dark! — But what was the power that had set me on the *Janet?*

"If your port's Bristol," I said, "I'll fare as I can in England. Or I might shift there to some Dutch vessel, and live and die in the Low Countries ——"

"And anyhow," he said, as if not marking me, "neither Scotland nor England's my destination at present."

"What is it then?"

McNaughton behind me gave a click. "Ye've got your impudence with you to be speirin' the Captain that! Fine fo'castle stuff ye air!"

As for William Bartram, he did not change his countenance, but wiped a drop of wine from the chart. He was a big man with his big nose and hawk eyes, and knew how to command. Stories of him were running around in my head, in motion after many years. There had been, I thought now, many stories. At last he spoke, in his reasonable, deep voice. "So you see, kinsman, your shortest way round might be just to step now into the boat and be rowed ashore!"

I said, "Will you row me ashore yourself, kinsman, as I rowed you across the loch?"

He put down the glass that was on the way to his lips, and leaning back appeared to study me afresh. Again I heard the water lapping. The air in the brown cabin began to move and hum around me, and yet no moving or humming was visible or audible. But I felt changes and decisions, and yet back of them something that neither changed nor decided. I spoke again, "When you said 'kinsman', sir, you said ' I'll not put you ashore against your will.' Now all my will is to abide with the *Janet*. You'll not regret. I'll work out the passage, wherever it's to, or long or short. The passage and the gold piece, too."

His beard twitched. " Aweel, as to the gold piece, I gied ye that. But I'm no objectin' if it heightens your appetite for wark." With that he rolled up his chart and called out, " Geordie! " whereupon the cabin boy appeared. " Glasses, Geordie, and another bottle and some biscuit." He measured me again. " I'm thinking that I've an old suit of clóthes that might nearly fit you. You can't be parading around in a guise that skirls out ' Runaway! ' " He rose from the table and crossed to his own cabin that opened into the great one. Now I saw more clearly what a big, muscular man he was. He vanished, and McNaughton gave another click. "I hope ye'll remember me, Mr. Scott, when ye're scattering moidores! What a thing it is to be daft about your ain kith and kin that ye see but seldom, and to find a braw example rising like Neptune out of the deep!"

I drew a long breath. "He's a fine man. I remember him so well now!"

"Aye, he's a fine man. No better captain in the trade! Aweel, your fortune's made. Dinna forget that 'twas I that pulled you out of the river!"

"I won't," I said. "And truly I thank you for it."

Captain William Bartram reappeared. "Go in there and change." I obeyed. There was a light, and he had laid upon the bed quite good enough apparel, better than any David Scott had worn this long, long while. We were both tall and big-boned men. He had more flesh than I, so that his clothes hung somewhat loosely. But they answered. As I dressed I looked around. His cabin was very neatly kept, with ingenious devices of shelves and cupboards and racks. There were arms, pistols and a sword and a cutlass, more pieces, it seemed to me, than would be usual for the master of a trading vessel. It might, however, be his fancy. Now David Scott had fought in battle and came of a fighting stock, and, occasion given, he could and did revolt, and feel somber, wild and hot anger and fight for his own. Witness all my life in Virginia for that! But I did *not* even then, not in Scotland, not at Culloden, not for itself, God knows, even in Virginia! care for battling and bludgeoning. I had rather reason it out, though I stifled that down so often, and fought. So I

looked at my kinsman's armory, but did not lust
for it. He had a shelf of books. I lusted more
for them, and I lusted now for the rum and
brandy which he must have upon his ship.

When I was dressed I rolled into a bundle
those wretched and ragged garments that I had
worn, and through the cabin window tossed
them into the dark and gliding water. And then
I returned to the great cabin and to my cousin.
Mr. McNaughton was now seated with a glass
of Canary before him, and the two had been
talking. Both gazed at me a moment before
speaking. No doubt my general air was im-
proved by decent attire and by hope and warmth
and kinsman and the taste of adventure that was
not tragic and despairing. At any rate, " Sit ye
down, David," said William Bartram and
poured wine for me. " Conditions cloak men
strangely!" Again he looked at me thoughtfully. " You've had a fair education? You
could clerk a bit at need? "

" I think so. Though for five years I've not
touched a pen and hardly seen a book."

" You like books? "

" I used to. Yes, I like them."

" I don't like all books," said my cousin.
" But give me the Ancients — in a translation
— and I'm as happy as the day is long." With
which he neatly picked up his talk with Mr.
McNaughton at the broken end. " You see, Mr.
McNaughton, it's not possible for a Bartram to

derogate his blood by putting it in the forecastle of his own ship. So we'll just name him a passenger and give him that bit hole in the side yonder. It may have been providential that young Smith was just no clerk at all and left me in Philadelphia."

"Whatever you say, sir. Your will's law here."

"Well, that's settled," said the Captain. "Have you had supper, David?"

Christian Todd and I had eaten at sunset, and I said so. "Then it's bedtime," answered Bartram. "We'll be lifting and away with the first blink of light."

The *Janet* seemed to me a roomy ship. The cabin that had been young Smith's who differed with the Captain and parted at Philadelphia, was big enough for me to turn about in, and I heard the water lapping, and seemed in a dream, and laid down a free man, and said the word to myself mair than once. "Free! Free!" and then I went to sleep.

I waked after hours of dreamless sleep, deep as the nadir or high as the zenith. In at the tiny window looked the pale dawn. Then the morning star was set in the round and vanished and came again. A hum and creaking entered my ears, and the cabin slanted slightly and righted again. For a little I lay, savoring the most strange drama of life. The *King William* passed before me, and Gervase Morrison and

Colonel Amory and Williams and Barget and
Nelly Barget and Judith Amory and Dick
Merry and Pickaninny and Eboe Sam and
Daniel Askew and others. I came down the
river with Christian Todd, and his flute was
playing. I was in Scotland, that now it seemed
my body would never be in again. During the
last three years the image of Mysie Johnston had
paled, the heart had despaired and altered and
ceased to beat that way. I thought now, " She
has forgotten doubtless, and maybe married,"
and the thought had a dull sound and was no
longer wholly unbearable. The star swung
again across the window and was gone.

Then Scotland no more! Well, then, where
was I sailing? I thought of the Bermudas, or
on the other hand, Charleston or Bahamas or
Barbados. If the *Janet* were for any of these
places, I meant not to leave her. I meant not
to leave her until she put me somewhere in
Europe. I was still a young man. All manner
of old, not all uncomely, ambitions stirred and
rose from the dead, from the slain and stamped
upon. I felt strength in me to make a name for
David Scott, a name that should stand for increase to all.

A hand knocked upon my door. It was the
cabin boy, and he held a tumbler of spirits and
water. "Your dram, sir." I took it and
drank, knowing that I had here a dragon to
fight, and postponing the combat.

Dressing, I peered out of my small round for air and light and saw no shore, but a green and rumpled sea and in the east saffron and purple bars of sunrise. The star had melted away. We were moving under a good breeze in the great bay or sea of Chesapeake. Quitting my quarters, I found the cabin empty of all but Geordie, who was setting the table for breakfast. It seemed that there was no shackle upon my movements. I might go where I would, so I went on deck.

The *Janet* was a fine ship, a four-master, larger, cleaner, finer, a better sailer in every way than had been that *King William* of weary memory, or that long-ago brig on which I had turned seaman through a northern summer. All my prepossessions of the night before strengthened, and a love of the sea and of this white, racing creature upon it shot up from some deep place within me. Oh, it was better than working Daniel Askew's tobacco!

The sails were piled to catch the light but favoring wind, and men yet worked aloft or upon the decks beneath those white billows. I watched and listened, leaning against the side. Seamen, passing, stared at me. But some word had been given, and they were civil when they spoke. Crew and officers, and myself as supernumerary, I reckoned that there might be not far from fifty men aboard. Some were Scots, but much the greater number English. Three or four seemed to me French or Italians, and I made out certainly one Dutchman. Sailors are — sailors. These seemed to me a good average, or — so sweetly did everything blow to me — slightly above the average. There would be good, bad and indifferent among them as among any fifty men anywhere. But there have been crews of scoundrels, and the *Janet's* was not such.

Cheerful were all the sounds of the ship, cheerful the golden sun that now pushed above the wave. I looked toward Virginia, and saw a dimness that I knew was land. It was vanishing. "Let it vanish!" I thought, and "New Life! I shall taste New Life!"

Seeing that I was the Captain's cousin, I mounted to the poop deck. Now I saw that the ship carried guns, three to a side. Just above me floated the great British flag. My eyes lifted to the mainmast top. There streamed another flag — it would be that of the owners — but I could not make it out.

McNaughton came up the ladder, saw me and stopped to speak. "I needna ask ye how ye're faring, Mr. Scott. Ye look like a bridegroom the morn. — Aye, it's grand, the sea and air and a good deck under a man's feet!"

I said, "What's the flag yonder, Mr. Mc-Naughton?"

He followed my gaze. The sky up there was now a lovely blue, and against it the flag gleamed richly, streaming in the blissful morn.

"Eh, the flag? The Royal African Company's."

I did not answer. Something crashed, as though a castle fell, and it was night, and a spectre arose. *The Royal African Company — The Royal African Company — The Royal African Company!*

I heard some one say, and it might of course be David Scott that was speaking, "We're sailing then to Africa?"

"Oh, aye!" replied McNaughton. "To Daga that's one of the Company's factories above the Niger. — And there's Geordie signalling breakfast. Will ye come along?"

CHAPTER IX

"SO that's where the wind blows!" said William Bartram. "I've marked you through the day, walking in a cloud, and I said to myself, 'What's wrong here?' and 'We'll have it out the eve.'" He leaned back in the great, fixed chair, in the cabin of the *Janet,* his pipe and glass and bottle before him on the table. He only drank after supper, and only wine, and no more than that leonine head of his could stand. The yellow lantern light fell upon him. I liked him, had liked him strongly, I knew now, when I was a boy; liked him to-day, and that apart from all reasons for gratitude. There was that in our two natures, for all our difference in years, that clung, that sounded together. There would be great differences too, but we should never escape, nor want to escape, from the liking.

"So it's as a servant of the Royal African Company that you're not liking me?" he said without anger. "And you're liking the *Janet* no longer, because she's built and decked and stocked for the slave trade?"

"I have been in effect a slave; I don't like slavery."

He answered from behind a cloud of tobacco smoke. "It's my own opinion that it will not last forever. But in the meantime it's the weary way of this weary world. We're all more or less slaves."

" Yes," I said. " More or less."

" I take your emphasis. But the ' less ' has always come on slowly and has had to wait on time. — As for Negro slaves, Pharaoh owned them, and for all we know, Solomon and David. Probably Pericles did, and certainly Alexander and Augustus Cæsar. When you come to know Africa, you'll see that it's just one great hunting ground for men and had always been so. It's recognized. Moreover, nothing would so break the public heart in Africa as not to be allowed to trade enemies or the useless or their own for what they want. When folk continuously enslave one another, there's no good shrieking about outside giants."

Eboe Sam rose before me. I said, " Still you think it will not last."

" I suppose one day we'll all grow up," he answered. " Europe, America and Africa. Grow to some kind of a religious level. But now we're in and of the present world."

" You tempt them."

" Aye, they're very temptable," he answered.

He drummed on the table. " I will tell you, David. The *Margaret* was my ship at the time when I came for a week to your father's house. I had had her then for three years, and I had her for four years thereafter. Seven in all.

She was a good ship, and I sailed her for the East India Company. London to Calcutta, Calcutta to London again. English goods and passengers going out, spices and ivory and fine Indian weaves returning. Seven years — I sailed her for seven years, and gave the people over me no trouble, and made the Company money. Sailed her well! I could not tell you all the storms and plagues I brought her through. And they praised me — they praised me in London and Calcutta. If a great man of the Company was going out to India, they used to say, ' Go in Bartram's ship.' Storms and fearful calms and plagues of kinds — those things happen in seven years — but I brought the *Margaret* and them in her safe to haven. And then in one night came a typhoon that broke our masts and beat us down. Our seams opened, the pumps were naught, we took to the boats. The *Margaret* sank before us. The boats parted company, two were lost that night. After six days a Dutchman picked mine up. Three men and I only were alive in it. We got at last to London. The Company had my record, and after six months it gave me another ship, the *Falcon*. I sailed her a year, then, passing Cape Saint Vincent, there shot out against us two Moorish pirates. We fought them a day, they grappled and boarded, we were afire. The officers and crew were slain or taken. I gathered my strength and burst from those that swarmed upon me and leaped into the sea. The murk saved me — the land was not so far — I swam and was carried and a plank came by, and at dawn I was ashore. — I'll not weary you with the long road for a penniless man to London. I got there and to India House and made my report, and old Hollingsbury said, as dry as Sahara sand, 'Your luck's not so good as it used to be, Captain Bartram.' I knew what that meant. It meant 'Nothing must happen to the next ship, if so be you want to continue with the East India Company.' But they gave me the *Good Adventure,* and inside three months she was driven in a gale and staved to pieces on the Irish coast."

He got up and walked the cabin twice and returned. "They who follow the sea know certain things. To be called a fortunate captain is summer and the fruits thereof. To be named an unfortunate captain is winter and the blast that makes you shrink. The East India Company departed from me. I had saved a little, but it wasna much. I had a hard year, David, a hard year.

"And then Murchieson and Murchieson gave me the *Rose of Lorn,* trading between Liverpool and Boston. And in a year, off Newfoundland, in a fog, the *Lydia,* a barquentine, ran us down. When I got to London this time I went to a woman teller of fates that I had heard of. She said that I had entered a belt of trouble that had been waiting for me, just as a ship might enter the doldrums or the Arctic seas. A star was adverse to me and a number was my foe. Why? — Well, as to that, the true I Myself had not been born in precisely the year 1720, as I had mistakenly thought. The true I Myself was old enough to have earned a world of good and ill. — And how wide did she think was the belt? — But that she could not tell though she held that it was thinning. I could not see that, David, when, after long, long waiting, I got just a poor brig, the *Hannah Lisle,* owned by the Alleynes and plying to Rotterdam. It was that or starve — and she burned at the wharf at Rotterdam, the boat next her carrying powder and a spark reaching it, none knew how. And what did it count that I did not set that fire, nor had the eye of God to foresee such a thing? I was done for, David, done for! — Did you hear no sound in all those years of my matters? "

" I was sent to school," I said. " I lived with my mother's brother in Edinburgh, and he was a bookman and a dreamer. And then my own life began to turmoil."

" Well, so it was," he said. " I had been a proud man, but that was over. I found a garret and grew gaunt as a wolf there, — as gaunt as you, David, when you came aboard. I knew owners and captains and seamen enough, and many I knew would have given me a crust or a crown piece, but I did not choose, as I did not choose to take my wage when my ship was gone.

What I had saved from my good years, having been always a free spender, was all departed. And I did not believe, David, that I would ever sail a ship again."

He was silent, then poured wine with a steady hand and pushed the bottle to me. "Then there came up my garret stair John Archibald that had been mate upon the *Falcon* and prisoner on the Barbary Coast whence in six months he got away in a Spanish galleon that carried him to Cuba, and from Cuba, by hook and crook, he got to Jamaica. He told me all about it. Then came into Kingston harbor the *Swan,* a Royal African Company ship, Captain Martin, wanting a mate. Archibald appealed to Martin and got the berth. Two years afterwards Martin retired. Archibald, who's a queer chield, had kinsfolk above him in station, with stock in the Company. He was given the *Swan* — is her captain still — I saw him last trip at Daga. Well, David, to get back to my garret! Once I had done him a good turn, and now he had come up with me again, and he had not forgotten the bairn Gratitude. He wanted me to go with him to see certain gentlemen. So I went, David, having no chance in the world of an East Indiaman which is what I would have much preferred. But beggars may not be choosers! And many are willing to serve the Royal African Company. — Anyhow, I went with Archibald. And like that, David, the luck turned! I came out of the belt of darkness that woman talked about! They took to me."

Color and vigor increased in my cousin's face. "They saw and said that those lost ships were not lost through me. They were willing to try me. They talked of the *Janet* that was building, that was nearly ready for the sea." Bartram's voice rose almost to a shout. "David Scott, in three months I trod her poop deck and took her down to the blue water. And she's seven years old, the *Janet,* and no man quarrels more with William Bartram. If a star was my antagonist, he has taken his war elsewhere!" Again he rose from his chair and walked the cabin, then stopped before the window and looked forth upon a dark blue night powdered with those orbs or beings or whatever they are. When he spoke his voice had sunken and was not addressed to me. "He is no longer in the sky; he is dead or obscured, banished as I was banished! But as for the *Janet,* she and I are one!"

He turned toward me. "Since the days of Elizabeth this trade's been going on. Tudors and Stuarts and the Hanover Family have all been able to put up with it! Parliaments no less — the Royal African Company has its parliamentary grants. And all the pillars of the world, the big pillars and the little pillars. If you could see now a list of the Company supporters! It's imposing, man, imposing!"

"I know the world is with the trade," I said.

"Well, the world maun live!" he answered, with a kind of fierceness. "It's all inwound — it's all so inwound. Things are built upon it to an extent you'd hardly believe. In all lands and all ranks. You ask the first merchant or lawyer, aye, or teacher or parson you meet! Planters, of course — but everybody beside planters. Fairly anybody."

"Custom and Gain."

"Aye, precisely. Custom and Gain. They're Rulers. As for me, I'm a plain sea captain, with my bread and salt to earn. I don't set up to be wiser or more moral than quarter-deck and forecastle of Society and they that own my ship!"

I said, "Yet you would scorn, for gain, to become a pirate."

He answered with violence. "You're daft! It's not the least the same!"

And I was so muddled in those years that I did not know if it was. The comparison would never have come into my mind but for Culloden and thereafter. And Culloden and thereafter were already fading away. I said dully, "I have been a slave, overboard in the rough sea, while the ship you call Society sailed by."

He answered, "You were a white political, sold into limited servitude. Africans are black barbarians, and all the reasoners will tell you that in the end if not just at the beginning, it's a happy exchange to the West Indies, let alone Virginia, New York and New England!"

He came back to the table, and suddenly he was entirely the reasonable and weighty person he had appeared in our earlier intercourse. " I would ask you, David, did you not see a good deal of happiness among them in Virginia? "

I saw Pickaninny dancing, and heard Old Joe fiddling and the negro women laughing, and the children squealing and tumbling about, and I thought of the suave self-importance of Colonel Amory's house servants, and of real contentment in good work in field and shop, and of religious ecstasies that I had witnessed. Even at Old Mill quarter that was the black books' quarter, I could remember jollity.

" Yes," I said. " I have seen what you may call happiness. But I never saw or heard of a black man or woman who had not been enslaved and brought from Africa against their will. They or their parents or grandparents. And if I have seen what looked like contentment, I have seen misery too. Always against their will and like animals, and still they are bought and sold and worked like animals. But they are men and women."

He poured wine and put it at my hand. And yet I know that he did not then know that this way lay one of my cities of destruction. I pushed it aside, and then I took it back and drank. And straightway the false, smirking lights began to play.

" You see, it's not the life I would have

chosen," said my cousin. "I don't say that I greatly like my errands, for I don't, but I do them. And I would have you observe, David, that my work begins and ends with the handling of my ship and cargo. The Negroes are already enslaved and in barracoons up and down the coast. It's the factors that collect and deliver them. The captains but see that they're brought as safely as may be across the water. And look you, if I were not sailing the *Janet,* another would be — and likely a rougher man, David, likely a rougher man! For look you another thing, David. D' ye know what I am called at Whidah and at Daga and Calabar and Bonny? 'Holy Bartram!' And that because the crew that sails with me and the blacks I carry are *not* ill-treated. Just as far as my power goes they are well treated, and that's more, man, I grant, than can be said for all slave ships and captains."

"I'm thinking," I said, "that I must go this voyage because I am here upon the ship. But at your return port I will leave you, thanking you for great kindness and hoping some day to repay it."

"You will do about leaving the *Janet* as you please," he answered. "As for thanks and payment, I'm not asking them, David. But I would not swear I was going until I had looked things over a bit. You're not very safe on land, and the sea gets a grip. If you took another vessel you'd have to give some account of yourself and to ship before the mast. Here you could render me a deal of help as my cousin and maybe clerk at times, with the sea to live with and my collection of books if you like them. McNaughton's got his points beside being a good officer, and our surgeon, Colley, that you haven't seen yet, for he has a touch of fever, is a man of parts. The old Guineaman isn't so bad, you know."

He ended quietly — asked if I would have more wine — said it was a braw night and that it might be six weeks and more ere we sighted the coast, and took up his cap to go outside.

CHAPTER X

THE sun rained gold, the sea ran blue, the wind in the rigging sang the very oldest song. I moved about the ship. The covers of the hatches were raised. I saw with a kind of shock that the openings beneath were grated. So were other apertures about the ship. I went to one of the hatches and looked down, but the strong light above showed little save darkness. I asked a man how much room would they have down there between floor and roof. "Six feet clear," he answered. "But the platforms divide it, you know, so each tier has almost three feet. The *Janet's* roomy compared to most. Roomiest Guineaman I know!"

"How many Africans does she carry?"

"Five hundred."

I stared at the darkness below the grating. The seaman — it was Jack Dannet — went on swabbing the deck beside me. I said, "Do you like bringing slaves from Africa?"

"I'm not paid to like it," he answered. "At first I didn't like it, I remember. But I got used to it. A man gets used to anything."

I thought, "There's always a little of him that creeps away."

Dannet, washing the deck, continued, "I've been in ships that I didn't like — any more than hell! Free English sailors get banged about in Guineamen as if they had been born without a rag on them, up the Oil River! But the *Janet's* got a reputation of being a regular old mother."

"But the Negroes — how do you feel about them?"

"Oh, them! I don't feel about them at all. Used to, maybe, just at first, but it don't last."

His continued swabbing put distance between us. The second mate, Pomeroy, came by. "Looking at our accommodations, Mr. Scott?"

"They're scant for five hundred," I said. "They're shallow for five hundred or for fifty or for five or for one."

"Why, there you're mistaken," he replied. "The ship has a name for commodiousness. At Whidah and Calabar and elsewhere you'll see them that I do think are scant."

He was a short, black-haired, bull-necked man with a fishy and prying eye. I liked Bartram and I liked McNaughton but I did not like Pomeroy. He was curious about me and I let him be curious. "Jamaica and Barbadoes are our usual ports. But we're just from Bristol where we've been refitting, and the captain had a fancy for anchoring by Norfolk. It's pleasant that we hit in with your plans, sir! I believe you have been on a visit to a relative who's a Virginia planter?"

That was Bartram's story! I laughed, I doubled up with laughter, but inwardly. "Just so,"

I said. " I've been visiting, Mr. Pomeroy. It's a good thing to see the world and all that's in it."

" That's a sailor's opinion, sir," he answered. " And you'll doubtless find things to interest you in Africa and the West Indies."

He went on about his business, and David Scott, being tired of standing and peering down through the gratings into the darkness of the empty slave deck, moved aft and found a place where he could sit and think, or not think but only stare at the sea that was growing more blue.

We are foreigners. I made the remark to myself that life was strange, and many other men have made, are making, and will make the like comment. For me, I was indolent and befogged and held in a Sargasso Sea, like to that physical one somewhere in this ocean. I said to myself that doubtless it would be difficult to leave the *Janet* in Africa, but at the first English island I would surely do so. And then came along Geordie with the morning dram for officer and passenger, and he seemed to regard me as both.

I drank. The sea sparkled, the wind sang. I began to love the ship. And was it so bad, this traffic that I had never particularly thought of and certainly never questioned before I quitted Scotland — *on a visit to a Virginia kinsman?* That ill gipsy Mirth, that I gave house room to, screeched at that. But as the rum worked the wry-mouthed started aside, and there came in General Benevolence, beaming on the slave ship and Whidah and Calabar and Daga and Camaroons and the other heathenish names. Then I grew judicial and thought I must wait to judge — *wait till I got used to it.* And I never saw the imp Self-Interest sitting on my shoulder, patting my head, his heel on my heart.

The dram was not so deep but that in an hour Daniel Askew — Eboe Sam — Old Mill quarter — returned upon me. But at dinner time there would be another.

The good breeze held and drove the full-sailed ship joyously. It was not hot or cold, but sunny and gay. And David Scott had no shackles upon him, nor had to go into the tobacco field. He began to think of his ambitions, and of how from, say, Jamaica, he might get to Holland, and thence into France where were Jacobite Scots not a few. Some kind of career — in a learned profession if he could manage that. He didn't want the army; not the Scots Company in the French army, not any army. He did not like the life of an idle soldier, nor the life of a soldier in action. He liked a book life and a life out with nature. He had, after all, that much good out of Virginia. Memories of the morn and the night, the sun and the air. Earth, water, air and fire, color, sound and the trees.

Scotland — Virginia; Virginia — Scotland. The Hebrides brig — the *King William* — the

Janet — Christian Todd's little boat and his flute coming down the river! And what would one do in France without money? Money, money, money, money. Rider without steed; sails without wind!

A slender, dark man, very dark, with blue eyes, approached me. I saw that this would be the surgeon, Colley, whom they had said at breakfast would be out to-day. He came up. "It's the Captain's kinsman, Mr. Scott, I believe?"

"The same," I answered. "Sit down, won't you? I am glad to see you better."

He took his seat beside me. "I got a nasty fever at Daga going in a boat up the river after sunset. I gave myself all the bark in the medicine locker, but it hung on. Up one day and down the next. But I've been getting better for a fortnight and I'll soon be all right. I feel finely to-day. — How did you like Virginia?"

"Why, it's got its good and its bad."

"Mixed feelings?" he said. "That's me. I regard most places with mixed feelings."

"The *Janet?*" I asked, then thought, "If I say things like that forever, I shall be disloyal to William Bartram."

He clasped his knee with long, bony, well-shaped hands — surgeons' hands with power and knowledge in them, and lifted those intense blue eyes of his to the topgallants. "I went in

debt to get through Surgeons' Hall. When I
was through, I could not get out of debt. Every
other man I saw seemed to be a surgeon running to a case! But I had none, or so few that
they could not get me out of debt. They seemed
all to be in debt themselves. Bread and cheese,
even, grew to be a problem. At length every
creditor was threatening. So at last I said, 'I
will go on a ship, for ships at least seem to be
always wanting surgeons.' So I answered ad-
vertisements of East Indiamen and others, but
always when I got there each berth had just
been filled. I was hungry and not far from
ragged. And there was one creditor who made
himself detestable. So I saw one morning that
the Guineaman, *Janet*, wanted a surgeon. Here
I am. — The pay's not bad, and your cousin's a
strong man and a good captain. I would drown
myself from most Guineamen I know, but I've
stayed on this. Three years. I've even paid the
worst of the damned creditors and mean to pay
them all."

"Shall you spend your life on a slaver?"

"No! No, indeed. Just two or three more
years till I get clear. The pay's higher than
elsewhere if you can stand the game."

"Stand the game?"

"Africa's a hot country," he said, "with
strange, old diseases. There's all the chances of
the sea — and there's Africa."

"I never gave all this a thought till lately,"

I said. "There are worlds within worlds like Chinese boxes. I suppose it *is* a sickly trade for all concerned."

"Grain Coast, Gold Coast, or Slave Coast; it is only a question of degrees. If you're merchant for inanimates — ivory, beeswax, palm oil, dyewoods, Malaguetta pepper or what not — still there's sickness. Of course it's worse in the *Janet's* trade."

"Yes, of course."

I looked toward the forecastle. "Yet he seems to have a healthy crew."

"These are the seasoned and the new hands. We lost fifteen men voyage before last."

"And how many black men?"

"Eighty," he answered. "There was a kind of pestilence. But all that's unusual. He's got an extraordinary record for a clean ship and little trouble."

"'Holy Bartram,'" I said, and then repented, for he had pulled me out of the river and I was going along with him. Colley's bright blue eyes flashed my way. "He's told you that? He's proud of it; he keeps it like a pot of balm on the shelf of his conscience."

I broke into laughter. "Then we've all got a conscience! You, too?"

"I've got a surgeon's conscience. I do my best."

I said, "I was not visiting a Virginia planter. I was a Stuart man at Culloden and was sold into slavery. I've got a personal, not a hearsay, knowledge of what it is to be bound. How much balm for my conscience should I have to have if I persisted upon this ship? At the moment, of course, I have a pot upon my shelf. I did not know what was the *Janet* when I came aboard, and I cannot go knock down the man at the wheel and alter her course."

He turned with vivacity. " I knew Mc-Naughton was holding something back! So you've had a history too! Aren't there a lot of them? And you're to be considered as just a bird of passage? I understood that you were to have Philip Smith's place. McNaughton said that the Captain had taken a personal liking to you and that as he's daft on family anyway, your fortune might be considered to be made!"

I laughed again. " What fortune?"

His blue eyes half closed. " Oh, all things are relative! But of course if you've got great ambitions ——"

" I do not know how great they are," I answered. " But greater than this. I'll go the first port I can."

" That won't be an African port," he said.

I reminded him of the ships that traded only for ivory and palm oil and gum copal and so forth. I might transship to one of them.

" It isn't," he answered, " the easiest thing in the world to do that! They aren't always in the same river mouth with us, nor are their times our times. From Sierra Leone to Camaroons is a long, long way, Mr. Scott. And you've got to go in parties in Africa. It's not a place for single souls to be trotting around! You'll have to wait, I'm thinking, for Jamaica. And maybe you'll change your mind in Jamaica. Unless you have influence with the Governor, or with some great sugar planter who buys what the Royal African Company has to sell."

I sat in silence, looking at the blue sea. Colley yawned and stretched his thin limbs. "Africa gets into the blood and bone. It's the climate and the sea and, it sometimes seems to me, an old, strange rhyme and routine. At first there's a kind of horror in the life, but at last Use comes in — though when you think of it there's a kind of horror in Use herself. But you grow indifferent. If there's any tremendous wrong in enslaving black barbarians it gets to be as invisible between Whidah or Calabar and Kingston or Bridgetown or Charleston as it is everywhere else in the world."

Colonel Amory rose before me and how invisible it had been to him and his easy and amiable like. How invisible it was to Judith Amory. How invisible it was to Scotland, whose merchants and wandering sons were everywhere. How invisible to England, with her ships upon the seas and her "royal" companies.

Something out of old school reading entered with violence into my mind. *The dyer's hand subdued to that it works in.* I left my seat and moving to the rail stared at sky and sea, then returned. "A little more or a little less of misery — good ships and bad ships — I'm not talking about that! It's the whole damned business, root and branch, white and black alike, that I'm meaning. Men enslaved and men enslaving everywhere, and they're twin brothers in wretchedness!"

He opened those intense blue eyes. "Oh," he said, "if you're a Quaker ——"

But I was nothing like so complete a man. I was an unhappy person with an imp upon my shoulder that was going to strangle me.

CHAPTER XI

I LIKED Colley, McNaughton and William Bartram. I did not like Pomeroy. I liked Geordie and the mulatto cook, Tom and his quadroon helper Don, which was short for Adonis. These two were free men, manumitted on his death bed by the planter their owner. They made a deal of it, carried it written as it were about them. Yet were they bound to the *Janet,* year after year, for one told me that they rarely went ashore in any port. I did not like Davis the boatswain. I liked Llewellyn the carpenter. Of the seamen whose names were quickly learned, I liked certain ones and certain ones I did not like and to others I was indifferent. There were no saints among them, but on the other hand few forthright scoundrels.

I knew now that that numerousness of her seamen which had struck me at the first belonged to her as slaver. She must have enough to allow for sickness and death, and enough to handle and cow those five hundred that would be brought aboard. I learned that many seamen signed for Slave Coast ships when they were muddled with drink or otherwise deceived. Llewellyn the carpenter told me this. "Wherever there's a sail and a mast and a hull, there's danger. Seamen know all that. Britain's

got her ships of war, and the Newfoundland
trade and the North American trade and the
regular West Indian and Bermudas trade, and
the East Indian trade and the Grain Coast and
Ivory Coast and Gold Coast trade and the Slave
Coast trade. Seamen don't wait to get old to die
— not on any ship! But seamen die quicker and
in more ways in the slave trade than in any going. And if they don't die outright, they move
ashore at last with some bad disease. And so
they die anyhow. I *have* seen old ones sitting
watching the sea that were on a slave ship in
their youth and manhood, but they aren't many.
No, they're few!"

But Llewellyn, too, said that the *Janet* was a
good ship. No man — no captain nor anybody
else — could have helped that sickness voyage
before last. "Yes, fifteen seamen — God rest
them!"

It was the first time I had heard that word
aboard. "Do you believe in God?"

"Oh, aye!" he answered. "Most carpenters
do."

"You lost eighty Africans."

"Aye," he said. "God rest them too!"

Days and days went by like beads on a string,
easily slipping beads.

As I had read Gervase Morrison's books on
the *King William,* so now I read my cousin
Bartram's. He had as many as fifty, the most
of them the Greeks and Romans done into Eng-

lish. But there were also modern books, poets
and philosophies and histories, and full in the
middle of his shelf a Bible. It had his name
written in it and the fact that it had been given
him by his mother, on his tenth birthday.

In boyhood I had read every book that came
my way and would go far out of my way to get
one of which I had heard. Then another life
rushed upon me and spoiled the old life. And
then I came to Virginia. One didn't read at Old
Mill quarter nor at Daniel Askew's. But now
the hunger returned and I read and read. — And
do not think I do not know that reading is an
opiate!

I read Herodotus, Tacitus and Livy, and I
read Homer in George Chapman's version. It
was so good a place to read — the *Janet* going,
not coming from Africa! Very clean she was,
with the salt air, warm not cold, searching all
her empty spaces. Cabin and poop deck were
free to me, and I had also the diminutive room
that had been Philip Smith's. I wondered sometimes about this man, and why he left the *Janet*
at Philadelphia where apparently, once or
oftener, she had touched. I had space and sea
quiet, with all the sounds of good weather. I
read and I read, and my hand went out for the
dram that Geordie brought. Or Colley, his
fever now only a memory, came and talked, his
intense blue eyes aiding. Or in the cabin after
the sudden dusk, when the yellow lanterns were

lighted, William Bartram talked. We talked in the cabin there about many things, but not about the slave trade. Early in the passage he had set his great foot upon that topic. "It's my business to sail this ship and see her laden and deliver her cargo as undiminished as may be. I'm no thinking of resigning. I loved the *Margaret* that I had so long, but she's dead and now I have married the *Janet*. And you'll please leave your reasoning and objecting alone! If I'm no for listening, I'm no for listening. And you'll kindly, David, do no preaching nor you-know-what-kind-of questioning among the officers and crew. It's not healthy for them nor any. I'll be obliged if you will take it that those are Captain's orders. I'll have no mutinies, David, even from one man."

He was captain of the *Janet*. I recognized that. "I'll make no trouble," I said, and saw not, indeed, how I could make it. And I spoke to my conscience that was not in robust health. "*It's but this voyage; we'll make a change when we come to Christian lands. We'll go ashore and stay ashore.*"

"And I'm noticing, David," he said, "that there's a lure for you in the wine and the dram. You're too Scots not to know that a hard-drinking Scot throws his soul away. I'd advise you to put the ship about while there's time."

"Have you seen it affect me, sir?"

"Why," he said, "not precisely 'affect.' But

you've a way of setting it to solve problems and I never heard of a one that it solved!"

I answered with moodiness. " It may not resolve but it makes one forget."

" It's better not to wish to forget. Face your life! At any rate don't make a dram your angel!"

He spoke with vigor, and Colley told me afterwards that he had a strong feeling upon the subject.

" He'll take wine after supper, but if it wasn't that there *would* be mutinies, I don't believe that he'd have a drop of rum or brandy in the spirit room! Drunkenness anywhere, land or sea, is to him the king viper. He's capable, if he didn't have the *Janet,* of going on a crusade to deprive the beast of his head. Sometimes he's funny ——"

David Scott thought, " Because the presence of some viper is on his soul. He's striking at it over yonder, when it's by his ankle, under the log."

But I ceased, in cabin, to question the backgrounds of trade, and when I spoke with Jack Dannet and his like I did not again ask, " How do you like it?" or "What do you think of it yourself?" Colley and I sometimes disputed, off to ourselves, with the wind singing and the blue sea sheering away. But one day he said, "You're here and I am here — on the *Janet.* Unless we are prepared to jump into the sea

let's stop the argument! You're just easing your
soul with it, anyhow."

And I saw that I was, and that it was taking
the place of action. Then I said to myself "Hy-
pocrisy!" and ceased to assert that there should
be no slave ships nor slavery. When I left this
ship then I might begin once more.

Moreover, after that talk with William Bartram, I had collared Geordie. "Geordie, a dram
in the morning and a dram at night, but no dram
in between!" and thought that I had done well
and killed the snake. I looked at Geordie severely, and he was a queer imp. He said now,
"Forgive me my sins, sir, and I'll try to do better!" and so elfish was he with light-gray eyes
and flaxen locks and slim as a reed in a bog, that
it passed, as did all his comments, for elfishness
and not impudence. So I drank less, though I
lusted for the foregone cups.

When I had been a week upon the *Janet* my
kinsman tried me out with a blank book and a
pen and a paper of figures and other matters.
Now it chanced that I had done some clerkly
work for that uncle with whom for a time I had
lived, and that he was particular and taught me
thoroughly. I could have clerked in Virginia
as well as Gervase Morrison, but I was bought
for a tobacco hand and woodcutter. But now
Bartram was pleased. "You're a better man
than was Philip Smith! I see that you may be
very helpful to me, David, if you'll leave strong

drink alone. There's nothing like kindred if everything else is provided."

After that I had an hour or two of work each day. He was upon — in the great blank book — a transcript for his owners of all the voyages of the *Janet*. In a month I became deeply learned in her fortunes and her trade. I had a kind of gift for this kind of thing. I could do it well and with the mind. I saw the pictures of all I was putting down, but I began to see them coolly. Even then, even so soon, feeling was dulling, Self-Interest, the promising devil, sitting fast upon my shoulder!

The *Janet* ran on, piled with canvas, through fair weather. A week, two, three, four, five. Sometimes at night, before I fell asleep, there filed before my eyes James River and Amory Hall and Old Mill quarter and Daniel Askew's and tempest-tossed forest wet as the sea and Christian Todd's boat under a sycamore. Going off, I heard now his flute and now a Scots pipe screaming a pibroch in a glen. I slid into dreams, some good and some bad. Once I dreamed that I lay in Sandy Scott's barn, and it was afire, and Helen Scott brought me a great book, and I said, "Now this will show me the way out for it is the book of Holiness." And I clasped it, but it turned into Eboe Sam, and we wrestled and tried each to throttle the other, and a great voice like thunder cried "The soldiers are coming!" And the fire that was laying hold

of the straw and the rafters began most awfully
to laugh. I woke and lay trembling, bathed with
sweat. There dawned a morning. I went on
deck. Pomeroy, leaning against the rail, turned
his bull head and spoke. "Africa, Mr.
Scott——" I followed his nod and saw the
mountains of Sierra Leone.

We coasted south by east, turned the great
hump at Cape Palmas and coasted east. There
were days and days of this, so huge is Africa.
We passed the grain, the ivory, the gold lands.
They all dealt in man-gold likewise; slaves
might be acquired in any bight or river mouth.
But the Slave Coast proper was our end, where
rose by the ocean the most factories or forts or
castles, French, Portuguese, Dutch and English.
Daga was one of ours, built seventy years before.
I knew much about it now from the great book
and Colley and McNaughton.

There came a day. The sea was strongly blue
and flowed in long waves. We had been standing in to land, were close now, could see the
fringing cocoanut palms and the low land behind and then hills, blue and emerald. Turning
a white prong of shore, we sailed into a deep and
narrow bay where emptied a sizable river.

"Daga Bay," quoth McNaughton at my
shoulder. "Yon is Daga."

The sea ran into surf against a shore of dazzling
sand. Drawn up on this lay a row of sharp-
prowed, narrow boats. The burning sand

stretched on and was met by palm trees. I, who had never seen a palm tree, knew them well enough. Stretched on and met palm trees and some low, green growth, hard and staring in the sun, and a big square of whitened masonry, big and low, with gateway and embrasures and guns in these, and under its shadow a huddle of huts. Only there was no material shadow just now. The sun stood at noon and all was blindingly light. Behind the walls rose a kind of keep, and from this floated the British flag.

And David Scott, an escaping prisoner, was back in Edinburgh on a wild night, a witches' night. There, there, I had seen Daga that lay now in my path!

CHAPTER XII

LACE was the factor at Daga, a corpulent man with a red face and a watery eye, and he had for assistant Berry, who looked for all the world like whom but Williams at Amory Hall? Under these were three clerks or handy men — Andrews, Hyde and Graves. The surgeon was Markham, a man of fifty and sour as a green grape. He was kept at Daga years and years, only, I think, because he was fearless. There are no more fearless men in this trade than in any other, and they are needed and are at a premium when found. Baker was the storekeeper, and he had Brown for helper. There were other white men at Daga, filling small offices of kinds. And there were four or five who filled no office, hangers-on, men with some claim on some one, or with no claim; sea-drift, withering and growing sapless of all that man might be. And there was Rathbone Lace, the factor's brother, a man of about my age.

Daga fort carried fifteen guns, but they were of old times and nowadays never used. But they could be used; shot was piled beside them, and Daga had an ammunition chamber, powder and muskets and cutlasses. Within the four walls a vast sunbaked square of court provided room for half a dozen buildings of kinds and yet left space for a caravan market or what not. And in the thick walls were hollowed passages and chambers enough — places of storage with heavy doors and infrequent, grated loophole windows. On opposite sides of the court stairs of stone led to the top of the wall that was wide enough for a coach and four, if ever there had been such a thing in Africa. From the wall, ocean, sand, wilderness — wilderness, ocean, sand, except when one looked almost immediately beneath, being then on the northern face. Here showed a baked, brown palaver ground and a haphazard and pell-mell assemblage of cane and plaster huts thatched with palm and sheltering the multitude of Daga's black retainers. Runners, hunters, boatmen, porters and so on forever. Women too.

On the eastern face also an interruption occurred, for here rose a sudden, small hill with what looked like a cart road to the top where, a hundred feet above the world, stood the fair-sized, broadly verandahed house of the factor with about it its own huts for servitors. With him dwelled his brother and he gave house room to two of the clerks. The cart track led directly from a postern door in the wall — nothing was more than a pistol shot from anything else. Markham the surgeon had likewise a house on this hillock, a small house under heavy and magnificent trees, where he dwelled solitary, a curious, bitter, hardened man. The remainder of the twenty or so white men at Daga lived in the fort.

This "castle", this African village, this wilderness, this white and sun-charged sand, this dark blue ocean! There was surf, but a barrier reef taking the most of it left only slight foam and low thunder for the actual shore. In the deep water beyond the surf rode the *Janet* and two smaller ships, the *Sherwood Oak* and the *Fancy* — Liverpool and Lancaster. It was now November and the climate at its best.

The *Janet* proposed to swing at anchor before Daga for no more than a couple of weeks. This was an orderly, big station that knew about when to expect the ships that used it, and that gathered and stored beforehand the cargos. Where such establishments lacked, a ship, if conditions were adverse, might hang offshore or in some river mouth while weeks slipped into months before the full tale of slaves was secured. But the proper factory made proper provision — never, in short, was without stock. Here were three ships, but the full crop was nearly gathered.

"Where is the barracoon?" I asked Andrews the clerk, who was showing me around. We were on the wall looking down into the square.

"Oh," he said and waved a hand, "there's room enough in this place! We keep them in the old stone rooms — dungeons, you know."

"Do they stay there day and night?"

"From five in the afternoon to sunrise,"
he said listlessly. "They've just been ken-
nelled." The sun hung low, a red ball. He
spoke in a weary, singsong voice. "The *Sherwood Oak* and the *Fancy* finished their lading
yesterday. There aren't but three hundred for
you here now. But we've boats up the river.
The rest will be down in time. This is your first
voyage and you're kin of Captain Bartram?"

"Yes," I said, and I looked at the sun, and I
saw the Negroes in the fields of Virginia looking
at the same red and sinking sun, straightening
themselves from their toil, turning their faces to
the cabins. And I heard with the inner hearing
Old Hannibal singing loudly:

> "When hab I done with de trouble ob de world?
> Ooo-h! trouble ob de world!
> My sins so heavy I can't get along.
> Trouble ob de world!"

I stared at the *Sherwood Oak* and the *Fancy*
and a kind of terror came upon me, and yet I
did nothing that I should have done.

Bartram and I were spending the night ashore
under the factor's roof. I might indeed spend
as many nights as I pleased, being lavishly invited to do so. But Bartram never, they said,
gave but the one and that grudgingly. The star
his foe might have traveled elsewhere in the
infinite room to journey, taking with him that
unlucky number, whatever it might be. He

might have come for all time out of the belt of
darkness. On the whole he thought he had.
But something nested still in his mind, for you
could not separate him from the *Janet* — not,
they said, until, every two years or so, she rested
in Bristol dock when he would go into the country for a while. But at Daga or Kingston or any
port a day at a time or a night at a time was all
he could be got to give. He trusted McNaughton whom he always left in charge, but when
pressed to stay he answered that Bartram's place
was with his ship and walked somewhat rapidly
to the boat that ever was held waiting for
him.

But first night at Daga was a custom that it
was politic to maintain, seeing that factors must
be kept friendly or captains of ships might meet
a thousand petty annoyances, to say nothing of
second or third choice in goods. So Bartram,
Colley and I had come ashore, leaving Mc-
Naughton and Pomeroy with the *Janet*. Bartram was smoking and drinking good wine and
conversing with the factor on the latter's verandah. Colley had been claimed by Markham.
Andrews the clerk would show me, the only
stranger, the sights of Daga.

The sun was going down. Somewhere a thin,
small drum began to beat, flat and fast and insistent and desperately unchanging, like the
drumming of a giant insect. "Tom-tom," said
Andrews. "The palaver ground's yonder. A

lot of black traders are in from up river and they're feasting. There goes their bonfire."

We came down from the wall and crossing the court went by the long storehouse and the ammunition house and the house where the white men slept, and through the dark, high, echoing passage and out at the castle gate. And here stretched the white sand and the ocean, endless under the red west. The west never stopped it; it came around again to the east. It was dusk, the air heavy and warm for all that sea before it, and the drums beat, beat, beat. — I have heard them so often; I have heard them too often!

Andrews was speaking, "I wish I were in Boston where I was born!"

"Boston in England?"

"New England. That's the country for me!"

I regarded his long, lank frame and his thin and sickly face. Everything about him languished. "Why do you stay in Africa?"

He answered with a weak and boyish violence. "Because I can't help myself! I got into trouble with the law — it wasn't so much my fault, I can tell you, as 'twas that of others! — but I can't go home. My father's part owner of the *Indian Maid* that trades here, so here I was shipped! New England ships come, and I can't go back in them. Back home. I'm homesick, I tell you. I'll die presently. If there's a melancholy hell it's Africa!"

"It's the trade you're not liking?"

He took me up dully. "The trade? No, it's not the trade I'm objecting to. But at home now the snow's beginning to fall, so white and pretty, and directly they'll be thinking of sleighing and Christmas."

We were walking now over the hard sand to the road that led to the factor's house. "Does every one here hate Africa?"

"Oh, no!" he answered. "The factor has been at Daga twenty years. He likes it well enough. He's got his comforts around him — he doesn't miss his family." He said the last in a curious tone, and I afterwards found it to mean the two Mandingo women and the children that looked now like them and now like Samuel Lace. "As for Mr. Markham the surgeon, he's an old hand too. He'd find verjuice wherever he went, so what does the place matter? And to listen to some of the others you'd think it the finest place! Of course you can have a good deal to drink and all the women you please. Only I don't like whisky, and for the other ——" he made a vague gesture of dismissal. "There's a farm out Concord way that I see forever."

By this we were even with those native huts and that irregular trodden ground of gathering where smoked and reddened and flared the bonfire and where moved and sat and kept up a great laughter and noise a number of dark people. We saw between stems of cocoanuts and other trees whose names I did not then know. "Let us stop for a moment and watch."

He asked wearily, "Do you find it interesting? That's long ago over for me, if it ever began." But he stood still and I with him under the heavy cocoanut fronds and the clusters of nuts the size of men's heads. A voice behind us spoke. "Listen to old Osuma holding forth! He's boasting now about how the King received him in Dahomey."

Andrews said, "This is Mr. Scott, Mr. Rathbone, who's kin to Captain Bartram and came in the *Janet.*"

"Glad to know you, Mr. Scott! I'll go along with you up to the house. I've been on the *Fancy* and so missed your landing. So 'Holy Bartram's' well and fortunate still?"

"Do you call him that here too?"

"Oh, yes! Behind his back. But no offense, Mr. Scott! He likes it when he hears of it. And coming in, just now, I admired the *Janet,* too, for the fiftieth time. The others in harbor can't touch her!"

There was still light in the sky, and also the back flare from the bonfire. I could make him out; rather tall, with a short beard and red cheeks, with a wide, straw hat and white clothes. His voice had oil in it, but also iron. Oiled iron. Between Bartram and Colley, I knew well enough the white inhabitants of Daga. So now I said, "Mr. Rathbone Lace?"

"The same," he answered. "Have you had enough of this? But if you will wait longer, I am at your service."

"They are traders who have brought in slaves?"

"A hundred yesterday. Small traders — Osuma and Banno and their men — and they'll feast and dance here till late. I see it's your first voyage. From Kingston?"

"No. I am a Scot, but I have come from Virginia."

"Ah, Virginia! I have been in Baltimore and New York. That's the one thing we miss in Daga, not seeing the world."

We went up the hill. It was low, rising from a wooded plain that stretched far inland. But there were mountains and great ones in Africa. I had noted them from the sea. We went up the hill in the hot dusk, the ocean faintly booming against the reef and the drums sounding behind us. I asked my question that was growing wearisome, even to myself. "Do you like your trade?" And Rathbone Lace's was the first full assent.

The others had misliked and inveighed and cursed though they stayed, or had found reasons for refusing to consider if they liked it or did not like it, or had seemed unthinking, or indifferent, or apathetic, or too dull to have tastes. But Rathbone Lace said, "Why, it gets hold of you! Yes, I like it." I was to come to know not a few who felt as he did, but he was the first. To like it for itself and in itself. To like black power as black power!

We went up the low hill. Lights were shining out of the factor's house. Andrews now left us, murmuring something about some errand and taking a side path with a small, lighted house at its end. We went on a few steps. Something came hurriedly from the bush and would have flitted across the way and been gone, but "Lalla!" he shouted and made after and seized and brought her back upon the white road that yet gleamed under a sky yet lighted. She twisted this way and that in his hands, then stood, a slight, dark-skinned girl, dressed in a scanty white robe with chains of beads about her neck. He spoke to her gibingly in a tongue I did not understand, and she answered thrillingly, with passion and complaining. He grew angry and shook her as he might have shaken a child or a dog; only needed a free hand perhaps to have struck her. She broke into a passion of speech, confused, hurried, and charged with some kind of woe, then putting forth a sudden, unexpected strength, dragged herself free, turned, and with a cry was gone into the thick darkness and matted growth. He thundered after her some threat, but there only came another cry and then silence.

He cursed, then laughed. "The devil! I'll pay her out!"

"What is the matter with her?"

"She's Fullah; that is, she's part Arab. Old Banno brought in yesterday five or six Fullah men whom he got from the King of Dahomey who had them as a gift from some Senegal chief. She's heard of it, and has taken a notion that among them is a member of her family."

Her cry still echoed in my ears. "Couldn't you release him to her?"

He stared, then burst into laughter. "Well, I confess *that* hadn't occurred to me! I'm more like to sell her to go along with them — the vixen!"

"Then she belongs to you?"

"Yes," he said, as indifferently as you please. It seemed to suffice to him to explain all things, for he immediately with profound unconcern began to talk of the trade goods that the *Janet* had brought. By now I knew as well as he that the *Janet's* port before Norfolk in September had been Bristol where she had refitted, and where the Company had loaded her heavily with wares for Africa. Only a small space of that slave deck was cavernous and empty, boxes and bales being stored through all the rest. To-morrow would begin the unlading and Daga be furnished for a year. And I knew that Rathbone Lace was supercargo or receiver here. He was speaking of trade rum, trade muskets, kegs of powder, tobacco in cask, hatchets and axes and small tools, beads and looking-glasses

and figured handkerchiefs, kettles and pans and
cottage crockery. I knew as he knew that the
muskets were none of the best, nor the axes and
hatchets and knives; nor the tobacco which we
had taken on at Norfolk, nor the rum, nor the
powder, nor the cloth, nor the more trifling
articles nor anything else. They were manufactured in England for Africa, and if the muskets burst and the powder was dampened and
the axes would take no edge and the cloth would
tear like paper, and if the tobacco was leavings,
and if rum and sugar and salt were adulterated,
what were the odds? Africa was not critical, or
if critical gained nothing thereby.

"A man," I thought, "to pay for a dull ax.
A woman for a glass necklace for another
woman."

I could think as my fellows were not thinking,
but I did as they were doing.

We were now before the factor's house, low
and rambling, untidy and yet comfortable. He
himself called to us from the verandah. "That
you, Rathbone? Is Mr. Scott with you? Supper is ready."

We went in. Bartram was here and Colley
and the captains of the *Sherwood Oak* and the
Fancy, Berry the assistant and Markham. A
table was spread — there were English dishes
and African dishes, rice and fowl and pepper,
cassava, yam. Two black women waited —
there were candles — it was warm. A vast bowl

of punch was brought and set before the factor. Tasted, one found it as strong as Hercules.

The captain of the *Sherwood Oak* was a man I should not wish to sail under. He drank hard and he would drink with each one, round and round. The captain of the *Janet* would not be tempted. "No, no, Captain Garth! You know my custom. But I wish your health all the same. Prosperous voyage, sir!" The captain of the *Fancy* was sailing before dawn. He said, "No, I must keep sober, Lace," and took but three cups of the punch. He was a talker, swinging from one subject to another, especially engaging Rathbone Lace, but bringing in Colley. The elder Lace, the host, promoted all as best he could and urged the punch. Bartram was speaking in his slow, reasonable voice to Berry the assistant. Garth drank with me again. The talk became general and grew thick with ports and prices, African and West Indian names, Company policies and niggardliness or the reverse, Bristol, Liverpool, captains, ships, fair weather and foul, storm, wrack, sickness, mutiny, loss and gain! In at the open windows came rhythmically the sighing, hot breath of Africa; the candle flames bent aside, there seemed wraiths in the room, then nothing but the punch bowl, big as a tarn, and the good, strong, West Indian rum.

Supper was over, I saw that, and the captain of the *Fancy* bidding Daga good-by, and it occurred to me that it was no loss to see him go. He departed, Berry seeing him from the house. Then the others drank again. Markham the surgeon appeared at my corner of the table, seated there, watching me. "You're drunk," he said, "but you carry it as though you were not."

"That's the way to be happy," I said, and indeed was so. I was "happy." And I sat quietly and did not seem to be drunken. When we got up from the table I did not lose balance or walk crookedly. I sat in a window and watched the room and its occupants, and it all seemed very large and filled with shifting colors and music. Time passed and sometimes I talked and sometimes did not. Time too had expanded and deepened till there seemed much of it and all worth while. And what we were talking of I really did not know, but at last I understood that the night was getting old and that we must go to bed. I thought that Colley was drunk, he and Markham drunk together, and going together out into the night, to Markham's house. As for myself, I proposed to return to the *Janet* just so soon as I should see William Bartram my kinsman safely installed in the room next the factor's, he in one bed and the captain of the *Sherwood Oak* in the other. I felt a joy of old romance when I thought of the *Janet* and the cool sea around and the star-powdered night looming above and between her bare masts. If they did not expect me to go and had not provided me a boat, I could swim.

Bartram and Garth and the factor had disappeared. Rathbone Lace had me by the elbow and was laughing. " Come on! I've quarters for you in the smaller house."

The smaller house was set behind and to the left of the greater one. There were trees and a roof and stars, a verandah, a door, a room. I thought that Lace had questioned me as to what book I had been reading lately, and I began to speak of Herodotus and his journey into Egypt that was in this same Africa that had been known so long and both favorably and unfavorably. I talked quite steadily and lucidly, as in a dream. He laughed again and said, " A Scot is a strange animal! Are you drunk or are you not? I swear I'm not certain which! "

But I was drunk and capable of wrecking a ship, my own or another.

The small house had the same guttering, blowing candles. By their vague light coming forth from the interior, I perceived two forms upon the verandah. As we stepped upon it, they moved with a kind of fluttering and a low, nervous, catching laughter. The one vanished around the angle of the verandah, the other remained. Lace put out an arm. "Are you there, Fanny? "

" Yaas, sah."

He drew her forward. " She's Fullah — like

Lalla. She's a good girl and has a little, a very, very little English."

He pushed her toward me, just sufficiently, so that her brown, warm arm came under my hand. "My room's round the corner," he said. "See you in the morning — but sleep as late as you choose! Only no one can really sleep after dawn in this place." With which he bade me good night and was gone, leaving Fanny's arm under my hand.

CHAPTER XIII

THE *Janet* took a fortnight for unlading, cleaning, mending and preparing for the Jamaica cargo. We all kept fairly busy, seeing that it was Africa. In my charge now rested merchants' books, lists, tallies, receipts. At some hour of the day I went over all with my kinsman in the cabin, but the actual clerkly labor and the actual supervision to a degree were mine. Bartram seemed satisfied and I was glad to do it. I had a power of work in me when I turned that way. After the first night I drank no more to excess of Daga punch. Bartram had said, " Mind you what you are about, David! I've seen many a tall ship wrecked on this coast. As for Rathbone Lace, I'm fair to hope he couldn't have been bred in Scotland! "

I laughed. " I've heard of Captain Mc-Kenzie."

" McKenzie's a changeling and a byword. He's not the least like any McKenzie at home."

McKenzie was the captain of the *Darling* and if Colley and others told true, there were oceans in hell and he had long been sea captain there. But the younger Lace did not seem to me quite of that energy.

I worked with him in the tally and transfer

of cargo to the Daga warehouse. Baker and Brown and Andrews and Hyde and Graves and others worked also. Sometimes we were upon the *Janet,* sometimes on the beach, sometimes in Daga fort, in the long warehouse, in the sun-baked enclosure. Work began early but stopped when the sun stood a little past noon. Except for an hour or so with Bartram, the rest of the time until dawn again was my own.

I remember the sands of Daga that were so white. The boats — the native boats — brought from the *Janet* boxes and bales and casks. Black men waiting knee-deep in the water lightened the boats and heaped the merchandise upon the sand. Black men, a line of them, shouldered the lighter things or carried between them the heavier, and bearing them up the sloping sand vanished with them through the dark and low entrance of the castle. They were powerfully built black men, naked save for the loin cloth, belonging to and serving the Company. Among them some worked mum as logs, others chanted and laughed and joked. So it had been in Virginia. They were naked here; they had clothing there. Here they used an African tongue, there they had learned or were learning an English one. Here was home, there another race's home. The sea struck ceaselessly against the Slave Coast. So they carried in the goods that were to buy for another continent their kind, maybe their immediate kith and kin; maybe, if they displeased any here, themselves. Muskets, rum and powder — tobacco, tools and gaudy cloth — crockery, beads and mirrors. I saw the English multitude toiling to make all this with which to buy, and that multitude themselves seemed slaves. And then I shut all such thoughts and images under hatches and went and drank with Rathbone Lace, and was myself — and not only in the drink — a slave.

At the warehouse toiled Baker and Brown with one or two nondescript whites and a dozen blacks to help. The warehouse was inside the castle, a long, shallow structure, stone against the stones of the wall. Around spread the baked earth, a square big enough for a town market. The sun beat on the stockade within the square where through the day was herded the *Janet's* lading that was to take the place of boxes, bales and casks. It was as large as a palaver ground. By dint of crowding, its citizens could make a space for dancing, for the beaters of drums, for exhorters and prophets, tellers of stories and starters of songs; space too for the serving of meals which were plentiful. It was policy to keep them cheerful. No one wanted pining skeletons for Jamaica or anywhere else. Their drums and lutes were given them; they were urged to dance, to sing, to eat. So far as their exhorters chose to encourage them, these were given full swing. The ordering of the barracoon fell to Berry the assistant and his helpers.

Berry was not a bad sort, but had a kind of wry joviality and a parental bearing. When he appeared in the place it was always to say, in effect, " How well we're getting on! Let's have a feast — but it's nothing, you know, to the feasts they give in Jamaica! "

Through the day, at intervals, the drums beat and there was singing and dancing and noise. Till an hour before sunset. Then the square was emptied, the drove vanished into those chambers within the walls, and all was still.

One morning, having an unoccupied hour, I found myself with Colley upon the wall. Hard by stood one of those guns trained within, and near to it talked among themselves three of Berry's guards, white men who looked much like pirates without a ship.

I said, " Do they ever rise? "

He answered, " Two or three times in ten years. When by chance there's among them some spirit of war and leadership."

" Wallace or Bruce? "

" Anan? " he said. " I don't think it goes as far as that. Anyhow, it's the most hopeless of enterprises! There's a tradition that once they burned and slew and swarmed away and were never taken, but it must have been very long ago."

I said, " In Virginia it was white slavery that was concerning me most. But is there any difference? "

He said, "There you go again! When I look at them I do not see white men and women."

"No, but men and women."

He swung round upon me. "Why, then, do you not make your choice? Yonder's a path into the forest and after a while another path and another and another! You come to towns, palaver grounds, chiefs' houses, black people, black merchants and traders, black princes and priests, thousands and thousands of black people, the land's so full! Why not go preach to them? Or, better still, why not preach in the factor's house this evening? Preach to white men and the Royal African Company?"

I answered him sullenly, "I am no preacher."

"I thought," he said, "that we agreed upon the *Janet* that we could not change the world. And I've thought at the factor's and with Rathbone Lace you were beginning to be fairly reconciled!"

I saw that I was, and I saw for a moment my blackness, I who had been a slave. — Then Fanny and the drink and Bartram and the ship and Security for David Scott, with clerkly work that did not come hard, and goodly books with leisure to read them, and coin in his pocket, and some seeing of the world after all, and friends. Security, friends, a good ship and the blue, salt sea. — *And at any time I might quit!*

I was not lost enough to say brazenly to myself, "I will not quit just yet." But underneath,

underneath consciousness, as it were, it was said. *"I will not quit just yet. Jamaica? Perhaps not even then."*

Immediately, there in the sunshine, things shifted a little. I saw the barracoon under a more favorable light. Under the light, in short, in which Colley and Bartram saw it. Yes, there was a woman weeping there. Yes, there sat a man in a gloom that darkened the sun around. Yes, that knot yonder was sending forth a chant that could only be likened to the one hundred and thirty-seventh psalm. Yes, there seemed some wretchedness in the barracoon. *But was it so bad after all? Nothing was idyllic in Africa, anyway. And one must live, and the shape of the world is past our changing. And of course nothing in any one else had the poignancy I found in myself. They did not feel as I felt.*

I said, "Well, they are laughing over there! And that girl who is dancing seems to enjoy her dance."

Rathbone Lace came up behind us. "We've missed you and Mr. Markham, Mr. Colley! You've been up the river?"

"Yes, up to Oil Palm village," answered Colley. "There's a man there with a melancholy Mr. Markham wanted me to see."

"Did you cure him?"

"It was to observe an interesting case. I don't think it is curable."

We leaned upon the parapet and looked down into the stockade. "Your five hundred," said Lace, " is about made up. Three hundred men, one hundred women, seventy young boys, thirty girls under twelve. There are a few lacking, but Gambo will bring them in presently. You've got an unusually strong, good lot! Mandingoes, Fullahs, Dualas, Soo-Soos, Ashantis and Coromantins."

Said Colley, " Coromantins and Ashantis are fierce and bold barbarians, Dualas and Soo-Soos are tractable as sheep, Mandingoes and Fullahs are, so to speak, gentry."

"Aye," said Lace, "but in the market all alike. — When do you begin lading? "

He spoke to me. I answered, " A week from to-morrow."

" Then we'll have time to go up the river for two or three days if you like. You've never been up an African river. We'll go up to Oil Palm village in my boat. Saturday? "

" I'll ask the Captain."

I did so. Bartram gloomed a little, then said, " Africa is biting you, David. Well, you'll have to have it over with. There's no saving a man from himself." He drummed on the table. " My self didn't come to me as Rathbone Lace, but perhaps as an ill a man."

I said that I didn't quite understand him, but the Inner Man did understand. The Inner Man is never less than clear-eyed.

Lace and I with five Negroes went up the Daga River in a boat carrying little food, for we would get that ashore, but with a great jug of Jamaica rum.

At first, to either hand there spread great coverlets of mud, forlorn with rubbish of the forest and the sea, and the water was dull and brackish. I saw here crocodiles and many a wading bird. By degrees, this changed to soil, black and loose and unfathomably rich. Here began the great trees and the marvelous blossoms. Here I saw parrots. The black men rowed us on, and now and then we drank. At times a forest overarched the stream so dense that there was as little seeing into it as into a stone wall. At times we passed clearings where there seemed to have been old cultivation. At times the trees were set as in a park, and a path ran by the water, a manifest, cheerful, trodden path. "Africa is full of paths," said Lace. "Even the caravans know in the desert the way to go."

"We are far, far away from the deserts."

"Yes. There are few people in the desert. But the Africa we know about is full of people, and these are their roads."

"What size is the Africa we know about?"

"God or the Devil knows!" he answered. "The size of Europe, maybe. Trade comes to the Coast from as far away as Russia — were we in London or Bristol. Down a hundred rivers like this and over a crisscross forever of forest paths."

"The Coast is their Ind or Ophir."

"You seem to read poetry. — Every black or brown kingling at any distance whatever, and every soul in the territory that he rides, knows that muskets and knives and rum and toys grow on the Slave Coast."

"The marvel is that they do not all see, having used one another for so long for money, that the day will come to each when he shall be used in like fashion. — But we do not see that either, in Europe. — It is like shipwreck, or plague aboard. Each seaman thinks, 'They die, but I shall escape!' Africa and Europe and Asia and America. Four seamen."

"You philosophize," he said. "I've never had time for it, nor for poetry. Negroes are Negroes and born to wait on their masters."

The five boatmen had among them a little English — all the Africans attached to Daga had so much or so little — but if they understood or did not understand was all one to Lace. They pulled the boat and had black bodies and faces, with hair unlike a Christian's.

David Scott had never dreamed of the trees and flowers and beasts and flitting birds and insects of these lands. Overpowering beauty and strangeness now were around him, up the Daga. Wonder came upon him, and a clutch of the land upon his heart. The Negroes began to sing. He knew that too — that there never were any people who loved singing more. Rathbone Lace yawned, drew his wide straw hat over his face and went to sleep. David Scott sat in a kind of dream between the pinions of strangeness and beauty. All along his life had been beginnings of sensibility here, but now on the upper Daga these gathered to a head, burst and expanded. Beauty! I came over the frontier, into Her kingdom — but yet was I unprofitable to Her — an unprofitable servant.

The moments passed, green and gold and purple. I could not follow the words of the boatmen's chant, but the air was now richly cheerful and now a wailing plaint — but from the one end to the other ran music.

It broke and ceased. The man in the prow said something in his African tongue, then all seemed to listen. Rathbone Lace took the cover from his face and sat up.

" Drums. They sound like Gambo's."

The Negroes acquiesced. " Gambo's."

" He's bringing in," said Lace, " the balance of your lading. Row on, boys, to the opening yonder."

We shot from a deep, gold-spangled shadow into full sun. It shone upon a narrow, grassy plain but little raised above the water, with a brown path running beside it. Now I heard the beating, as of quite a little host coming.

" Do they bring them in with drums? "

"Why, they come more quickly so," he answered. " Everybody walks better to drums and horns. They keep time. And then, it's for Gambo's importance."

A long, wooden trumpet blared as though in confirmation, and out of the shadow of cotton trees and palms and bamboo emerged into the tawny meadow a procession headed by Gambo with his musicians and tailed by half a dozen of the trader's armed men. In between moved perhaps seventy men and women and children, divided into three squads and tied one to another with rope. Each squad had for guard a couple of men with muskets and cutlasses. They came on without at first seeing our boat masked by a clump of canes. The great sun lighted their almost naked bodies, their faces, intelligent and unintelligent, the rope about their necks and their wrists. Only the children were unbound. Nine, ten and twelve-year-olds, they trotted beside their elders.

Slaves under thirty are the valuable slaves. Men and women, most of this band were young, though Gambo had acquired a few at middle age. They seemed of different tribes, for some were charcoal black, and others deep brown, and others light brown with almost straight hair. Some were low-browed, flat-nosed and thick-lipped, with a great, protruding jaw, and some had by no means that coarseness but were well featured, with a black or brown comeliness.

The figures of many were strong and fine. The young boys and little girls had grace, forlorn or impish as the case might be.

The drums had ceased to beat. All moved a few paces in silence, when a woman with a high, quavering voice, burst into a chant of parting. A man joined in, then a woman, then others, men and women, till all the company of bond-folk were singing as they marched to the slave ship.

They sang upon the brown, African road an eerie, wild and tragic chant. David Scott sat in a dream listening, for it linked to that perception of Beauty. And again he was hearing Negroes singing at Amory Hall, singing at dusk, in the quarter, after work, singing before and after the white parson's religious instruction, singing at funerals. The tongue was changed but the music was the same. All the rolling ocean was an illusion, this land and that neatly joined.

The chant broke. One viewing the river had made out our boat. Gambo's powerful, unctuous voice rolled out a command; all halted. The armed men made motions with their muskets. Lace, standing up, shouted, " Daga, Gambo! "

The boatmen pushing the boat head into the bank, we jumped out, Gambo and his lieutenant Big Man — I never knew his real name — affably assisting. The company of slaves was no longer afoot but sitting and lying amid the grass, instantaneously resting where rest was to be had.

Lace and Gambo talked in a fearful mixture of English and African that I could not as yet completely understand. I gathered that the trader was discoursing troubles and expenses.

Big Man moved back to the sunken troop and I went with him. A woman with a child beside her, roped as she was, managed to fling herself in the dust and grass before me. Her hands touched my ankles, she laid her face against my shoe, then gathered herself to her knees and cried to the white man to be let to go back with her child to her village and her hut, where two children screamed for her. Big Man, when I asked what she said, got through to me with that much. He also offered to beat her away. I prevented the blow that was falling, but I said, "Tell her it's useless — that I can't — that I have no power," and I drew myself from her grasp and removed a few steps, when a man began to cry to me, "White man master — white man master!" There followed gibberish to me, wildly and energetically spoken. I turned and found Lace beside me. "What is he saying?"

"He says he is from Calabar and was in the employ of the factory at the mouth of the Camaroons River. He says he has favorably known white men and white men have favorably known him, and that he was their interpreter when any journeyed up to the mountains. Then he went home to Calabar, and there happened a great war — three years ago, I gather — and since then he has been a slave of a king on the Benwe. The king sold him to an Arab slave merchant — he escaped and swam a river trying to get home — a second caravan captured him — he escaped again, and has been far up Daga River for a long time in a village, the same, he says, that the woman who has spoken lives in. Then lately there fell a war, what war he does not know, but it was for slaves. The village was burned and its strong men and women carried away. It was all in the dark, and the leaders in the war quarreled, and one marched away with no more than a dozen out of the village and he among them. That was a month ago, and a week ago he was sold for a knife and some powder to Gambo. The moral of it all," said Lace, " is that having worked for white men and done, he says, his best, he thinks that white men can hardly mean to put him on a ship." Lace laughed. "*I* don't listen to their stories, bless you! But you are new to it, Scott, so I translate."

" Have all of them stories? "

" Any one can make up a tale. I have known funny ones in my day! But many are as dumb as cattle. — Pshaw, they *are* cattle! "

He looked the company over with the supremest indifference as to certain things, but with merchant keenness upon others. " Gambo's done pretty well! They're a mixture. He's bought from King Timbu who collects from all quarters. But they seem sound. — Big Man, club that fellow if he will not hush!" The man from Calabar subsided. The woman with the child sat with her head upon her knees. "A lot of them have been slaves before. Gambo says that there are two witches also and three women sold by their husbands and a thief or two."

I looked at the witches, two young, thin, great-eyed women, more heavily bound than the others, as though for stigma. Their companions seemed in part to shrink from them and in part to feel a dim enchantment and a hope that if they were propitiated something to the good might yet happen. Their village had sold them for the good of the village and for rum. The three wives seemed much as other women. Perhaps they had brought scandal and commotion and strife and adultery into the family and were justly punished, or perhaps newer loves and jealousy and revenge had somewhat to do with it, or perhaps the husbands merely ached for muskets and tobacco and rum. What the couple of thieves had stolen did not appear, but here they were, going to the sugar islands. I have known in England of a boy hanged for taking loaves of bread, and it's not so long since in Scotland we burned three women for witchcraft.

The woman and the man were not the only ones to find voice. Two thirds of the troop were making appeal — a distressful noise of many in trouble. There was a clamor around us until

Gambo, Big Man and two or three of theirs began to lay about them with whips and the butts of muskets. — David Scott turned and walked away. He went back to the boat and sat there with a stony face.

Lace returned at last. "Gambo's a jewel! With a little direction he'd make a great merchant. There's a small world of native traders in Africa and he's of the best."

"Are they going on now?"

"Yes. There are the drums."

They were beating and the long, wooden trumpet blared. I looked through the cane and saw the squads in motion.

"How many are bought or caught and shipped overseas in a year?"

He considered. "If you take all the factories from end to end of the Coast — British, French, Portuguese, Dutch and so on — it's a big number. Seventy thousand or a little above, I should think."

"A year!"

"A year. We British have any number of factories, a few large like Daga and many small ones, and more than half the trade. All the English ports together may send out not so far from two hundred ships, big and little. Perhaps the British total may be between thirty-five and forty thousand Negroes a year. Ships and seamen, manufactured goods, establishments on the Coast and so forth — I don't know how many million pounds are invested, nor the number of investors. It's very great."

The drums beat, beat, beat. Gambo and Big Man and the armed others, the drummers, the trumpet man, the three groups of slaves for the *Janet,* passed across the meadow and vanished into the shadow of gigantic trees. "Get on, boys!" said Lace. "It is hot here in these canes. More rum, Scott?"

That afternoon we reached Oil Palm village, named so by Daga of old time because of its many of these trees and the oil they furnished. For long it had been a kind of pet place, rendezvous of traders, depot at times for merchandise for the interior, provider of guides and go-betweens, center of intrigues, under the protection of two or three factories, a supple favorite of many years. The chief or head man was a creature of Daga, the four or five hundred villagers bowed with the chief, and the surrounding clans kept hands off the " white man's people." Daga maintained here a big clean hut, and had often on the ground a clerk or other emissary. Oil Palm village flourished to the eye and grew sleek and prosperous, without fear of damage, under the gracious shadow of that great tree, the British. A good many vices grew up with its prosperity. It had somewhat the function, for wearied traders and men from the factories, of a Capua. A bland, suave, dusky, noisy place.

Here Lace and I abode for two days and nights. There was plenty of rum, and there were women.

CHAPTER XIV

WE began to lade the *Janet*. She was clean and stanch and as all had always sworn, roomy. Our seamen, to whom Bartram had given just as much shore leave and license as his name for a " good " captain obliged him to and no more, were all home again and fairly fit. The officers no less — McNaughton who never seemed to take a holiday, Pomeroy who took all of it that he could hold, but who had a bull's strength, Colley who took with moderation. As for Captain William Bartram, his holidays were of his own devising and within his own mind and spirit. Tom and Don, the cooks, had been three times, I think, ashore. Once I had encountered them on the wall, staring down into the barracoon. Those therein had surged toward them with shouts and appeals. They had answered back, but their tongues were not pure African and did not seem to be understood. The barracoon had begun to laugh and to jibe, and then it seemed to menace spiritually, seeing that it had no material power. The two from the *Janet* cried something back and left the place. Again I had seen them at low tide, sitting on the beach, upon a piece of a wrecked boat, staring into the west, where would be Jamaica. If anywhere was home to them it was Jamaica — and the *Janet*.

If anywhere was home now to David Scott, it was the *Janet*. Scotland was fading. A time would be when all its tint would come again, but now it was fading.

Davis the boatswain and Llewellyn the carpenter, Hamilton that was surgeon's mate, Benjamin the steward and Geordie, Jack Dannet and all his fellows, poop, midship and forecastle, we were all aboard. The sun was shining — the hatches were open — one looked down along shafts of light into that depth that, quite clean and airy and empty now, would soon be not the one nor the other. Colley said that the Captain had them up from it an hour earlier and into it an hour later than any other that he knew. " He's got good customs."

McNaughton, standing by, put in, " Aye, he gaes tae kirk inside. At times it gets into the way of complete effeeciency."

" I don't agree there," said Colley. " I think he's more efficient for it."

" Aweel," answered McNaughton, " there's room for a difference of opeenion. — But yon's the first boat."

He moved to the side. William Bartram was on the poop deck. I went to him there and watched with him the oncoming boats, two or three between us and the shore. They were the long, native boats, made of the greatest trees;

they had many rowers and were packed with slaves. On the white beach beyond showed a number of Daga figures, the factor and the assistant and Rathbone Lace and others; and squads of naked slaves were issuing from the barracoon and Daga castle, driven forth and down to the water where waited boats. The sky was the bluest imaginable, there was a sweet, singing air. The scene had beauty, but there was horror too.

On the *Janet* a certain number of our seamen were armed with cutlass and pistols. " There's a fear and despair at first," said Bartram, " that makes them dangerous."

The foremost boat now touched the shadow of the ship. Men stood by with rope and the long, cleated, landing board. This boat had women and children, mostly silent, ashy with fright. They were taken aboard — the boat pushed off — the second took its place. Again naked black women, naked young boys and girls. In Africa many tribes wear some slight show of clothing, some light and partial attire in a land of heat, but Africans put upon a slave ship are put there naked — nor could it be otherwise, the conditions given. If they felt it or did not feel it, I do not know. There was so much else to feel. In this second boat there was wailing and praying.

Bartram descended to the deck. He stood among those women and children and hon-

estly tried to comfort them. He had, as had all
at Daga, a rough and ready acquaintance with
African tongues that were all, so to speak, vari-
ants one of the others. Now I made out that it
was:

" Stop greeting, you women; you're wringing
your bairns' hearts! Nobody wants to eat you
— nobody's going to hurt you in any way if
you're good! Ship — this is a good ship — fine
ship. Men — these are good white men.
You're going to a good country — plenty to eat,
houses, good folk. Plenty your own kind there!
— Now, here comes another boatful. See if you
can't get up a laugh to meet them! "

The third boat — women and children still —
came alongside and gave to the deck, Pomeroy and half a dozen seamen handling the
cargo. I had followed Captain Bartram, and
now in the momentary lull while the company
aboard watched those coming aboard, he spoke
to me and with feeling.

" I'm looking to you, David, to follow my
ways and Mr. McNaughton's ways, not Pomeroy's ways nor Rathbone Lace's ways. I'm fain
to treat these poor souls, just as far as 'tis possible, like kindly Scots folk torn from hame by
poverty and trouble and gaeing ower seas. I've
seen greeting amang women at Glasgow and
Leith when first they came to the white ship
that was to take them away. Not loud greeting
like these poor, naked children of the sun, but

greeting. In the end greeting's greeting, sorrow's sorrow, whatever the color of her claiths." He sighed, " There's many a cruel necessity, David! "

From out the women from the third boat started one, taller than the others, vigorous, with a deep and intelligent eye, with a dark fire running well-nigh visibly through and around her. — David Scott had in his time felt anger too deep for any shaken voice or idle movement, and he recognized it. She spoke, and she checked attention and held it breathless. We did not know her tongue; she seemed a Negress from the mountains. Maybe she had been a prophetess or a queen. Beyond doubt, by nature she was something like that. Her speech straightened the cowering groups and for a little made it to seem that the captors cowered. There was a strange illusion. — David Scott, at least, saw as in a mirage a great dark figure, out of space and time, standing as judge.

The voice of this woman thrilled through the *Janet*. She cried upon God — presumably ours and hers alike — to show us through suffering. We did not know her tongue, but the ship understood. Through suffering.

Then I, watching, saw and heard something strange. It came as it were from the inner sky, out upon her visibly. The dark fire changed hue, became rose and sapphire, then a golden flame. Her arms were lifted, she seemed tall as a mast, her voice sang and was universal as the wind. "Show! If it must be through suffering, then suffering, but show! Show!" That was her saying, though I knew not the words. I do not know if what I saw and heard was caught by any other, though Bartram beside me shuddered slightly as though one had passed over his grave. But David Scott heard it and felt it for the *Janet* and all ships upon the seas, and Africa and the rest of the earth. Show! Show!

It stayed with us a moment, that enchantment or that Truth. Then, Bartram having nodded to him, Davis the boatswain seized the prophetess and threw her reeling among the dark crowd. "You'll stand watching, for it's you that bring about risings!" She fell to her knee, caught by one of the women and stood up, but spoke no more. I saw her now as only a tall negress with the air of one who held rank. Her voice sank away, now and for this voyage. She died the third week, and we dropped her body into the wave.

The boats that were coming now held men. The sun blazed over Daga. The whitened castle and the many palm trees, the river mouth, the village, the factor's hill, the white beach and the ant procession out of castle, out of barracoon — and again there flashed to me Edinburgh and the Luckenbooths. A naked black man, first of his boatful, stepped upon the *Janet's* deck, and for all the world he looked like Pickaninny.

CHAPTER XV

A LL night and every night five hundred beings lay as close as herrings in a cask upon the *Janet's* slave deck, under the *Janet's* grated hatches. Men were shackled, two together at the ankles. Women and boys lay ungyved. Each and all had just enough space in which to lie their length, or almost their length, and their breadth without turning or spreading. Bodies touched and rubbed one another. Overhead was scant, scant space. The hatches were kept uncovered, but still was it suffocating down there — and fetid beyond believing. David Scott, who knew an Edinburgh prison, yet had never dreamed of anything like it. It steamed up through the gratings. He thought he saw it, one hot night, as a cloud surrounding the ship. It was black in that sighing, grunting place, black as the pit. Sounds came up all night long. Out of five hundred always some were sleepless, always some in anguish of body or mind, always some breaking out into wrath. They remonstrated with each other, they seemed to curse God, or now and then to be praying. Sometimes would come a wild and sudden cry. The watch on deck paid no attention, unless the noise grew and a certain note came in. Then a threat was cried down through the gratings.

In the morning, " an hour earlier than other ships ", the gratings were lifted, and they poured up the short ladders to the light and air. The deck became covered as a sugared board is with bees. They gasped, they stretched themselves, some leaped up and down; they stared at sea and sky and each other; their tongues were loosened. Water was given them and a sufficient breakfast. Divided into companies, they sat and ate from great platters of beans and rice. Now you might hear, out of one group or another, a guffaw of laughter. There is something in the Negro ineradicably cheerful. But there was never much or lasting laughter, not even on the *Janet* that was so " good " a ship!

The slaves stayed on deck all day long. Two hours before sunset they had their second meal. The allowance of water was a pint and a half in the twenty-four hours to a man, less to women and children. This seemed great hardship and was miserably felt by these who at home drank when they wished from a thousand springs and streams. But the Middle Passage took long weeks, and tempest or dead calm might at any time make it longer. Among the ghastliest stories were those of slavers without water. The five hundred black folk were given sufficient for some degree of health and no more. A little thirst spaced through the voyage, said Bartram, was better than empty water barrels a hundred leagues from land. Certainly he wished there were room for more barrels.

" If we carried fewer Negroes ———"

" The Company thinks we should carry more."

He had his rules for the day. All ships had pretty much the same. There must be exercise, and it was best got by a kind of dancing. Fettered men still could shuffle and sway, and the women and boys were free of bonds. Dancing was good for the body and the spirit. Singing was good too, so that it leaned to the jovial and not the melancholy. All were encouraged to dance and sing. They might sprawl in the sun and sleep. They might converse and tell stories. The surgeon came and looked them over every morning when they emerged from the blackness, every evening before they returned to it. If there were any truly and really ill they were removed to a corner that was called their hospital. All wanted as few as possible to die. A certain number might be expected to go between Daga and the sight of Blue Mountain in Jamaica — half a dozen out of a hundred perhaps, in a decent ship like the *Janet*. Much more than that would mean some calamity. So soon as they were forth in the morning, salt water enough was sluiced about the slave deck, swabbing poles were used and it was dusted with purificatories. The Middle Passage was a time of labor for all but the Negroes, and as for risks and anxieties, slavers had them in abundance. A prime need always was to keep the cargo well and reasonably content, or if not content, submissive. Every interest led to kindness with firmness. Not only were the owners served by carrying their goods undamaged, but to secure as many lives as possible there had been devised head rights. Captain, first and second officers and surgeon had each so many shillings or pence out of the price of every able-bodied slave delivered to the agents in the ship's port. Every interest led to reasonable kindness in Virginia. But there was Daniel Askew! And at Amory Hall, that meant kindness and in a degree achieved it, I had not loved their kindness.

The *Janet,* to many slave ships, was as Amory Hall to Daniel Askew. I will give her credit, and I will give Bartram credit, and McNaughton and Colley and many more. I will give David Scott credit. We were not demons. We were perplexed and erring men, calloused by this work.

The first week we lost nine. The first week, they said, was usually the worst. There was more despair, and there was the universal seasickness. Two suddenly, at sunset, jumped overboard, and though sailors leaped after them they were not rescued. One refused to eat and though at last Bartram ordered the cat, and

though the third day Colley supervised the forcing open of his mouth and the pouring down of
broth, neither did any good. He determinedly
died. A man and two women died of some disease. Two children died. A boy died, apparently of mere homesickness. The second week
saw less mortality. It had its toll, as had every
week that followed, but we kept the fair side of
calamity.

Time out of mind two things are most dreaded
by slavers — plague and outbreak. The *Janet*
was helpless before plague, except inasmuch as
she strove for what cleanliness was possible, and
what order was possible, and had drugs enough
and a good surgeon. But as to outbreaks, William Bartram kept the probability or the possibility of that as low as might be. And he kept
it so to an extent by being a good captain, not a
bad one.

The story was that he did not sleep on the
Middle Passage. It is called that because a
ship's original course is England to Africa —
Africa to America — America to England
again. And so it is the Middle Voyage, the
Middle Passage. Bartram slept, of course, but
he slept little. All day he was wary; cool, just,
according to canon, and wary. Throughout the
night, any hour, he might be found going about
his ship with his padding step, like a tawny,
watching, desert lion. The watch had no chance
to grow drowsy, the man at the wheel, the mate

on duty, found him silently beside them one moment, then gone. He stood at a grating and harkened to the sounds coming up, and gauged their importance; he studied weather of whatever kind. Then he might go and sleep a while and return again. A tall, robust man with tawny hair and beard, big-nosed and keen-eyed. When he and McNaughton walked together, there were two tall, red Scots; when David Scott was joined to them, there were three.

He kept his seamen with his eye and his slow, full, reasonable voice, and the character behind both. They did their work, they made or took in sail, they sat aloft in the rigging or swabbed away the filth and refuse of the slave ship, or stood as guards over those five hundred prisoners; they toiled, watched, ate, slept and played, shouted, cursed and laughed, were sick and well, grumblers more or grumblers less, as seamen are; but they gave no fear of mutiny and the *Janet* sailed her way.

The *Janet* sailed her way. It was the winter and the heat not as it is in summer in the Middle Passage. But there was heat when the deep wind failed and the sun stood overhead. Then the sails hung slack, the sea became a hot blue floor which never might we cross; the ship seemed to fester, to fester and to groan. Then the wind blew again, the sails filled, and life revived.

Twice we met tempest, once bitter and prolonged, the greater part of a week. A mast broke, the seas washed over the sides, the ship was tilted and played with like a walnut in a boy's hand. For three days and nights the Negroes must be kept below hatches. That was frightful. Eight were dead when the sun shone again and the waves stilled themselves. We lost also two seamen, Jonathan West and Walter Bigger.

Barring this week of storm we had a fair and uneventful voyage, day after day of good wind and bright, blue sky. We sighted two British Guineamen, a Spaniard to whom we gave a wide berth, and a craft that we could not make out. Africa now was far behind us and the great West coming nearer, though still it, too, was far, far away.

In some sort a part of the Negroes grew reconciled. I saw brutalities aboard the *Janet*. Pomeroy could be brutal, and Davis and certain of the sailors. But the ship's intention was not brutality, other than the brutality of being there at all, a fetcher and carrier so, in the eye of day. Harshnesses appeared; punishments and intimidations. It is a problem of high difficulty, the ruling of five hundred barbarian captives crowded for long weeks on a ship upon the sea. What harshness Bartram exercised, or let the mates exercise, was always to him a necessity, done to save from worse things. But the same plea would be advanced by the captains of the

Sherwood Oak and the *Fancy,* or by that Mc-
Kenzie of evil name, men of less judgment as to
good and ill and necessity than the Captain of
the *Janet.* When it was thought to be needed
the whip was used, or other punishment such as
deprivation of food and drink, detention under
hatches by day as by night, or chainings to the
mast. Disobedience and turbulence were the
crimes. Some committed them, others did not,
and Bartram strove for justice. And when he
could — or thought he could — he showed much
kindness. Only there was so little room for
kindness on that slave deck!

Yet, as I had heard laughter in the Tolbooth
— as I had known men to laugh at Daniel Askew's — so I heard laughter among the black
men and women on the *Janet.* For such is the
human spirit. Laughter at times, weeping at
times.

CHAPTER XVI

AT times David Scott's stomach turned against this work and he waited but for Jamaica and freedom. At such times he saw that he and Bartram and McNaughton and Colley and Pomeroy and the others were slaves; aye, that the Royal African Company, supporters and Parliamentary grants and all, was a slave. Daniel Askew was a slave. Colonel Giles Amory was a slave. — David Scott was in slavery.

At such times he sent Geordie for a dram, and then, for such a length of time, he saw things differently. It was not so bad a life. All life was a picture and a play and great emotions surged through it!

Again, he might be as cool and as much himself as the Tron clock. From Africa to the Indies was a small hell. Granted! But there had been and might be again the great empty ship from the Indies to Africa. He liked that, and there would be the ports, the Indies and the coasts of America, England where he might risk it, and Daga where was none so bad company. A man must live! If there were iron walls against him where he might wish to live and prosper, then he must even live and prosper where he might.

Because he had been a slave and knew, there-fore he must not enslave.

He said to himself, so cool and at himself, that he was not enslaving. That was the Company, Daga, England, America and the earth. A man was a puny thing and must go with the crowd! And the slaves being enslaved anyhow, they might even profit by having for slaver among the others one named David Scott. He saw things that even Bartram could not see, how to combine kindness with rule. They might bene-fit. So he reasoned, the losing soul, so cool and clear! Had it been a shipload of white slaves — had he been an ancient Roman bringing slaves from Britain, slaves enslaved in much the same ways, it would in the end have been much the same. *He* was not responsible, but the order of affairs.

And other moods possessed him, and chiefly, "Let sleeping riddles lie," and "Take it as it comes."

The golden and blue days, the starry nights went by. Over-thronged, foully smelling, with some sound of mourning always, the *Janet* that I had thought so clean and light ploughed her way. Bartram gave me work to do — kept me at it, not unwilling, for it killed the thinking when I could not drink. Under his apparent self-sufficiency he was a lonely man, craving his own, missing son or brother or friend. I came to meet a need, having the same blood as himself, understanding his liking for books, understanding his wish to be kindly, and his passion for the native land, understanding his pride and his self-ponderings. We could journey together, talking little, but sticking no thorns one into the other, and on occasion giving each other help. He troubled me no more about wine, rum and brandy, though his eye was watchful there. Nor did he argue any more about the *Janet* and her freight, nor did I argue any more here. The action is the thing that has the clarion voice. I did Philip Smith's work. Once I asked McNaughton why he left at Philadelphia.

The mate looked at me from under red tufts of eyebrows. " Ah, he was a brittle chield! He developed scruples."

" You call that being brittle? "

" If this is your wark and your living, Mr. Scott, I do. Aweel, he's doubtless howked himself to death in an almshouse. He wasna fit for much when he left us."

I slept in this man's small, small cabin, and at times I felt him. And at times, waking in the night, I felt the slave deck below, and the fetid blackness, and the bodies close, close to my own, sighing, pressing, straining for space where was none. — But then the comfortable dwarf within me slammed the door against that silent calling.

The stars rose, crossed and departed my window. The cold dawn, the solemn dawn, rode into the field, and then, his mood brightening, decked himself with the violet and the rose. The golden cap of the sun parted the purple sea. And here was the day, to better or to worsen.

At first the horde we carried had seemed all of a piece, sex and adult or youth the only distinguishing marks. All were bare; all had a jargon that only painfully was I learning to interpret and find a language like my own; all were dark, dark of skin though with shades in that nighttime. All were crowded, all were captive; the same destiny was to all; they were already slaves. At first the one looked like the other. But at last the observant eye parcelled out even in that swarm. David Scott had vision to use and must use it. He watched the cargo and could not choose but watch it.

It had been so in Virginia also. At first one had seemed like the other. Then it had emerged that Old Hannibal was not Joe, nor Joe, Pickaninny, nor Pickaninny, Eboe Sam.

Colley sometimes stood beside me, gaunt and hollow-eyed, for there was something, he said, in every voyage that poisoned him. "Then quit it!" I answered one day. "Spring to the first shore and run!"

"Take your own medicine!" he said. The sun was shining, the rigging humming. We look down from the poop upon a corner where naked men were playing some game with a kind of dice, bits of wood that they had secured somehow and most ingeniously marked.

" In God's name what have they got to dice for?
They can't even sell themselves any longer."

A young man, all clean bronze, threw and
leaned back and laughed. Another, sitting
cross-legged, cupped the bits of wood in his
hand, shook and cast them. Four others, thick-
lipped, with woolly heads and bandy legs, sub-
servient somehow to the main two, laughed and
jabbered and clapped their shins. " Two great
lords gaming," said Colley, " and their followers
and cup-holders. I've seen the same when I had
a look one day at White's."

" This ship makes you sardonic," I said. " I
don't know what it makes me."

" There is," he said, " a thoroughly abomina-
ble two months or rather less, followed by a
somewhat longer term of comparative happiness. I live for the comparative happiness. We
all do."

I was looking at a woman seated with down-
cast eyes, a child of nine across her knees. Now
I saw that it was the woman who had cried to
me up the Daga River, who had two children
at home. If she felt me staring at her I do not
know; perhaps she did. At any rate she raised
her eyes and stared back. She was hollow-eyed,
her face and frame were thin, her breasts hung
lank. A dark light as of recognition entered
her countenance and turned into hatred, blank
scorn and hatred. She stared at me leaning
there, then with a most deliberate insolence

slowly moved her body until I had only her dark back and shoulders and her face was for the sea.

Colley had followed my eyes. " I thought she would die, that Eboe woman. She would have gone, I'm pretty sure, but for the child. I worked it so. I said — black lingo — ' You don't want to leave her, now do you? ' and it worked like one of their ju-jus." He finished reflectively. " Mother and young one like that are usually bought together, but not always so, by any means. So it may be that she'll have to leave her anyhow."

In the middle of the swarm — the deck was black with them; they had little room to move about — a man was laughing, a rich, subdued, whole-hearted laughter.

" That fellow there must be clean of sin."

" You laugh and I laugh."

" Not like that ——"

" If he's clean of sin there's one there — and there's one there — who is not."

It was a sullen and violent brute to whom he pointed, and a crafty and apelike one. " Yes," I said, " they are mixed."

Those nearest the barricade began to speak to us clamorously, men and women. They made appeal for increase in the water ration, for more and other food, for a little rum, for license to stay, when it came dark, this side the hatches, for medicines, for news of where they were and where going, for release, for return to Africa,

for justice and knowledge and joy and freedom.
They made no discrimination — we were white
men — it was enough. We were in the magic,
wizards and evil kings, all! No one ever knew
when gusts of passion and of desperation would
take them. Something of this kind happened
now, appeared and spread and mounted. From
a few many become involved. There grew a diz-
ziness of faces and upswung arms. Voices ran
the ladder of excitement into a deep-throated
yell. Like a levin flash came a certain tension.
Colley raised his voice. "'Ware, Michaelson!
'Ware, Dory!" A man above us shouted "Mr.
Pomeroy! Trouble here, sir!"

Pomeroy was at hand, McNaughton came
running. The deck showed now a ferment
as of determined bees. A leader started forth,
then with a yell there came, as a comber comes,
a dark mass against the barricade where they
thought it weakest. Then I saw Bartram, tawny
as a lion, with a lion's roar.

"Too late for soft words, Mr. McNaughton.
The tall one, you, Dory! Fire!"

Dory fired, and the tall one, the leader, fell.
"Burke! Take that man yonder!" and the one
to whom Colley had pointed fell. The wave recoiled upon itself, broke. A moan ran through
and over like the moan of foiled waters. Bartram shouted to the insurgents in their own
tongue, "Who'll die next?"

This way and that they looked into the mouths

of pistols and muskets, and upon cutlasses that flashed and dazzled and made dread, and beside these there was only the shoreless sea. They feared the sea that was their severing foe, they feared the ship — sailed and tiered ships being the highest magic, — they feared the white men's guns and swords. Blight struck them, they wilted, withered, sank into an abject, wailing or silent mass.

The two dead men were lifted and thrown into the sea, and the blood mopped from the deck. There was no further punishment. Bartram was not sanguinary, nor loved in any way immoderation.

Days and nights — days and nights — days and nights, and the reeking ship went on. Week on week until we had counted six. The log showed an average voyage. There had been better, said Colley, and there had been much worse. We lost three seamen, two in storm, one from sickness. Others were ailing, but it was always so. There were four hundred and seventy slaves on deck or under hatches. The loss of that thirty made for them that much more room, but still a stranger would have wondered where that thirty could have been stored.

We were now upon the Indies. I remember the cry of "Land ho!" and how it thrilled, for there was none upon the *Janet* who did not now wish land.

CHAPTER XVII

AND yet it was days between the sighting of the first of the Windward Isles and the vision, like enchantment, of the Blue Mountain of Jamaica that was twice as high as Ben Lomond.

These days were different from those before them. The run was all but over, many dangers overpassed. The ration of water was doubled; the slaves might have all they wished to eat. All the object was now that ills be forgotten and the cargo seem and indeed be in the fittest conceivable shape. It was Daga's triumph to ship stout slaves; it was the *Janet's* or the *Sherwood Oak's* or the *Fancy's* to deliver whole and stout as many as might be. Ours were fed and cleansed, and given oil to rub with, and at the last the most were unshackled. And they were told tales of the goodness of the Indies.

There is something in the Negro of a vast good nature and a knowing how to live. Tragic was this ship to him, and his own land was left behind forever and forever, his land and kin and ways and tongue. He had not left it of his own will, but was stolen, forced, dragged, wronged. He was going to a world strange to him as the moon, and into slavery, and the slavery he was already tasting was not sweet. And yet Great Nature gave him humor and mirth, and the moment, on the *Janet,* physical pain and oppression lessened, up and out they welled, like springs from dark hillsides. Not from all but from many. And another thing. He is a barbarian and a heathen, with images of stone and wood, but behind that mask and that childhood yet, he is religious. David Scott found that out of old in Virginia, and nothing ever changed his conviction here. Not that it shows in every man and woman. In many it shows not at all or most fitfully. But in the whole there is the tincture and the mark. Even on the *Janet* it rose in many or descended upon many, and out of the black present sprang a bloom, a sense of a Future that was different. David Scott saw that happen, and deep, deep in him something knew what it was. It was there, behind or above all the flows of passion, all the sluttishness. — Something in them, as in the Africa they were leaving, dark and rank and strong, incredibly old and incredibly childish. Something mirthful, despite the world. Something savage, something grotesque, something shallow as the skin and deep as the bone, something foolish, something passionate, something delighting in music and drama, something religious, something warm and kind, something good, something wise, after one of Nature's many ways of wisdom. It was all there; it showed on the *Janet* as elsewhere.

Some were credulous of the tales that were told, some were not. John Dory and Benjamin the steward were the ones set by custom to tell them. Our slaves would like to have heard, I thought, from Tom and Don. But Tom and Don avoided Africa, naked and chained; as little as might be went that way or looked that way.

John Dory and Benjamin had been afoot through Jamaica, Barbadoes and Trinidad, and on the steed of imagination across the Spanish and French islands. I listened to them telling preposterous marvels of fat and ease and plenty. One or the other or both sat cross-legged atop of barricade and dealt out fairy tales in a mixture of Negro tongue and sailor's English. The four hundred and seventy listened, and woebegone faces shortened and white teeth showed. What was dearest to them was that they would meet a lot of their own folk — a lot of black skins — and that these were universally happy, and that they, too, would be happy. A woman shrilled at John Dory, " They won't part me and him? " " Lord, no! " said Dory.

We passed by the Bahamas, and saw the mountains of Cuba, and the mountains of Santo Domingo and at last the mountains of Jamaica. The *Janet* was made as clean as was possible, the sick sailors seemed to recover, fiddles sounded in the forecastle. The officers smiled; around Bartram played like a beam of light, *The star that warred does not return!* The Middle Passage was gone over, the voyage made, the luck fair.

The shores of Jamaica are gorgeous to see, under the golden light, under the rose and purple when the sun is low. I gazed and gazed at the peaky mountains and the vales between and thought I saw a paradise. Dusk gathered, stars swam above the purple land, it seemed to me that there was music. In the cabin after supper, McNaughton and Colley having gone on deck, Bartram put out a detaining hand. "We'll anchor presently in Kingston harbor. And there, David, what is your will? Will you be leaving me?"

"I hope the *Janet* may be my home still," I said, "until I know."

"You do not know?"

"No."

Opening a box beside him he took out golden guineas. "Here is what I would have paid Philip Smith — a little more, maybe."

"I'll take just what you would have paid him. — Thank you, sir."

"The *Janet* will stay two weeks or more. North, that's the agent here, has a good enough house and decent connections and is a safe man. If you want to see Jamaica he can put you in the way of it. It will be best just to say that you're my cousin who came out with me from Bristol."

"You're very good to me, Captain Bartram."

"Of course it must be 'Captain' before the

warld of the ship. But when we're like this,
David, it might be ' Bartram ' — for all that I'm
a wheen aulder than you."

I said, " That's as the warld counts it, Bartram. Inside, there's no telling which is the
auldest or the youngest."

" Guid! " he answered. " Have you a purse
for your money? "

At midnight we anchored. At dawn all the
slaves were let upon the deck. The east reddened and threw a light against mountains and a
broad coastal plain, blue water breaking against
the shore and a host of cocoanut palms leaning
from the land over the wave. We saw bright
green patches of sugar cane. The air breathed
balm, one made out a kind of houses among
trees, and the crowing of cocks came faintly to
the ear. All the upturned dark faces! — It was
not hideously, fearfully, unlike Africa. — *It was
like Africa!*

The sailors were making sail. Up came the
anchor to a chantey. A steaming breakfast went
to the deck, and, with the Captain's compliments, a dram for each man and a smaller one
for a woman. Afterwards abundant water was
given with which to bathe. They scrubbed
themselves and each other, while the cleaning
gang below made the slave deck sweeter than
it had been since we laded at Daga. The wind
blew fair, the *Janet* went hummingly, the great
sun laughed on flag and pennant and sails. Bar-

tram sent Willy the fiddler to play for Africa.
Then out of the storeroom came cotton breeches
and shifts — slaves' clothing, since English and
Christian countries must not be shocked by
nakedness — even black nakedness, which in itself, so comfortably has Nature arranged it,
shocks much less than does white nudity! In an
hour the slaves were clothed; they only needed
now to be baptized.

We entered Kingston harbor, that is a goodly
one. Ships large and small rode at anchor, and
before us, flat upon the plain, sat a fair-sized
town, all embowered in tropic trees. There are
shoals and reefs and spits of land. A pilot came
to us, and he was white but his boat held black
men. Ah! — and ah! — and ah! Africa to
Africa.

The town enlarged before us. There showed
a wall and a long and low stone building and a
wharf that ran out toward us like a giant's
finger. All grew until we could see the moving
crowd that watched us — watched the *Janet,*
known to Kingston, coming in with hundreds of
Negroes. Her wings were folded.

> " Oh, heave her down,
> Oh, heave her down,
> Heave her down ——"

Her anchor grappled the white sea floor. Another boat appeared under our bows. It had in
it a medical man who stood up and flourished a

fine hat. "Good day and welcome, Captain
Bartram! Have you smallpox, or any plague?"

"Good day, Doctor Cawthorne. We've no
smallpox and no plague."

"Then I'll come aboard," said Cawthorne,
and doing so, greeted Bartram and Colley standing beside him. "*We've* the yellow fever," he
said. "But that's a matter of course."

A third boat appeared. "That's North, just
behind me."

Mr. North came aboard. Geordie put wine
and glasses on the cabin table. Captain and
first mate, the port doctor and Colley and the
Company's agent and Mr. David Scott, cousin
to Captain Bartram, drank to one another, to
the *Janet* and Jamaica and the market and so
forth. Cawthorne and North both were tallish,
thin, yellowish men, somewhat drawling and
weary in speech. They asked of the voyage and
the cargo and the luck, and gave the news of
Jamaica and of England from a man-of-war in
harbor.

We went on deck, to find small boats enough
around us, chiefly oared craft. The rowers were
Negroes, naked to the waist, with cotton drawers, and some with a shirt beside. They had
fruit and wares for sailors, and all around the
ship pulsed a chanting, shouting noise. The
four hundred and seventy from Africa were not
silent neither. A strong light beat, the plain
shimmered, the mountains behind melted into

misty greens and colors of heather. Bartram
and the others were talking, talking. David
Scott thought, " How old is the world, seeing
that this has been going on since old time, and
yet is but a moment? " And it seemed to him
drawn out like a long, long violin note, yet there
was silence on all sides of it.

That very day we transferred cargo to the
long building that was the Company's barracoon. The Company had a fleet of boats. Load
after load the four hundred and seventy were
ferried ashore. They left the *Janet* without
seeming reluctance. A man, standing up in the
first boat, shook his clenched fists toward her and
shouted something that Pomeroy translated for
me. " ' Stinking hell! ' he's saying. ' All evil
to you, stinking hell! ' If I had him here, I'd
flog him to a mask of blood for that! "

Pomeroy's red face grew redder. And David
Scott too had a kind of love for the ship — left
from her outgoing — and resented the black
man's words. But then he had not spent his
nights on the slave deck.

CHAPTER XVIII

NORTH'S house, a commodious enough one, built of plastered stone, had a verandah that commanded Kingston harbor much as the factor's house had commanded the far smaller haven of Daga. The climate was not so different, nor for the matter of that the landscape and the tree and the flower, save that tree and flower in Africa were vaster and more varied. And the ocean struck here and the ocean struck there. Ocean, Ocean, Ocean, just the same, striking Virginia, striking Scotland.

Colley and I stayed with North but went back and forth to the *Janet*. Bartram stayed with the *Janet,* but came and went ashore and to North's. McNaughton I met at times in the street. Pomeroy had, they said, a wife or a mistress in a tiny, deeply shadowed house. And for our sailors, there existed the waterside and the town at large and the Seaman's Delight.

The uneasy spirit within drove David Scott to the sun-baked slave market beside the barracoon. I saw our cargo sold, and only long usage could make that selling less than frightful. Back I was upon the *King William,* and they were selling me!

At North's there was always punch or brandy

neat, and servants and servants to wait upon one. Colley and I slept in a great airy room, with a net over the bed to keep out mosquitoes. North had no wife, but a brown housekeeper. His table groaned, and at supper was always company. Down by the water stood the house of the Company, with clerks and ledgers and a great lounging place. North's days were spent there, and this was the place to find ship captains and traders and outfitters and often sugar planters.

I saw little of Bartram these days. He seemed willing to give me sea room in which to make decisions.

With Colley or alone I saw the scambling, hot and dusty, not so big town that was Kingston. We were put in the way of getting horses and so rode over the plain, between sugar fields and through untrimmed forest to Spanish Town, where was the King's House and the Governor, and some kind of Parliament, and an Assembly room and a theater and a great church and an inn. We put up at the latter and saw the sights. Spanish Town was once, they said, St. Jago de la Vega, before Cromwell put the Spaniards to the sword and took the island. The old port town was Port Royal that a great earthquake swallowed only sixty years ago. Then up came Kingston in its place. Earthquakes still happened, earthquakes and hurricanes and yellow fever and the pox, and threats at times from

Spain and from the French in Santo Domingo; and pirates infested the surrounding seas.

There were British soldiers in Spanish Town — two or three companies, I should guess. In the inn we found their officers gaming and drinking. By degrees they began to speak to us at our small table, and when they found an intelligent ship's surgeon and his companion, to draw us in to the general company. We did not meet the consideration which would have been ours had we come from the man-of-war in the harbor, nor the consideration due to a stately East Indiaman, nor even to a general merchantman in the American Trade. The slaver had a dark mark over the world, though the world demanded that she persist. She was like a prostitute.

So they used a certain freedom and condescension of tone. It irked Colley, I saw, but God knows it seemed only to put me back into Virginia, where I had been a servant and laborer.

They wished to know of the sea and the cargo and Africa, and if we had seen so and so who was upon the Guinea station. Colley would hold his gentility and so minced in and out. But David Scott did not care. For a moment he had been in the great parlor at Amory Hall, where there was a fire burning, and a dance and young men and women laughing. And then he sat thinking.

There entered a couple of men who also had been riding and who, greeted by and greeting our officers, seemed folk of consideration, Jamaica owners of the neighborhood, sib to English squire or Scots laird. One seemed an amiable man enough, languid and drawling like North, but with an educated tongue. The other was of coarser stuff. They drank and the talk went on. The Captain of soldiers — a fine young buck such as I might have found opposed to me at Culloden — mentioned our names to Mr. Dalrymple and Mr. Crabtree, "Doctor Colley and Mr. Scott. From the *Janet* in harbor."

They seemed to know the *Janet* and asked of Captain Bartram, "Holy Bartram," said Mr. Dalrymple with drollery. A military man of superior rank entered the room; the officers present rose and saluted and then all sat to drink again. The newcomer proved an authoritative, talkative person, just back from Kingston and from dinner aboard His Majesty's sloop of war *Nemesis*. Wishing to talk about the posture of affairs at home — they all, Dalrymple and Crabtree and the soldiers, called England "home" — he talked and the others deferred or put forward just the starters he wished. He talked of the French and Prussia and Austria and the Ohio Company and Pelham and Pitt and Ireland and Scotland. His remarks upon the last-named were intemperate. I said, "I am a Scot, sir. The country is poor but not villainous."

He swung himself around in his chair and stared at me.

"And who the devil, sir, are you?"

"I am from the *Janet*," I answered. "The country is poor but not villainous."

Mr. Dalrymple intervened. "A nephew, I believe, Major, of Captain Bartram of the Guineaman *Janet*. You know how are the Scotch, sir! He means only properly to stand for his own."

"I mean," I said, "that the country is poor but not villainous."

The Major swallowed. "Well, sir, it is villainous in part. You, doubtless, are an exception."

"Every land is villainous in part. For instance, England——"

He suddenly roared. "Yes, England too! Haven't I just been saying so? In short, I don't feel like quarreling, Mr. whoever you are from the Guineaman!"

"David Scott, sir."

"Well, Mr. David Scott, I don't think the *waur* of you for finding good under your own rooftree! I'm supposing, of course, that you were not 'out'—as the saying is—in '45, or that you were 'out' on the right side?"

"I was 'out' on what I considered the right side——"

Colley's voice, that was a clear, penetrating one, made itself heard with suddenness and completeness. "A soldier with the yellow fever. As we came into Spanish Town ——"

"Another!" exclaimed the Captain.

"I don't think I could be mistaken," said Colley. "He had every sign and was making for the hospital. Have you ever thought, sir, of moving the men bodily to a mountain top? The higher you go, the less of the fever."

Mr. Crabtree followed him, though certainly without any notion of serving David Scott. "I've thought the same. I've thought of balloons — and I tell you what I've thought too, Doctor. I've thought it is the mosquitoes."

"The mosquitoes!"

The soldiers laughed and no one picked up again the former topic. As for Colley and me, our eyes met and said, "We'll sit just long enough to show that we're not chased, then pay and depart." The company now was upon a ball to be given at King's House in honor of the officers of the *Ariadne,* upon the ball and the fever and the sugar crop and the Maroons, which last word I think I first heard here. We were about to rise when a young white man in a very poor dress, who seemed to have been riding, entered the room. He had in hand a package, and standing by the door he coughed twice and at last attracted the attention of Mr. Dalrymple.

"Bulkeley! What are you doing here? Oh, did I leave that behind?"

"Aye, sir. Mr. Robinson, he sent me after

you with it." Advancing to the great table, he extended the package, which seemed of papers. The planter took it.

"All right, Bulkeley! Wait outside. I'll have a note to send back to Mr. Robinson."

Bulkeley in his poor dress touched his forehead and went out. He was, I saw, a white bondsman, indentured servant in Jamaica like those in Virginia. Dick Merry rose before me.

When Colley and I had bowed to the company and paid our score and left the inn's big room, we found him leaning against the wall outside. I wished to stop to talk, but Colley said, "For God's sake, David!" and whistled to the black hostler who brought our horses. We mounted and rode through Spanish Town, past the cathedral and the other wonders. At last we found ourselves out upon a road running between groves of logwood in blossom and the harvest field of a fabulous number of bees. We had it to ourselves, save for a wagon drawn by four oxen with three or four black men walking alongside that was disappearing into the distance.

I said, "I considered it the right side. But now I think Tory and Whig are just on the same side and that it's not a particularly important one!"

"I think," he answered, "that in another five minutes you might have found yourself apprehended. What possessed you?"

"I don't know, Colley," I said, "except that I love Scotland. Listen to the bees in all that yellow stuff!"

We rode on. "Mosquitoes!" he said. "How could it be mosquitoes?"

Leaving these trees, we came to a great planting of sugar cane, many acres, breathlessly still now in the drop of the wind. Half-naked black men were cutting, cutting, a large gang of them, dim and dimmer down the rank field where the cane was head-tall. They felled the stalks with curiously shaped knives, somewhat like a short cutlass. We made out two armed white men standing watching, and in a moment a third, on horseback, came along the road that seemed an unfrequented one, and stopped at our greeting. I recognized an overseer, with some of the marks of Barget, but harder.

"Good day!" quoth Colley. "The cane seems prime."

"'Tis so, sir." He stood in his stirrups and shouted something to the nearest white man, who shouted it in turn to the next. In the distance rose the tall chimney of a sugar mill, and there was a movement toward it across the great field as of a monster serpent, a dragon of antiquity. We seemed to catch a sight of oxen too, and of heaped wagons.

"New slaves?" said Colley.

"Just so, sir," answered the man on the horse. "Out of the *Silver,* no longer ago than Christmas. Coromantins, too. The worst of the lot!"

"But they're in demand."

"They're big and strong as an ox. That's why," replied the overseer. "But, God! they're hard to tame! And when they find that they can't kill you — unless they wish to be burned alive — they run off. Clear away to the mountains and feed the Maroons! We've been breaking these in for a month." He had pistols, a knife and a great whip, and his white helpers were similarly armed.

"Are they broken yet?" I asked, and he answered with satisfaction, "Pretty well!" and I saw Eboe Sam who also had been fierce and haughty.

He departed into the field, following the line like a serpent. Colley and I rode back to Kingston, to North's house, to the verandah and the hammocks and the bowl of punch. It was an easy, easy life and it attacked with the power of a tiger. To lie and dream, to lie and think that you were thinking!

Two days after Spanish Town we rode into the Blue Mountains, starting before sunrise, our destination a "pen", as their plantations are called well up toward the clouds that hid the purple heads. The owner was a Mr. Browne, a connection of North's, and the latter had suggested our going, but indeed Colley had been before. It was not a sugar plantation, but

Browne experimented with coffee. And as planters are as hospitable as Highland chiefs, no need for forewarning. It had been so in Virginia and was so in Jamaica.

When we left the plain and began to climb, the road grew profoundly poor. But all around was beauty — around, above, below, where now the plain and harbor spread, a shield all vert and argent. We saw the ships, could make out the *Janet.*

"There she is!" quoth Colley, and "There she is!" I followed. Still we climbed while strange trees pressed about us and rich and strange flowers, and we heard water falling. From shoulder to shoulder we saw, in an amber light, the plain and the mountains and the sea. I said, "It is a beautiful island!"

He agreed. "A man might live here very well if he had means and place."

"There would be forever warmth and light, even if you had neither."

"Yes," he said. "But toil. Warmth and light and toil."

The day was well on when back among the hills we came to cleared land, to growing coffee and to flat, stone drying-places called barbecues and finally to a house of wood and stone that was Browne's Folly, where we were going. At once the great shady bloomy yard before it seemed to swarm with Negroes. A great bell rang, we dismounted, a Negro house servant, not at all unlike several I remembered at Amory Hall, appeared to tell us with unction that "the Captain" was out but would be in ere long and that we were at home. He showed us a big untidy room, and a blowsy mulatto girl brought us water for our hands and faces; and the butler, if that was his denomination, returned with glasses and a squat bottle of rum. There seemed no hostess. "I don't know if he ever married," said Colley. "He's an old man now."

We sat awaiting the Captain — Colley did not know how he got the title — in deep and comfortable chairs on a verandah with a great view. Some kind of quarter seemed to extend from the house at the back, or some kind of cultivation to go on in the immediate neighborhood, for numerous voices made themselves heard, rich Negro voices, men and women. I said, "They sound mighty gay and cheerful."

"This pen's got the greatest name for good nature. Browne's an oddity with some notion in his head. North says he has money in the funds at home or he could never do it. He says the place makes him nothing. Rather he's always putting in ——"

"All these Negroes speak English after a sort. They don't seem recent."

"They aren't. Browne believes in their breeding and so keeping up the stock. Most planters go the other way about. When their number is worked off and getting low, they buy more out of Africa.   North says Browne hasn't bought for a long time.   There are some here who were born in Africa, but they've almost forgotten it.   He doesn't work them hard either; there are always two or three to a one-man job."

" How old a man is he? "

" Browne?   Seventy, I imagine, though he doesn't look it.   He came out to Jamaica young."

" What does he do when the population grows too great? "

" Sells, I suppose," said Colley.   " Yes, of course.   Junia at North's was raised here."

I listened to the laughter somewhere beyond a thicket of fruit trees.   " I should think that they would miss it here when they're sold."

" Yes," he answered dreamily, " I should think so."

" They have no say in it," I said.   " This island is like Virginia, only a deal more so. That's the climate, I dare say, and the fact that it's an island, and the history of these seas."

" These seas and these islands have a terrible history," he said.   " Well, that is man! "

It seemed not to trouble Colley, or not to trouble him at that time.   And David Scott, upon this mountain shoulder, with the tropic day about him, the light and the air and good-natured sound, with a long deep chair in which to stretch his limbs, with drink at hand if he wanted it, wrapped in leisure, wrapped in balm, said No! to his eternal querying, said, "Don't trouble me now — don't trouble me ever, if you can manage it!"

Browne came home and proved to be a white-haired, strong old man, with a round face and a kind of perpetual beamy look not unmixed with whimsey. He greeted us hospitably, the Negroes grinned when he spoke, the dogs sprang up on him and a parrot flying down from a mango tree perched upon his shoulder. "Universal Benevolence!" I thought. "Father Christmas!"

We had supper of an untidy abundance but well cooked. One hardly counted the attendance, but saw dark countenances come and go, and that one and all seemed happy enough. After supper, we sat upon the verandah in the warm, rose-shot dusk and smoked and talked. He had an easy, old man's loquacity. He wanted to hear about the *Janet* and Daga and Bristol, Liverpool and London, but with a touch of disinterestedness.

"I said to myself forty years ago, 'This thing ought to be better managed! Buy enough women — make them all, men and women, comfortable and happy enough — and see what will happen according to Nature! In short, raise your own Negroes and don't be forever spending fifty pounds for a raw Ashanti or Eboe stark from the Slave Coast!' So I began with this place and thirty odd, male and female, and a

few children. It's paid. They'll tell you, of
course, in Kingston that it hasn't, that I make
nothing. But I do. I make the satisfaction of
seeing a theory *work* — and as you know, young
men, there's nothing in the world like that! If
the Indies and the Continent, North and South,
would go about it my way — be indulgent to
them and give a feast for every baby — there'd
be enough right in America in a hundred years
to cultivate all the fields we're likely to want
cultivated. Then all the cost and worry and
loss of bringing them from Africa might be
stopped for good and all. Turn the slave ships
into spice and oil and cotton ships. That's a
deal healthier trade for all concerned! "

I said, " You'd stop the warring and kidnapping and buying and bringing them. But you'd
keep those who are this side the ocean slaves
forever. Those that you have, and their children, slaves."

"Yes," he said. "Treating them always
kindly. There isn't any other way to get the
work done."

" No, I suppose not," I answered.

*Who would clear the land, who would tend
tobacco and coffee, who would make the sugar,
who would make the rum?*

The rose dusk changed to violet dusk, with a
beat as of wings and the dry voice of an army
and an army of insects. A white and glowing
star set itself above a palm tree. Voices

throbbed from the hidden huts of black men and women and children, mellow voices, voices that laughed and sang.

I said, " Set them free and if they will work for you, pay them their wages."

The old planter knocked the ashes from his pipe. His face was round and pleasant as the moon and on the whole as unenergetic. " That's for Utopia," he said. " No, no, they're children! Best to own and command them like children. But children are not sent us to be harshly dealt with. That's my point. I like children and like to see them happy."

He was a still more benevolent Colonel Amory.

One might live rather happily in an island within an island, with a vast household of " children ", with a soft abundant Nature dropping flower and fruit around. Be happy, lose edge, become rounded like a pebble in a river bed. Be happy and at the same time pretty good, making happy " children " around one, not over-working them or over-punishing them, giving them their little pleasures.

After all, they were barbarians — as the Romans said we Scots were. God knows how long we had been barbarians there in the northern forests when the Romans came. White — black; black — white. Red, yellow, black, white. If Great Nature loved the white so, why did she not make all white? White marble is beautiful, and copper and bronze and ebony are beautiful.

"No, no!" said old Mr. Browne, as though he had answered my thought. "They are naturally inferior and of course we must recognize it. But make them happy — make them happy!"

We soon went to bed. Colley said he was dog-tired and slept, but I lay awake, and the tune in my head went, "When the *Janet* sails, do I sail with her? When the *Janet* sails, do I sail with her?"

Had I money I could live like Browne, who had begun this life when he was as young a man — live as kindly as one might, considering all things — live in a Jamaica of wonderful colors and tumbled mountains and forever summer — live with black folk around me whom I would buy and at need sell, but whom I should treat kindly in the meantime — kindly, with only just such hardness as would ensure their working. But I had not money, so why dream of all that?

I might, through Bartram's influence with North, obtain a situation as clerk in the Company's house, with the ledgers and the other clerks, and the coming in of slave ships and the tallying and recording. But so I should have changed naught, being still with the Royal African Company.

I might become clerk or bookkeeper or overseer to some planter — be as Barget or Williams.

Somewhere on these mountains, on unoccupied land, I might build for myself a hut and thatch it with palm, plant yams about it, and there live as a hermit, a solitary, an eccentric; now and then earning a little from some greater neighbor, enough to buy rum with, a little meal, a gun, a suit of clothes a year. And I liked that better, but not well enough.

I could earn somehow doubtless — enough to live doubtless — and somehow keep a still tongue doubtless — and the years might pass like heavy lilies, growing on the edge of mire, falling, falling, one by one, upon the mire.

The sea and Bartram. The sea and Bartram and the *Janet*. Turning in bed, I made that choice, flung my arm over my eyes and went to sleep.

But waking in the night, I heard as though it were the echo of a deep voice. "There are other ships than slave ships coming, going, and you might go upon one."

I said back, "I should not be so advantageously placed. I should be under much more restraint." And turned upon my side and went to sleep again.

Before dawn I woke once more and that same deep voice was saying, "God." Just that, just the one word. It should have been enough. But I at once grew deaf to it, putting what I thought to be David Scott's needs between me and it.

CHAPTER XIX

THE beginning of the second year on the *Janet* saw a change in my relations with rum and brandy. The body had its reasons doubtless that only reached the mind as recognition of an alteration in taste. I began a course of drinking not at all or more sparingly even than Bartram, for something like three months precisely. That time out, I then with deliberation drank myself into a kind of lucid drunkenness in which I saw a strange world and did strange things therein. For the better part of a fortnight I moved in this perpetually renewed mirage. Then I slept two nights and days on end, and came out of the cabin of Philip Smith a sober man. Three months of the one state, a fortnight of the other, and over and over again. Out of the cabin of Philip Smith, or out of the small house back of the factor's house, deep shaded by palm and pepper trees, on the low hill at Daga.

On the *Janet* I became accepted for what I was. At Daga there was that latitude that no one cared. Rathbone Lace liked me better drunk. Then I was like a sleepwalker, and sleepwalkers did all manner of odd and entertaining and daring things without winking. When he suggested I followed, though now and then I did the suggesting myself.

But on the *Janet* obtained a different version
of latitude. And nothing in the world but Af-
fection caused Captain William Bartram to
keep David Scott upon his ship. He did good
work and was satisfactory throughout the three
months, but those two weeks might come down
at sea, in storm or danger, or in good conditions
and make a danger. And if the stuff were shut
away from him, he grew more of a madman
than with it. So Geordie was told off to watch
him, and Colley kept an eye over him, and William Bartram suffered him where with another
he had hardly waited for port to say, " Begone
this ship! "

Bartram looked grim upon me but I answered
him out of another world. Then I slept twice
around the clock and came to supper like a lamb.
He kept me after McNaughton and Colley were
gone and said, " So you're hame again with your
better man? "

" Is he a better man? "

" He's got the power to ask questions anyhow.
David, you're like your grandfather. I've heard
about him. He was verra responsible and somehow big, except just once in so often when he
sold himself to the devil."

" Just once in so often? I'm not certain that
I'm so like there, Bartram."

He answered dryly, " For all your way of
looking at it, I don't hold that you've sold yourself entirely. Your grandfather sold himself

like you, for short terms. But in one of them
he took a torch and fired his own barns and
byres, and it spread to the whole house and it
was burned. He tried to get through to a room
where was a child, but the rooftree fell and
slew him."

" I've heard the story."

" Then I wish you'd lay it to heart. For
you're like him, David. I've seen his picture."

But I did not wish to talk about torches flung
in barns and byres, and even as I thought that,
saw the flaming barn of Sandy Scott, smelled the
smoke, and marked the cover and the leaves of
Helen Scott's Book begin to move and curl. I
said, " What are you reading now, Bartram? "
For it was the voyage out, and he had time to
read.

" The ' Odyssey ' again," he said, and fell to
speaking of the Phæacians.

One year, two years, into the third year upon
the *Janet*. Counting that first involuntary one
from Norfolk, five voyages.

Pomeroy was dead, knifed by a seaman —
Eldred — whom he had thrice flogged. Bartram hanged Eldred. Hamilton, the surgeon's
mate, was dead of smallpox in Barbadoes, Davis
the boatswain of flux at Daga. Of the forty seamen whom I watched that first day out from Norfolk, more than half were sunk away from view.
Dead, disabled by disease or accident, or simply
gone, vanishing in port towns, saying that they

would reappear but never doing so, spirited
away by their own desires or by those of others.
Bartram accepted losses, filled his number as
best he might and sailed on. More than other
merchantmen slave ships must be forever renewing their crews. Even the *Janet* with William
Bartram for captain.

Her second mate now was Edward Black, and
he was more than a little like Pomeroy.
Wheeler was the boatswain, and a better man
than Davis. Out of the seamen a dozen would
bear watching.

Five voyages. Twenty-five hundred Africans,
men, women and children, taken on at Daga.
Twenty-two hundred delivered to Company
agents in Kingston, Bridgetown and Charleston.
Three hundred dead and given to the sea somewhere in the Middle Passage, or dead in port
before they could be landed. It was all down
in the great book, how they died and when, the
most of that smallpox which we found among us
the third voyage. On the whole, for five voyages, the fortune was good.

The *Janet* had been a long while from Bristol
in England, from her berth there and any true
overhauling and renewing. Under Bartram
what could be done at sea, at Daga, at Kingston,
was always being done, but for all that she was
growing old and worn and sere and foul. When
the next lading had been delivered at Kingston,
he would take her home to Bristol and give her

full time there in which to be made new again.
He himself would go then into the country, or
even, it might be, to Scotland. He would rest
through those months, repose himself, forget
what it was to be captain of a Slave Coast ship.
And Colley would go to London — pay his last
creditor — and like enough settle there and return no more to the hot, blue sea between Africa
and America. McNaughton would surely go
to Scotland, to Stirling where he was born. But
he would come back to the *Janet,* or to William
Bartram, for the two were interlocked in Mc-
Naughton's mind.

What should I do — what should David Scott
do?

It was eight years since Culloden, and if I
changed my name and grew a sailor's beard,
should I not move in safety, even if — even if —
I went to Scotland?

" Aye, you may, man," said Bartram, " if only
you'll time your veesit. It'll never do, David, to
choose the time when the devil has you. That's
the day you should seek the *Janet* or at the worst
a Bristol lodging house I'll give you the name
of. There, with Geordie at the door, you can
bide till Auld Nick and you are weary, the tane
of the tither. But if you meet him in Scotland,
he'll betray you to the Whigs, or you'll betray
yourself and it's the same thing! "

He looked at me with an anxious fold in his
broad brow, sunburned into the hue of one of

his old brown books. " I'd feel safer about you,
David, if you'd bide in Jamaica that while.
Leave you at Kingston, find you at Kingston —
and the old berth on the *Janet* and the books and
the sea and all ——"

" I want to lie on the green grass by Arthur's
Seat once more."

" Well, I'm saying what I think is best, but
you're your ain man."

The full moon that night made of the *Janet's*
sails mountains of pearl and caverns of ebony.
We were going toward Africa. The ship was
clean, was silent save for the ever music, where
we gave it harp strings, of the wind that put us
forward, and the sound now and again of seamen's voices; was spacious. A full sea was running and under the moon there were crests of
light and caverns of night. I watched them,
and Bartram's words kept running through my
head.

" My own man. I am my own man. — David
Scott, you are your own man. — Then why the
devil am I so unhappy? "

It was not necessary to show that I was unhappy. Before Bridgetown in Barbadoes I
overheard — a great water cask on deck hiding
me from them — the steward Benjamin describe
me to Black, the new second mate, just signed
with the *Janet* and a former acquaintance of
Benjamin's. The latter had doubtless been picturing Captain and first mate and surgeon and

all. I came in only for myself. "And there's Mr. Scott——"

"Who's he?"

"He's kin of the Captain. God knows, I think he'd been in some horrid strait in Virginia where he picked him up! Killed a man maybe, or maybe 'twas a woman. — He's a stark, tall Scot with a glint of the Captain about him."

"What does he do?"

"He clerks for the Captain — and the Captain's been always a perfect sea lawyer about putting things down. But he can handle a ship too. He wa'n't no novice there when he came aboard, though he might be what you call rusty. If he'd 'a' wanted it he could have been second mate after Mr. Pomeroy was killed."

"Well, seeing that you are aboard, Benjamin, I'm glad that he didn't want it!"

"We were nearer Cape Verd than we were to the Indies when Eldred killed Mr. Pomeroy and was hanged for it. Then up comes all of a sudden a terrible blow, regular small hurricane! Mr. McNaughton gets struck by a boom — knocked senseless and didn't rightly come to himself for two days. Enduring that storm Mr. Scott was mate and there's no denying he did well. The *Janet* never had any one do better. He's rash and he's not rash — that kind."

Mr. Black demurred. "Give me the kind that's steadily not rash."

Benjamin, who had a turn for analysis, would

not relinquish me. "Yes, poop and forecastle have got a liking for him, but he's got curious ideas about slaves. — Yet he has a slave girl at Daga and he stays quite calm upon this ship."

"Curious ideas?" said Black and spat. "My only idea is they're cattle!"

"About every two months," continued Benjamin, "he gets drunk in the entirest way. The strange thing is that you don't know if he is drunk or is an extraordinary person doing extraordinary things. You tell it at last because there doesn't anything useful come of what he does. They're just fantastic."

"Well, if he drinks that way, he oughtn't never to be mate."

"He's the kind that's more like to be captain, and God knows there are drinking captains enough in the trade!"

"Captain of the *Janet,* you mean?"

"Why, no captain's immortal! If Captain Bartram was to go, he might say to the Company, 'I recommend my kinsman for my place,' and they might listen to him. Mr. McNaughton don't want it. He's been first mate so long that he'd rather die as he's lived. I talk that way," said Benjamin, "but Captain William Bartram ain't like to die yet, and his kinsman will have to stop his particular kind of drinking before *he'll* put him over the *Janet.* That's *his* care for seamen and slaves."

McNaughton called, "Mr. Black!"

" Aye, sir! " and the second mate and steward departed that quarter.

It was true that there was at Daga Fanny. I bought her to make her safe while I was from Africa. She was Fullah, that is, mixed Negro and Moor, from the country where the caravans over the great desert change sand for forest and where the Negro villages grow Mohammedan. She said " Allah " as often as she said " God ", but when she was really moved she used the Negro word for the same Being.

Fanny!

CHAPTER XX

WHEN I was away from Daga she lived with an old woman in Daga village; when I returned she came to the small house among the heavy trees. She was slender, quick, with beautiful black eyes and features rather Moorish than Negro. She could sing richly and sweetly, and I loved to hear her sing. She was merciful to small lives about her and would go out of her way to do a kindness. Once I found her passionately crying and learned that she had been down the hill and upon the beach and had watched two hundred men and women driven from the barracoon to the boats of the *Sharon,* a Boston-owned brigantine.

" Do you care, Fanny? "

" Do you think I am devil? "

" So many of you don't seem to care."

" How do you know? How do you know? How do you know? "

I did not entirely know, though I thought that I knew it of some. The great trouble in this matter is that we say at once, " They are different! " and so leave ourselves no way of seeing how like they are.

Fanny rose from the ground and went off into the shadow of the tree and I did not again see

her cry for the filling or the emptying of the
barracoon. Yet she may have done so many a
time, or cried in her heart where it could not
be seen. Her name was Aja before the factor's
hill at Daga named her Fanny. She might be
twenty when I bought her. Three years before,
being in a boat with others on a river in her own
country, slave hunters set upon them and took
all. She received some hurt and when at last
after long travel and change from hand to hand
she came to Daga, it was seen that the factor
would reject her. There were always a certain
number thrown back upon the hunters' and traders' hands. These were sold for little or nothing
where they might be, or if no one wanted them
and they could not even travel if they were set
free, then they were taken into the bush and
quietly killed. So it might have been with
Fanny, had not Markham the surgeon observed
her and thought he could cure her, and undoubt-
edly felt compassion. In this trade, vast through
time and space, over and over again occur individual emotions and acts of compassion. But
they do not stop the trade. Markham bought
her for a trifle from the trader, put her in Daga
village with old Bembe and in a year she was as
strong as a young palm tree. Markham left her
in the village where she cooked and wove with
Bembe, but not long afterwards, taking the fever
and believing that he would die, sold her for
her own protection to the factor. He might

have freed her, but at Daga she would have been little better off for that. He stipulated good treatment and that she should not depart Africa against her will. I bought her on the same terms from the factor my second time at Daga.

She was a young, barbarian woman, comely, clean, at times affectionate, at times deeply sullen. She had a quick apprehension, a kind of deep tact. There was much in her that I never fathomed, much that I fathomed only afterwards. Each time I came to Daga I found her at the small house.

So it was all around me. Only Bartram, when he came to Daga, paid no visit to Daga village, or to a further village in the bush, or to Oil Palm village up the river; took no woman from one or all of these or from the barracoon. Upon the slave ships, the anchor weighed, any and all intercourse in this sort was straitly forbidden. Between Africa and America, on the broad blue sea, by written and unwritten law, the women of the cargo were cargo only. But in Africa, with Spaniard and Portuguese and French and American and Briton far from home, it was otherwise.

Once, twice, thrice, four times, five times. I saw from the blue Atlantic below the Line the foaming bar, the gleaming beach, the palms, the castle and the flag that I had twice seen with an inner eye before ever I saw the *Janet*. — Daga met that which was evil in me, and the two in-

tertwined.   There was a side of me that cohered
with Rathbone Lace.

I seemed to rush forth to myself in Africa and
to cry "Hail fellow, well met!"   I laughed and
I caroused, but I was not happy.   Markham,
that dour and acid man, once told me as much.
"Unhappy — I seem to recognize in you an unhappy man.   I'm not myself a happy man and
like knows like."

"For why?"

"For why aren't we happy men?   Ah, that's
a question that goes far back on the road!"

We were seated at sunset on his verandah.   I
was waiting for the boat from the *Janet*.   In the
east hung a great moon.   "You do not see me
carol and bubble with joy," said Markham.   "I
do not feel joy and years ago I gave up the
empty carolling and bubbling.   But you still
whistle and joke and stride along, outfacing
yourself."

"Outfacing myself?"

"I suppose so," said Markham wearily.
"Yourself or Justice or Something."

I sat with my eyes upon the round and golden
moon.   Presently I said, "Markham, have you
ever known any one improve in this trade?"

He considered.   "No, I am fair to say I
haven't."

I thought to myself, "Even Bartram, Mc-
Naughton, Colley and David Scott.   Even Bartram, McNaughton, Colley and David Scott."

He had been smoking. Now he laid down his pipe and locked his long, thin, parchment-hued hands. " It is not only this trade — this trade is just a part of it. It is not only African slavery — African slavery is just a part of it. There is something that is needed, for and in you and me and others. I don't know what it is; it is, perhaps, something like light and something like a command. I can see that they ought to come to me, but they don't come to me. Maybe they will to you, maybe not. I only know that to lack them is to know hunger and thirst and nighttime and purposelessness. I have that knowledge of myself that I am an unhappy man, and I have the like knowledge of you. That is all. — There is the boat."

The moon shone upon us so, the boat was picked out by it so, the fifth time at Daga. The *Janet* would presently be sailing with a fine lot of Coromantins, Mandingoes, Fullahs, Ashantis, Whidahs, Eboes and Dualas. The cargo delivered at Kingston, she was for home, for England. It might be a year and more before she came again to Daga. And as yet I did not know if I should go with her to Bristol, or if I should stop in Jamaica. And if I did the latter I was not sure — I might never again come upon the slave ship — not, that is, to sail with her and be part of her. It might be true farewell to Daga.

There was Fanny. I spoke to Bartram. " She is mine — I am fond of her. If I should stay in Jamaica, I could keep her there. I do not want to leave her here where any and everything can happen. Does it matter to you if I carry her with me to Jamaica?"

"That's against the rules, David. I might have McNaughton or Colley or any one speaking for such a permission. It's been over and over proven that it does not do."

"I know it's a general rule," I answered, and proceeded to argue for an exception, showing how it could be managed and she be reckoned both with and not with the *Janet's* lading. He listened, pondering, and at last, though with distaste, he agreed that I might take with me my slave. There would have been no difficulty had I been willing for her to be shipped simply with and like the five hundred, no difference made from Daga to Kingston, and only there, in the unlading, pointed out as my property. But I was not willing; I had rather leave her at Daga.

He agreed, but when he had done so and we had turned toward the factor's hill — we had been walking upon the beach — he stood still and looked at the *Janet.* "Something came athwart me then, David! — Did you ever think how the stars are always there, behind the day?"

Eight days later we sailed.

Fanny made no objection to going to Jamaica. When I told her what I thought of and why, she looked at the sea and at the palms and to the northwest where, far away, was her country, then squarely at Daga castle and barracoon. She waved her hand. " I go like them? "

" No, more comfortably, Fanny." I described how it would be, and that the sea was only six to eight weeks wide, and then I spoke a little of Jamaica, where was sea and white beaches and mountains, and trees and weather much like trees and weather here and where were great numbers of her people. " Those that have gone away in the ships. Mandingoes and Fullahs and others."

" I think that a lie. All of us think that a lie. Why do you never bring any of them back? They say in my country white men's ships all go to a place where they sacrifice dark men and women to their gods. White men have just one god, and he says, 'Give me dark men that I may eat them! More dark people, and more and more!' "

As she looked at me with large eyes, her years at Daga where she heard all manner of other statement than this appeared to roll from her. She was back in her old village, in the forest where it touched the desert, a young barbarian, believing all things so that they were fearful enough. Her eyes widened, she shivered, her hands went up, palm out. I laughed at her and took pains to tell her many things that might alter her opinion. At last she laughed too, and an hour later I heard her singing over her work. But if her mind altered or not — or if it altered and acceded only to alter again and hold to the forest opinion — I do not know. — Or rather I *do* know. I know that it did.

When I bade Rathbone Lace farewell, he said, "Come back — come back next year, David Scott! I'll miss you to-morrow, going up to Oil Palm village — the rum in the boat and you not there! Good-by and Good Luck!"

Bartram heard him. I caught his muttered, "It's a strange, sad thing, I'm thinking, Rathbone my man, your full definition of Good Luck!"

The *Janet* sailed. Slave ships sail at night, so that all the slaves may be below. If they are above hatches they grow frantic, seeing the African shore stand back from them. So many may be trusted to leap overboard.

At sunset our five hundred were induced, urged, thrust, beaten, naked and the men shackled, down upon the slave deck, where they must lie rubbing sides, the feet of one row touching the heads of another, and above small space of heavy darkness between them and the platforms on which others lay, or between the platforms and the deck. Began the continuous sound of the night coming up through the gratings, and presently the reek. It is hot, hot, in Daga harbor, before the wings unfold, before one beats out from the shadow of the land. The multitude below hear the seamen's running feet, the making of sails and weighing of anchor, the shouts they do not understand. The swell rocks the ship; sickness seizes them who have never been to sea, many whom, a little while ago, had never seen the sea. They do not know where they are going or to what fate, except that if it is in the middle and in the end as it is in the beginning, it must be terrible. Their prison becomes a cavern of mere terror and pain and misery. Night passes, that is as long as a year. Gray light filters down. White men appear at the gratings, the gratings are opened.

"Out with you now! — Nearest first — So!"

They come thick up upon deck between poop and forecastle. Overhead are the spread sails, around is the empty blue sea, astern are distant mountains that may be Africa. — Even then there will be attempts to leave the ship.

One first night and morn from land are much the same as another. So with this time on the *Janet*. The only woman who did not fare quite as the other women was the girl Aja or Fanny, who was known to belong to me. She wore her cotton dress; at night when the others were herded below, she curled herself upon the deck upon a coil of rope and slept there. But throughout the day she was with them all, men, women and children. They were hardly strangers to her, for they had been collecting for weeks and months into Daga barracoon, and at times parties from Daga village might go to the stockade and watch and talk. The fate was so common all over Africa — one might hear news and see known faces from tribes and villages with which one had acquaintance. Each time the traders brought in parties, Fanny went with old Bembe to see if there were Fullahs.

From the poop deck, from time to time, I marked her in the crowded waist, finding her by her scanty white dress among the unclothed forms. She was there all day. The weather was good, the ship sailed steadily. Bartram had followed his wont and standing with the cargo before him had assured it of good treatment, as long as it itself was good, of safety and food and just as much water as could be spared, and of ultimate content in the Island of Jamaica. Colley had made his round and sent two or three into hospital. We kept a store of native drums and castanets and several of these were tossed down to them with the suggestion that dance and song were good for the body and spirit. When I looked that way again, she was dancing. A small space had been cleared; two men, seated on the boards, were beating drums with a rapid, insistent and wild rhythm. Aja, another girl and two or three boys danced. The shackled men, the women, watched absorbed, squatted or standing close together around the cleared floor which must be small, small, in so thronged a hall. Hardly smaller, though, than I have seen in some Highland gatherings. Highland dances mean something, and I thought that this one

did also. The boys ceased to dance, the girl
stopped, but Aja danced on. She had now a
castanet in her hand; the drums and that
sounded all the time, continuous as water falling or wind on a roaring day. The noises of ap-
proval or indifference ceased; all became quiet.
Those who could not see appeared to take the
sight from others; all could hear the drums and
the castanet. I began to feel a tension and to
pick the meaning. The first dancing had been
ancient love dancing, mating dancing. This had
ended. The woman dancing in the cotton dress
was expressing another theme. Bartram came
beside me on the poop deck.

"That's a religious war dance. — Mr. Mc-
Naughton!"

"Aye, sir, I understand!" McNaughton
went forward.

"David, you'll tell that wench the eve the
kind of dances we'll have here and no other!"

"I'll speak to her."

I did, when the sun was underneath the sea,
and the west all a carmine flare, and the five
hundred below, and the usual dull sound and
stench coming up through the gratings, and the
now darkened sails of the *Janet* flapping like bat
wings in a fitful and sunken breeze. I came to
her where she was sitting, her knees drawn up
and her hands around them, her eyes fastened,
not on the flaming west but on the east that we

" Fanny! "

" Yaas."

" Don't let us have any more dancing like
that! All these Coromantin and Mandingo men
are to be quieted, not stirred up. You have
sense, and you've lived long at Daga and understand. — You understand, Fanny? "

" Yaas. — I did not mean to do wrong."

I left her seated there, not far from a grating.
An hour or two later I marked her in her corner,
apparently asleep, her arm under her head. As
I turned toward my own quarters, I met the
boatswain Wheeler whose watch it was. " A
hot night, sir! One of those nights for African
dreams."

" African dreams? " I answered. " Just what
are they? — But I think I know, boatswain."

" They're when you seem a considerable way
back upon the road. You're yourself, but you
seem a considerable way back. The road's familiar — that's the kind of dread in the
dream —— "

" Yes, I know them," I said. " European or
Asian or African. — Good night, Wheeler! "

The next day was again a hot and listless day.
Only among the Negroes did there seem much
life, but there went on jabbering and dancing
and singing and a good deal of laughter. It was
quite beyond what was usual — but each voyage
provided its own difference. Each five hundred
that we conveyed struck, so to speak, an altered

note, or — despite its being classed as all of a
hue — changed in color. It depended in great
measure upon the natural leaders within the
swarm, but also on the subtle variations within
each breast. What seemed evident after the first
day and night was that the *Janet* had not, this
passage, the woebegone and listless crowd that
sometimes she carried. But all this day the
drumming and singing and movement, in so far
as there was room for movement, remained
cheerful. From the morning on, Fanny was
with and of it. I remember thinking, "It's a
good part she's playing — to help them on so."

So light was the wind that three nights out
from Africa the mountains, faint and blue, yet
kept the eastern sky. It was hot, the ship foul
to the nostril; again to my sense, and this time
to Colley's also, was a haze, a smoke, a cloud
about her of what she was. All sound above
man height was fallen to a droning and a flapping. All Negroes save Tom and Don in the
cook's galley, and Fanny, stretched motionless
in her appointed nook, were under the gratings.
No more complaint than was usual came up
through these. Rather less than usual. I heard
McNaughton say, "We've got a quiet, jolly
lot this making — just a wheen too jolly
maybe ——"

The strong watch was set. McNaughton himself had the decks to-night. In the forecastle
Dory was playing the fiddle — an old jig called

Money Musk. This ended, those who could sleep slept. Bartram went his rounds with his long padding step like an old lion, then retired to his sleeping cabin, where ran his shelf of books with the Bible in the middle, and hung in their rack pistols and cutlass.

I was quite sober — had been so for a fortnight and would be so throughout this passage. I lay in my small, small cabin where still at times I felt Philip Smith. I felt him to-night, then I passed from him to Christian Todd and his boat coming down the James River, and I thought, " I will let his flute play me to sleep." I slept and waked. It was very hot. I saw by the stars out of the window that midnight was near. I slept again and dreamed. The flute was playing — but it changed to pipes skirling and dirling in a purple glen — and then to a hammering and hammering that the guide that goes along in sleep informed me was due to the putting up of Hawley's gibbet in the Haymarket whereon to hang, not Jacobites, but easy old Bartholomew Browne, up in the Blue Mountains above Kingston. That seemed to frighten me, for I awoke and the sweat upon me was cold. For a moment I lay listening to the echo of the dream — a continuing hammering. Next I became conscious that the sound did not belong to the inner but to the outer life. I sat up in my bed, then left it and stood uncertain. I heard a pistol shot and a shout, "Watch!

Watch! Watch!" and then a wild yelling from a hundred throats and knew whose throats they were.

When I reached the deck, the gratings had been forced upward from below. There were the lanterns, and some one had fired the great cresset provided always against trouble in the darkness. We had light enough, though none too much. Coromantins, Mandingoes, Ashantis were pouring up and out. In some way they had freed themselves from their shackles; they brandished these now for weapons. They were yelling, they came forth thick as bees, strong and furious men, and ever as they swung themselves on deck, others pressed behind them. The *Janet* turned into gigantic noise. Her seamen too were shouting, running for arms. Bartram's voice came towering.

"Are you ready? Fire!" A dozen muskets flashed. The *Janet* seemed to shriek. There fell almost as many Africans, but what was that to hundreds, wholly desperate? Had those who were forth hesitated, those behind had pushed them on, coming up as it were through the ship from the depths of the sea.

I saw Bartram — McNaughton — Black — all seamen in their places. The barricades were manned — cutlasses, pistols and muskets — and the boys and Tom and Don behind to take and load and pass. The night was not dark. It drew toward morning, there swung a quarter moon in the sky, and the ship's cresset and lanterns gave light beside. Bartram had one barricade, McNaughton the other. I saw Colley with the latter; I stood with Bartram. The air rocked with the din. Below hatches was a volcano, belching dark lava, lava that parted and rolled upon this barricade and upon that.

" Fire!" shouted Bartram.

We were above them and fired down. Men fell, there rose shrieks, the torrent recoiled upon itself. " It won't last," said Bartram. " They're thoroughly up! We'll have to kill half of them." A huge Coromantin, moving, gesticulating, where the light struck him, held my eye. He was brandishing both arms, and one hand grasped the iron shackle loosened from his ankles and the other a file!

A slave cargo comes searched and naked into the slave ship. — But there are files enough in the stores at Daga. And as I thought that, I saw another in a Mandingo hand, kept for weapon where real weapons were none. — There was one slave who came aboard clothed, who even had with her a small bundle of her toys and fineries. — I looked for a glint of white cotton and I found what I sought.

She was with them, in the middle of the storm. Other women too. In Dahomey the king has women soldiers, a great guard of Amazons. It is not likely that any of these were aboard. But there were women who came with the men out of the deeps and fought.

With a great and frenzied cry, all bore against the barriers.

" Fire! "

Crash and smoke and shrieking, and many were down and trampled. But they came on and swarmed up and over, naked and weaponless, and clutched and locked with men who had cutlasses, who had firearms. What was their vision? Their vision was the seizure of the ship and the death of all white men, save only just enough maybe to show them how to put about the ship, how to bring her again to Africa, not to Daga but some lonely place. Then, then, kill all and leave the ship — take the boats, and swim, and get ashore, and burst away from the sea, inland, inland, and get maybe to the old villages; or if not that, make a fastness in the hills and live there. It invited from the slave ship; it beckoned and smiled.

The vision of the fifty white men was life, even if the cargo were lost. We slew and were slain.

But we had all manner of weapons and their spears and knives were far off in the African villages.

Victory crossed to our side.

A cold light lifted in the east. We leaned against the barricade and twelve men were dead, their own weapons wrested from them, turned against them, and twenty had their wounds. But the deck below us was a shambles. We had shot and shot them down, and what the gun did not, the cutlass did. Under the dawn lay thick the dead and the desperately wounded. Less than a hundred dark figures raised their hands and cried for mercy. These and the women with children who cowered beneath the gratings were all that were left of our lading. No great number of the wounded were like to recover. Eight thousand guineas easily must be thrown into the sea.

I saw white cotton, torn and blood-stained, Fanny lying dead, near the big Coromantin with the file.

CHAPTER XXI

THE house, stone and fairly large, faced the sea, across a quarter mile of cane that was bright green, that rippled like the sea, that sent up, here and there, pale, purplish, feathery heads of bloom, ghostly in the twilight. Along the sea ran a narrow beach of deep, soft, ivory sand, and bordering the sand and the road went a ribbon of sea grape and cocoanut trees; and where streams ran into the ocean, or it was marshy and shoal, stood mangrove that is a desolate growth. The cane stretched like the sea right and left of the house, but behind it a wood ran up into hills and the hills into mountains. Palm and mango and allspice and the cotton tree and mahogany and many others. The mountains had beautiful shapes; a troop of them, joined at base but above sharply separate, peaky, horned and rounded forms, clothed with an amethystine, a dreamy light. The sea was superbly colored. An Italian painter could give it there no hint, must take the hint from it. A highway ran between the sea and the cane — the cane of My Fancy, for so was the estate named. Diverging from this the plantation road struck through the cane and then between thinly planted trees to the house, but there, bending, went toward the sea again and found, halfway, the sugar mill. The

sugar mill had a tall chimney, and the smoke
went out like a gray plume and all day long it
shredded away with the moving air. A stone
aqueduct of many and many an arch ran up into
the hill and fetched water thence to grind the
cane. About the mill grew a cluster of long
and low buildings, and the whole did not lack of
making a picture. The heaped wagons and the
empty wagons, the white, wide-horned oxen
came and went, to the mill, from the mill. At
a stone's throw, on either side the dripping aqueduct, were strewn, haphazard, the huts that
sheltered at night the slaves who cut the cane and
made the sugar.

These and the oxherds and stable men and
boatmen and nondescripts and the house servants in their own quarter back of the great house
constituted, men, women and children, the
nearly two hundred out of Africa owned by My
Fancy. Out of Europe were eight indentured
white men, "servants" as against "slaves."
And there were three "bookkeepers", who in
Virginia would have been called overseers, and
a manager and his assistant. Fifteen white men
in all.

The owner, Mr. Godfrey North, a connection
of North, the Company's agent, was gone with
his family to England, his object to put his son at
school and to marry off his daughter. He pur-
posed an absence of a year. His old manager
in whose charge My Fancy must be left did not

please him — there was a change — a new man must be sought. North in Kingston brought him and Bartram together. I was spoken of. — At last I came to supper with North and his kinsman.

I was the manager at My Fancy, engaged for the term of the owner's absence, with a fair salary, a free hand, the great house, emptied of all its former inmates, to dwell in, between the hills and the sea.

The *Janet,* the blood stains scrubbed and holy-stoned from her decks, the relation of misadventure, unforeseen and occurring despite all care and good conduct on the part of officers and crew, duly entered in her log, duly drawn up in a memorandum for the Company, sailed for Bristol.

"Will you go or will you not, David? You know this thing makes no difference to me. You've got a star, too, man. — And as for ill luck continuing and some discovery of you being made, and its coming as a back-blow upon me also — why, you see, man, William Bartram will risk that! — I dinnae think," he said in his reasonablest voice, "that after almost ten years the danger's mair than you can carry."

But I had made up my mind not to involve him. I said that I would stay in Jamaica and that I preferred it so.

The *Janet* sailed. I watched her forth from Jamaica Harbor, and then, walking back to

North's, found there two horses from My Fancy and a mulatto boy — they are all " boys " though they are fifty — who was to return with me. My belongings went into two pair of saddlebags. I said good-by to North and two or three others in Kingston, and an hour after sunrise started for the northern shore and the western end of the island, for it was there lay My Fancy. It was like riding across Scotland from Inverary to Dundee and then by ocean side from Dundee to Dornoch. — It was not Scotland, but a sugar island of the West Indies, and the sea the Caribbean.

The *Janet* had sailed three months ago. I lived in the great house alone save for Atkins the assistant and managed My Fancy. For the sugar manufacture I was soon instructed there, and as for labor and the handling of it, behind me lay five years in Virginia. Tobacco or sugar, what was the odds? And though there I had been among the handled I knew well enough by observation the other side. The sea and the *Janet* also gave training. And to move among and be over Africans was no novelty.

Atkins, a short, sturdy, curt, efficient person, five years my junior, had the immediate supervision. I looked at affairs from two or three steps above him, parcelled my time and gave or withheld my presence as it seemed good. Yet I was not idle, and all matters of real dubiety came before me. Atkins, fortunately, took a liking to me and I to him. It was an old, long-established place — My Fancy — just as had been Amory Hall in Virginia. Old, that is, according to colonial notions. All things went on smoothly enough after the lavish, loose-end, colonial system, lavish and loose-end at least in warm climates and where there is slavery. A full two thirds of the My Fancy Negroes had been born in Jamaica, and of the remaining third very few were recently from the Slave Coast. In consequence there was little turbulence. And by and large the treatment was kindly, just as I could now see that it had been kindly at Amory Hall — "kindly" being a word of a high degree of relativeness. Of course they must work, and not for themselves. Two or three hours' toil a day would have provided, in such a climate, all that they, as yet, desired for themselves. But to make sugar for the world and ease and luxury for one family, they labored from sunrise to sunset. Of course, being property, they must not be idle and they must not run away. Of course, if they were guilty of either, they must be whipped as that was really the only way to teach them. If they were incorrigible more and more pain must be heaped upon them, and if they deserved death the law would see that they got it. But all this provided for, there was not at My Fancy and there was not at Amory Hall wanton cruelty, but rather, in the interstices of the system, kindness, or what was meant for that; what, relatively speaking, was that. At any rate, at My Fancy, one heard a great deal of genial Negro laughter, of good-natured talk and singing. — But the thing rested slavery.

The eight white men likewise were enslaved, but for a term of years only, and they had sold themselves, and were called servants, not slaves.

The great house had cool, large, mahogany-floored and panelled rooms, high-ceiled, slightly furnished and echoing, a wide lower and upper hall, deep windows and a porch from which I saw the sea of cane, the mill, and then the utter ocean. The whole was mine to wander in. Atkins had a room that made a jut from the main building. The two of us together were supposed to keep the house from damage or entry, having abandoned for that purpose the mana-ger's cottage. There also slept, in a small cham-ber next to Atkins, a powerful mulatto named Dick, who had been born upon the place. And there were two strong and fierce dogs, Nero and Cæsar.

Three months. When I had been at My Fancy something more than six weeks, at twi-light one evening, sitting smoking in the stone porch, I spoke to Atkins of that periodic shift of mine to another level of feeling, thinking and doing, warned him that it might begin in a day or two, and told him what to ignore in me, what to acquiesce in and what to override. " Mr.

Godfrey North knew about this before we signed. For all I know, you may know too."

"Yes, Mr. North told me," said Atkins. "But you see in this country the difficulty is to get men who don't drink all the time. He snapped at you!"

Well, I drank, and for a fortnight became a crazed spirit moving among dream landscapes. Then out I came, and found that Atkins and the mulatto Dick had kept me from wreaking any especial mischief. When I had ordered fantastic things they had said "Of course!" and when my back was turned disobeyed or substituted. I always thought that I was a kind of sultan.

Well, I came out one afternoon and took a great dip in the sea, and was David Scott again.

The months slipped by, bead on bead.

All these "great houses" in Jamaica as in Virginia practised to their own color and class a boundless hospitality. The inns were few indeed and wretched. Who rode on the highway and found himself toward eve too far from his destination, or who merely wished to break his journey, noon or evening, turned, as a matter of course, into some plantation road. He might be a planter or a merchant or a lawyer or a clergyman or a doctor, or he might be of simpler estate, but if he were free and white he had entertainment. To these lonely estates he was news, he was society. Such a guest occasionally rode up to the great door of My Fancy.

But they were not many.   In all this island,
which is a large one, there were not, I suppose,
eighteen thousand white persons.   Strew these
over so great an extent and save in the towns
there are few indeed in any ten miles.   Lonely,
lonely, the plantations are lonely, each by itself,
a small world in space.

Yet they stopped at My Fancy, one alone or
two or even three together.   Perhaps once in ten
days I had company for dinner or for supper.
All the months together I saw the planter and
the trader and the lawyer and the doctor and the
sea captain, and the clergyman and others —
more of the planter and the merchant, less of the
others.   And one and all they had to me the
mark of something less than the good, and David
Scott had and knew he had the selfsame mark.
Yet many of them were what you call amiable
and honest.

They assumed the system upon which and in
which they lived.   They assumed that it was
Deity's system, wherever Deity lived.   Slavery
of dark Africans, benighted, childlike heathen!
Servitude, over the world, of white men and
women if they were born by the sea of poverty
and trouble.   And very strangely poverty and
trouble were both God's good will that it were
blasphemous really to try to overthrow, and the
error of the individual man or woman who must
suffer for it — need not be overmuch compas-
sionated, seeing that they were but getting their

deserts. And the moral of it all, " Nothing can be really changed. And why should it be? for on the whole it is a pretty good affair."

So the planters, merchants, captains, lawyers, doctors and clergy.

But none that rode by My Fancy and asked for a meal or a night's lodging were in straits for either. None who rode by My Fancy had been slave or servant, or if any one had come out from home as the latter, he now strenuously forgot it.

But I had not forgotten. I had not forgotten the Tolbooth, nor the *King William,* nor Amory Hall, nor Daniel Askew's, and I knew Daga on the Slave Coast, and I knew the slave ships. I had not forgotten, and the mark of something less than good was upon me plain and I knew it. Plainer than upon them, who were only unimaginative.

CHAPTER XXII

IN a small room at My Fancy I found a few
books, and among them " The Faery Queen."
During these first months I read and reread and
read again this volume with a kind of desperate
clinging to its beauty. It came to help me, to
give me a kind of gleam.

I saw in a sort of moonlight how general was
the problem, how general and how deep, and
how it allied with all other delays and struggles,
how they were all one, mere varieties of one
another, and how both ill and remedy might lay
somewhere in that mysterious other-world called
" Within."

I saw it, I say, as by moonlight, but it went
then no further. Instead, when I had been six
months at My Fancy my soul entered Egyptian
darkness. Outer life went on as it had done, but
within I sat in blackness, and before me sat the
Sphinx, and I did not move and she did not
move.

There was a bit of beach, a lonely place, that
I haunted in these months. At dawn I went to
it to bathe. There were no great breakers, but
I swam and floated, and then came out and lay
naked upon the bone-white sand.

The sun rose, but my soul was dark and my

mind a treadmill. And there was a narrow estuary, sluggish water and shoal, winding between mangroves. I came down through the cane to this and found a boat and on winter days that knew far more heat than summer days in Scotland, rowed myself up and down or sat idle in a shadow from the dismal growth. Here and yonder stood a long-legged wading bird, motionless as I. Crabs scuttled over the mud; at low tide the oysters were visible fastened to the mangrove roots, the forlorn forest of them; where the soil was firmer tall trees overhung the water that mirrored an azure, empty sky. It was not so unlike Africa, but I lacked Rathbone Lace. I did not want him; I wished now to be alone. Sometimes I rode into the hills but not often. At long intervals I rode three leagues or so to the nearest town, sat for an hour or two in the inn, wine before me that I did not always drink, then rode back to My Fancy. But it was the house itself, the house at eve when Atkins had said good night, the house in the night time — I slept, then I waked. My room was large, with a bare, stained floor, with a couple of tall presses, with three windows giving upon the cane and the sea. I rose when I could not sleep and paced this floor or took my station at now the one and now the other window. Sometimes when the moon shone I opened my door and paced barefooted the great upper hall or wandered in the vacant rooms. These windows were closed. I returned and from my own heard the wind in the cane and the surf upon the shore.

It was now the world, not one part of it but the whole.

It was now, *What am I and what is He?* not a particular year and plan in the so-called existence of a so-called David Scott.

It was a deep and large place, not the Slave Coast nor the slave ship, nor Amory Hall, nor Daniel Askew's, nor My Fancy, nor the *King William,* nor the Tolbooth, nor Culloden Field where white men shot one another down, though all of them were in that ocean and that whirlwind and that mountain of fire.

The place was dark, the fire was dark. At times there were plains of ashes and then I thought, " Why not kill myself? "

But I was not the kind to kill myself. Had I been so I should have done it at Daniel Askew's.

There I had been the slave. Now I was, so to speak, the master, being manager for a master. There I had thought, " Why not kill myself? " Here I thought the same. For all the worldly difference, the state was the same.

I could leave My Fancy and I could leave the *Janet.* But others would step into my shoes as I had stepped into theirs. I did not know then what I felt, but now I know that I felt the General Man and his self-destructiveness.

Up and down, up and down, I walked barefoot up and down. I walked the long hall as it were the deck of a ship and saw the moon framed in the western window, and each time I faced that way it was nearer the sea. — As I walked the old Lykewake Dirge came and walked with me.

This ae night, this ae night,
Every night and alle,
Fire and sleet and candle light,
And Christ receive thy saule.

I read it with Mysie Johnston in the glen at home, and the bird was singing in the thorn. — Then I was at Daga and in the Oil Palm village, and a desolate wind howled in my soul. I saw the *Janet,* and Fanny lying dead upon the heaped slave deck. — O Mysie Johnston and the throstle in the white thorn! — O the gross, thick darkness!

To Brigg o' Dread thou comest at laste.

It was not my own fortune but the world's fortune. My own and the world's were one fortune, and it was bad.

From Brigg o' Dread when thou mayst passe,
Every night and alle,
To Purgatory fire thou comest at laste,
And Christ receive thy saule.

The moon hung just over the sea. I stood in the window and watched it, but my soul was away with the Sphinx.

If ever thou gavest meat and drink
Every night and alle
The fire sall never make you shrink. —

If meat and drink thou never gavest nane,
Every night and alle.
The fire sall burn thee to the bare bane. —

What was meat and drink?
" To do the will of Him who sent me." That
started out. Who sent me? What am I and
what is He? *The same, and I feel my own
wounding?*

The fire sall burn thee to the bare bane.

The moon touched the sea. Cæsar began to
bark. A voice outside was calling. I went to
the window at the rear of the hall and heard
Dick quieting Cæsar, then Atkins' " What's the
matter there? "

" It's a child very sick, sah. Maria's child.
She say for Jesus' sake give her some medicine! "

Maria cooked for us and lived just by the
kitchen across the yard. I called down, " I'll
come, Bob."

A torch lighted the hut. The child lay con-
torted upon a mat on the earthen floor. I
thought it was poison and went back to the house
for remedies out of a big closet that looked and
smelled a veritable apothecary's shop, then re-
crossed the yard and got the stuff at last down the
child's throat, after which we made a fire and
held him by it, rubbing his body. The medicine

worked, he vomited, the small twisted frame relaxed, he opened his eyes, gasped and began to wail. Maria gathered him into her lap, I gave him a spoonful of weakened rum; he hushed, stretched himself, then curled into a ball and went to sleep.

" He's all right now."

Maria laid him upon the mat, then stood up. She was a slender, charcoal-dark, dramatic creature. Now she raised her hands to heaven, then spread them abroad, then curtseyed to me not once but thrice, each time more profoundly than the foregoing, just as, I think, she may have seen the young ladies of the North family practise for the Governor's ball in Spanish Town. " Thank you, master! Maria thanks you, master! May the Lawd Jesus stand for you at the end! O Maria and Bob and Little Bob thanks you, master! May the Lawd Jesus step up to the Big Chair and say, ' I was a little black boy and I took what was bad for me, and this white man worked over me and brought me through! ' — Yaas, master, what you want you just say ——"

David Scott went back to the great house. He had seen abundant small kindnesses, abundant small, right actions through life. A kind of surge of these everywhere and in all times came upon him. But there rose to meet it a corresponding wave of cruelties and stupidities. — Something, something was needed so tall that it saw through and over both and built another sea!

I threw myself on my bed and slept and waked unhappy. I went down to the mill and did a round of things, and then I rowed again among the mangroves, and felt again oppressive night, more deep, more black than before.

Another week and the time came round to drink and forget in a paradise not without horror.

That two weeks was over. I came down to the sea at dawn, stripped and plunged in and swam across to the reef. And here I sat and watched the coming of the sun, and all the world was still and dry and empty to me.

After an hour I swam back to shore, dressed and came up through the screen of sea grape to the road. A man walking by turned his face toward me. A white man, rather tall and plainly dressed, with a long, pale, quiet face, broken and made animate by very bright, dark eyes. He seemed to have been upon the road some time, judging by the dust upon him and his broken shoes and an air of not being fresh from bed and ease. He carried a staff and leaned upon it when he stopped to greet me. "Good morning, friend!"

I answered "Good morning!" and made to cross the road toward the My Fancy opening.

"Can thee tell me how far I am from the town?"

"Three leagues," I said, and noticed again his weariness. "Have you been walking through the night?"

"Through much of it, friend."

"Do you want breakfast? This is the My Fancy estate. If you will go to the house they will give you bread and meat and coffee."

He stood as if pondering, his hand upon his staff, his eyes level, then raised. "Why, friend, if thee will I shall be grateful."

"Come along then. I am going there myself. The family is from home."

For a few paces we moved together upon the highway, then turned under the huge cotton tree into the road through the cane. He looked at it, on either hand, tall and waving in the early light.

"Thee grows so green and high! Thee, too, gives praise, and thy great longing is to give full and innocent praise." He turned his eyes upon me. "What is thy name, friend?"

"David Scott."

"Then, David, if thee did know how empty is my stomach, thee would be glad thee has the means to fill it!"

"Why, hunger is hunger," I said. "I have been hungry. 'Thee' and 'friend' and 'David.' Are you a Quaker?"

"So thee calls us," he answered cheerfully.

"I have met two or three in my life," I said, "and found them very good folk. But there are few of you in Jamaica, and I seem to have heard that you are not particularly welcome."

He laughed. " Thy qualifying word is not strong enough! I have been five months in Jamaica, and truly, David, thee is the only man, apparently in authority, whose voice I have heard say ' Quaker ' and yet continue friendly. Thee is in authority? "

" I am manager of this estate."

" If thee asks me to breakfast will thee not get into trouble with thy master? "

" I do not precisely call him master," I answered. " Besides, he is in London."

We walked on between the cane shaking in the morning wind. I did not care if he were sectary, Jew or paynim. My likes and dislikes did not depend on these things. Presently we met two great wagons and their oxen with half a dozen men bound for the Five Trees field. Some were riding, some walking, and all cheerful enough in the bright air and free with " Morning, master! Morning, master! " We stood aside to let all pass, and when they were by the Quaker turned and watched them into the distance.

" I gather, friend David, that it is a kindly plantation. Good the child in the arms of Giant Ill."

I did not answer. The house now rose before us, and from the rear was blown a great conch shell.

"That sounds sweetly!" he said. "I do not suppose thee has been in Africa?"

"Yes, I have. Many times."

He looked surprised. "As a trader?"

"Yes. On the slave ship *Janet.*"

Checking his long, deliberate stride, he stood under a palm — we now had left the cane — and looked at me with a new interest, but hardly a flattering one. "Ah!" he said. "And what made thee do that?"

I answered, "Needs must when the devil drives."

"Is thee sure he drives?"

"Not wholly but sufficiently sure," I answered and preceded him up the ten stone steps to the door.

At breakfast I proposed to him that he rest with us until to-morrow. He was evidently footsore, had been walking, he said, for the better part of a week. Now and then he met with a lift but not often. In the town to which he was making lived a brother Friend who could give him certain information. He was going to get this, and then return the length of the island to Kingston in time for the sailing of the *Mary Pembroke* for Liverpool. I asked him why he had not bought or hired a horse, and he answered that in the first place he was a city man, little used to horseback, and that when they talked of mountains and rough paths instead of roads a voice within had said, "Thee knows two feet. Rest content without six." In the second place he was short of money and must save where he could in order to spend where he must. The enterprise in which he was engaged, he said, had been more expensive than he and others had reckoned. "That does not matter," he ended. "But I must skimp between here and Liverpool."

"What is the enterprise?"

We were seated, just us two, at the mahogany table in the hall. Atkins was gone to the mill. We had eaten and drunk, and a boy that we called Puck was taking away the dishes. My guest waited till he was out of the door at the back, then he said, with his bright, dark eyes very full and quiet upon me, "David, we who are Friends are at many points not of one mind with the world around us. One of those points is the propriety of that very slave trade in which thee has been engaged. Two years ago our Society resolved to send a member into North America and another to this island to the end that it might have certain first-hand observations. I was chosen for Jamaica, and I have been going about the work with quietness for a year and more."

"My wonder is," I said, "that being so free-spoken, you are not spending your time in some gaol."

"I am not always so free-spoken," he answered serenely. "There was a little trouble at

Spanish Town where I was accused of preaching sedition and inciting slaves to rebellion. But the Lord's hand was over me and I escaped."

We rose from table, and I showed him a room where he might rest. It was next to mine. We paused together by a window. "Will thee go again, David, on the slave ship?"

"Yes. In a few months' time."

"Things are strangely written," he said. "Perhaps it is to some good that thee goes."

"Do you Quakers think to end human slavery?"

"It is the Light Within, not us 'Quakers' that will end it. It may be a long time, David. There are instruments, of course. And times and seasons. As for African slavery it may continue a long, long time. Where it is established. The parents and the children and the grandchildren and their grandchildren. Those who are already brought and the born in the land, and they who shall be born. But it is borne in upon Friends, David — and others, too; and others too — that the Slave Trade itself might cease. The making and bringing more across the sea, continually and forever. The tearing them from their land and forcing them here. It might cease, and cease in our day, David. The Light has grown that much, it seems to us. It will grow further, of course, but not for a time. — So, David, thee may not be chained to thy slave ship forever."

"Am I chained? It is said to be the Negroes who are chained."

"Oh, thee is chained!" he answered cheerfully. "Thee and thy ship captain and crew. Thee is chained here, my poor David. Can thee not see and hear thy manacles? *I* can. Thee wears thy manager's chains, and the owner here wears his chains."

I said, "This is the first time I have ever heard it determinedly said that the traffic with Africa for slaves should and must stop. I know men who would secretly welcome that, and I know men who would rouse the dogs and beat you forth.—Yes, I am chained, but to something else and more than My Fancy and the *Janet*. Something larger and darker. I am chained to living, and the devil and myself."

He jerked his hand toward the shining cane and the sea and the road between. "The Voice said back there, 'Lo, a poor, chained one!' So I came with thee, David."

I broke into laughter. "So I and not you are the fed? Well, let your pride have it so!"

He put out his long hand and touched me and his dark, bright eyes came again fully into mine. "Both of us are fed, David, both, both! Thee has done unto me and I have done unto thee. The chain is in thy laughter and thy slavery is deep, including as it does all slavery. But thee will come forth, David! Thee will lift the gravestone and come out and up."

With that he made a strange, wide gesture and turned from the window to the cool quiet room and its bed. " I was walking the most of the night, and yesterday too was tiring unto me."

I left him to his repose and went to the mill. Things there proceeded as usual. I caught up the threads of work neglected or done awry by David Scott during his two weeks. I was busy, and so partly buried my Quaker and his errands, and Daga and the *Janet,* and that dark idleness inside me where I sat with the Sphinx. The conches and horns blew for dinner. I returned to the house and found him still sleeping. Atkins and I ate together, and I told him just that I had sheltered a Quaker who seemed a good and harmless man and would depart if not to-night then in the morning.

Atkins looked at me shrewdly. " Aye, they seem harmless, but to most of our folk, Mr. Scott, a pirate appears the luckier guest! They're a curious lot, with their ' thees ' and ' Call no man master ' and ' Go not to war ' and their ' Voice ' and ' Inner Light.' Mr. North can't abide them. Not that there are many in Jamaica! "

" This man came from England and is going back on the *Mary Pembroke.*"

" And that's a good thing for him to do! " said Atkins, and pushed back from table. " Of course he can't poison the house while he is here, and I just wouldn't say anything about him in the letter to London this month."

He was cautious, liking My Fancy and meaning to abide there. David Scott did not intend abiding, but he recognized responsibility. "He will go in the morning at latest," I said, and went to my own room for the afternoon rest, then to the mill, then again, an hour before sunset, to the house, and found him sitting in the porch, his bundle beside him, his staff across his knees and his eyes upon the very splendid clouds in the west, above the sea. "There will be a good moon," he said. "I will eat with thee, David, and then thee shall set me on the road and I will trudge to the town and ere midnight knock at Friend Thomas's door."

I said, "If you care to pass the night ——" but he shook his head, and I did not press it. Puck gave us supper in the hall, Atkins absenting himself for his own reasons. He told me certain things that I had not known, having to do with his Society and with individuals out of it. I had not known there was any conscious attempt anywhere putting out, however faintly, force against the Slave Trade. But he said there was a growing feeling, that it would come to a head, and some day the whole matter would be brought before Parliament. He took from his pocketbook a slip of paper and laid it under my eyes. It was the copy of a Resolution passed by the Yearly Meeting of Friends.

" We fervently warn all in profession with us that they carefully avoid being any way concerned in reaping the unrighteous profits arising from the iniquitous practise of dealing in Negro or other slaves; whereby in the original purchase one man selleth another as he does the beasts that perish without any better pretension to a property in him than that of superior force, in direct violation of the Gospel rule, which teacheth all to do as they would be done by and to do good to all, being the reverse of that covetous disposition which furnisheth encouragement to these poor, ignorant people to perpetuate their savage wars, in order to supply the demands of this most unnatural traffic, by which great numbers of mankind, free by nature, are subject to inextricable bondage, and which hath often been observed to fill their possessors with haughtiness, tyranny, luxury and barbarity, corrupting the minds and debasing the morals of their children, to the unspeakable prejudice of religion and virtue and the exclusion of that holy spirit of universal love, meekness and charity which is the unchangable nature and the glory of true Christianity. We therefore can do no less than, with the greatest earnestness, impress it upon Friends everywhere that they endeavor to keep their hands clean of this unrighteous gain of oppression."

I read and gave the paper back. " It is enwound in every civilized country with commerce and revenue and private interest, ambition, pride and gain. It is like back and front — I don't know the thunderbolt that will split them!"

"Yet God will launch it," he answered and put up the paper and said no more at all upon this subject. Nor did he question me upon conditions at My Fancy, but put the whole aside and turned, it seemed to me, in a strange and intimate fashion, to the inner plains and keeps, mountains, tarns and sea of David Scott. At first, moving from the house toward the high road, we moved in silence. The night was quiet and beautiful with a half-moon riding high, and golden Venus. in a west still flushed with color. We heard the sea and the forever-ever slight rustle of cane and frond. We walked in silence, he with his bundle and stick, and with his thoughts, whatever they might be; I with mine. I say that and yet, strangely then to me, still we seemed to be conversing. We walked so to the great cotton tree and stepped upon the gleaming coast road that should take him to the town. Across from it ran the thin belt of sea grape and cocoanuts and the white sand and the blue water. I said, "Let us go through and look at the sea." He nodded agreement and presently came upon the beach. Before us streamed and flowed and held the enormous sea.

> This ae night, this ae night,
> Every night and alle.

I said, "There's a slave ship that I am upon — beneath the gratings, in thick hot darkness, with All That Is pressed against me. — It's not the *Janet,* and this is not the sea, and color of the skin does not come into it. — I was there at times in Virginia where I was a bought servant. I think I may have been there at moments when, so young a man, I lay in prison in Edinburgh. But I was there, too, when I ranged free. Then it was at moments, but now almost all the time. And if I were in London or Paris or home in Scotland, it would be the same. If I had never come upon the *Janet,* or seen Daga on the Slave Coast; if I had hardly seen a Negro or a formally named slave in my life; if I thought not of them, if I were lawyer or schoolmaster or tenant or laird, all now would be the same. There is a Great Ship of slaves, and slaves are in the shrouds and on the poop deck, and I am a slave in the depths of the ship."

"Aye, aye," he said. "Aye, aye! Such is the perception and the emotion — and neither do I speak of physical enslavement, though that is of it, too."

He stood leaning on his staff, his bright eyes upon the sea. "David, the slave both cannot and must free himself, and there is your para-dox ——"

I laughed and it was dreary and mocking laughter.

"To find in the dark, without fingers, a catch

or spring that may or may not be there — there being everywhere!"

"That is just it," he answered quietly. "There is everywhere."

"I am tired of riddles that are never answered."

"Never is a long word."

He turned upon me in the moonlight, with the voice of the sea about us. "You cannot be helped further at this time. But I say unto you, You will find the way."

With that he turned from the sea back to the road, and presently I parted with him, and have never, with my bodily eyes, seen him since. With the other eyes I have.

CHAPTER XXIII

THE *Janet,* her second voyage after refitting at Bristol, carried a cargo slightly differing from her usual one in that it represented Negroes from the Zaire and Africa beyond the Camaroons, a vast back country that Daga did not ordinarily drain. But Daga, ministering to twenty ships, had this time thrown her net in that direction and drawn. These Negroes were heathenish to us; from afar, very heavy and black. The Coast tongues, north and south, and the back country tongues that we knew did not meet their case. We handled them more like animals than was the *Janet's* wont.

Daga lay three days astern. —

My Fancy in Jamaica lay to me more than a year astern. Back I had gone to Bartram and Colley and McNaughton and the ship.

Colley had paid his debts in London, but here he was again. He had even had a fair offer of a practise — but here he was. "You know it ruins you, David, this life! ruins you for anything else. At last you don't know how to treat any other world, and it doesn't know how to treat you. — Well, here's a right good company too!"

And it seemed that we did cling together, Bartram, McNaughton, Colley, David Scott,

Tom and Don, Michaelson, Llewellyn the carpenter, Geordie, Jack Dannet and Dory and other who still lasted from the *Janet's* population that autumn night when I climbed her side from the boat of Christian Todd — and later ones too, — Wheeler the boatswain who took Davis's place, and others. Benjamin the steward was dead. Black the second mate had left us for the *Sherwood Oak*. In his place we had a big, slow Dane named Olafson. And every year saw changes, many of them, among the seamen.

She had come into Kingston Harbor, white and trim from England, all her sails so lovely, and strong new masts and rigging, her decks and her hold and her cabins sweet again, her figurehead, a sea goddess, restored, her flag and pennant new — the big and fair ship, the *Janet*. In her hold and boxed upon her decks she carried stores as she had carried them when first I knew her, all manner of trade goods for Daga. She came in with a kind of music, and David Scott had a warming of the heart to see her, the Enchantress, the good and evil one together! She had been away a year; he had been at My Fancy a year. He knew about when she was due, and had ridden from the north and the west through the great island to Kingston, having resigned his manager's place at My Fancy, given it back to Mr. Godfrey North who was home from England, and who would have kept him on. But

David Scott was restless, and his own unhappiness had tainted for him My Fancy. So he returned to Kingston and North the agent, and the *Janet* was sighted and swam into harbor like a mountain of pearl.

That had been a successful voyage to the Coast and back. Going out, it minded me of that first voyage from Chesapeake Bay. Returning, we had only the best luck, weather, health and all, and landed four hundred and ninety-two out of five hundred slaves. This time our port had been Charlestown in South Carolina.

Said Bartram, " All in all, David, taking all my years together, East Indiaman and Guineaman, they may call me a fortunate captain! We have our ups and downs, but that one ghastly ribbon has been spun off the spool! " But as he spoke he put out an arm and touched wood. When he saw that I saw it he laughed, then drew a kind of long, sighing breath. " Eh, man, eh, man David! Life's a strange bird that goes across the sky and who'll say whence or to where? And then, you see, there's yon net of stars up there! "

Back at Daga and Rathbone Lace and his boat up the river, to the Oil Palm village.

Markham the surgeon asked me about Fanny. That luckless voyage was of course known in all detail at Daga, but such things were never stressed. The accidents of the trade — they were the accidents of the trade — and all trades

have accidents. But I went to Markham's
house — Colley chancing to be somewhere up
the river — about a cut that I had received upon
the arm in the bush, and when he had dressed it
he asked me the question. I told him briefly.
He nodded, was silent a moment, then said, " I
find it natural enough."

" I am quite of your mind," I answered. " I
think it was so."

" They were her people."

" Yes. — It's all the same, Markham, all over.
— God knows how we can be One Thing that
hates and hurts itself so, and can't give messages
to itself from itself! But so I come to feel it
is. One Thing. One tragic, pitiful, insane
Thing!"

We came out upon his verandah. Daga lay
in the afternoon light. All suddenly castle and
village and ivory beach and native boats and
palm trees made again the picture of that
witches' night in Edinburgh, long ago now, long
ago! It passed, and I saw with distinctness a
mournful, human Face — and whether it were
Fanny, or a girl in Barbadoes, or Maria at My
Fancy, or old Melinda at Old Mill Quarter, or
Eboe Sam, or Old Hannibal, or Pickaninny, or
Tom and Don, or all together — and I think it
was all together, all these and many more together — it held, it overwhelmed and drowned
me. Then it was gone.

" What is the matter? " demanded Markham.

"I don't know. — I saw a vision."

"Don't do it!" said Markham. "I began it once. But I stopped them off."

But I made a gesture and left him, going down unseeingly to the sea.

That was the first time at Daga after the *Janet's* refitting. The second time, for two weeks, I was drinking and altogether for and with Rathbone Lace, and what I did or left un-done one day I may pick up and stare at with affright. I came back into sobriety, and all of Rathbone's power could not make me drink. He laughed and gave it up. "But it won't be al-ways so, David, it won't be always so! No wall that you've built but shall crumble! Then you'll stay at Daga, and find rum good every day in the year, and we'll go forever, my boy, from Oil Palm village to Oil Palm village!"

At times, from the first, I hated him. And then Daga again, and we sought each other out.

This second time the *Janet* had swung at anchor long weeks before Daga. There were trade troubles. A war that had been expected to send down streams of slaves, that had indeed been fomented for just that purpose, had failed of bursting. Other chiefs were demanding more and more and more for their villagers, and the factor had made a stand against such exor-bitancy with the result that here, too, befell a temporary drought. Add to this that a rival British company had lately established a factory no distance at all up the Coast and was making glittering promises. Trade, diverted, flowed that way as well as to Daga. And other things had happened. We had been not far from two months at Daga when like a flood tide came traders with those Negroes from the Zaire and beyond Camaroons.

We took them and filled the *Janet* with them. They seemed to us brutish, with their heaviness and unknown tongues — we handled them at last in the piece and with no ceremony. All at last was done — the water was in — all was ready — we should get away that night. In the harbor about us lay the *Sharon* of Boston, the *Waterlily,* the *Blake* and the little *Frances Fynes,* the *Sharon* taking too of those southern and inland Negroes and almost ready to sail, the others just in. When the factor came aboard before sunset to bid Captain Bartram farewell the captains of the *Sharon* and the *Blake* came with him, and all had wine in the *Janet's* great cabin.

" Here's to you, Captain Bartram! "

" Thank you, Mr. Lace. Thank you, Ross. Thank you, Jenkins! "

" The best of voyages! "

" I'm thanking you again. If it's like the last it will be good."

He was not convivial — " Holy Bartram." They knew it and secretly winked that the bottle was emptied and there would not be another. A little further talk, and out they trooped and down into their boats and so away — and that night about three we sailed from Daga.

Africa lay five days astern.

I came in the early morning out of Philip Smith's cabin into the great one to find seated at the table Bartram and Colley. The latter was speaking in a low voice. Bartram, looking particularly tawny and big, sat staring out of open door. The sun was just up, the sea ran sparkling, a brisk wind filled the sails. I remember the blue and gold and white, the humming, the thrilling salt, the cool and lift. I made to pass through the cabin, but Bartram spoke, "Come here, David! There's trouble walking beside us."

"What is it?"

"It's sickness."

He moved his big frame, put his hands behind his head — a way he had — and stared through the door at what showed of his ship. "Five dead this morning."

I asked Colley, "What do you think it is?"

"God knows! *I* don't. I've never seen it before. We bought it with these Negroes, and where they bought——" He described the sickness. "It's one of the old plagues."

"None but the Negroes ——"

"Yes. Jack Dannet's got it."

Bartram stood up. "We'll do as we've done before — the best we can! Say nothing of its

newness or anything else. Say it will presently
stop. I'll order an extra dram for all."

" All " meant the *Janet's* officers and seamen.
No one told or could tell the freight that it was
not serious and would presently stop.

Seven days out from Daga. There had been
half a dozen more deaths, and another seaman lay in the ship's hospital. But that was
not so bad — we could weather it at this rate.
Then suddenly like a tiger the thing jumped.
On a hot morning, the sails lank, we brought up
and cast into the sea fifteen bodies. At noon
Dannet died, and in the evening Jonathan Williams. Between dusk and dawn three more
were smitten in the forecastle. It settled down.

McNaughton's opinion was that we should put
back to Daga.

" What for? " asked Bartram, with reason.
" The sea opens for them as easily here. We
can't send them back into barracoon and poison
all there — and for us white men the *Janet's* still
the best hospital. If it's bad, better to be bad
keeping our course. If it's an evil that's got a
term, what's the object in turning tail? What's
to be will be, McNaughton, and we'll go on our
way."

The next day panic appeared, in the black
and in the white. Bartram quelled it, shamed
it, dissipated it, so that at least it came into
bounds. In both colors arrived the drawing
into two camps: they who feared and gave all

way to fear, and they who feared but kept their manhood and banded to help themselves and others.

We ceased to drive the Africans at night under the gratings. The most of them stayed night and day on the deck and they began to die like flies. It was fearful, their noise; and fearful their stillness. In every throng of black men and women as in every throng of white, there will be so many who are better, braver and wiser than the others. They are smothered under until times like this. Then they come forth and are seen to be tall and strong. So out of this mourning or desperately silent mass sprang at last their own helpers. When we saw who they were we picked them out, gave them freedom and told them as best we could what to do, then left it to them.

When we were two weeks from Africa a third of our cargo was gone. Seven seamen were dead. Hardly any one who was taken recovered. It was malignant from the first.

Add that there now befell a calm. Day after day of it when we hardly moved. And each day dead men and burials, and the sea hardly seemed to take them away.

Bartram apparently did not sleep at all. The old lion went padding at all hours through his ship, strengthening here, strengthening there. Bartram, McNaughton, Olafson, Colley and young Winter his helper, David Scott, Wheeler the boatswain, Llewellyn, Dory and Wat Allen,

Geordie, Tom and Don and some others feared, but worked.

Then Winter was taken and died, then Geordie, then Llewellyn. Three weeks, and half the cargo was gone, and out of fifty white men aboard were left not thirty-five. The dead calm held. The sea was brass and the sky was brass, and the sharks swam beside the ship.

It was middle of the night. It had been my watch; Olafson had relieved, and I came to my bed, to throw myself upon it and sink into dead sleep, forgetting for three hours the stench and the cries and the heat. But as, half-naked, I touched it, I heard Bartram's voice at the door, "David!"

I knew, I knew, what it was. I knew it in his voice. When I reached him, he was supporting himself against the table. " It's the number and the star, David! They've come again — they've come again!"

I got him to his bed and went for Colley, who presently stood beside him. " Captain, Captain! You're stronger than us. You pull through! We need you."

But Bartram regarded us with strange eyes. " You've got McNaughton. — William Bartram is sending in his papers, and crisscross and blotted and torn they are!"

We gave him water which he at once began to call for as they all did, and McNaughton came quietly and took his orders which were short.

"The best you can, McNaughton, the best you can!"

It was to be kept from the *Janet* as long as might be, which was short enough, we knew. There were three dying men in the forecastle. Colley, thin as paper, with hollows and shadows under his eyes, returned to his enormous work; McNaughton to his. I stayed beside Bartram. His speech was rapid and dry; now and then he groaned, and his hands moved over the bed or with strange signallings in the air. "Is it dawn? Is it dawn?"

"It's coming, Bartram."

"There was to be a wind at dawn. A right wind. And land at dawn! Land, land, land!"

He struggled to sit up. I pressed him back. "Lie down, Bartram, lie down!"

His wits came back. "Ah, David, man, a sair trouble — but we've known so many! I'm fortunate in McNaughton. That Dane, too, is a good man."

"Yes, he is," I said. "But you're the best man here, Bartram."

"Na, na!" he said. "And I've got a star to fight."

With that he began again to toss and speak at random. Colley returned and looked at him. "No worse and no better than the others. The same boat, we're all in the same boat, captain and crew." But by dawn he was worse. The very strength and bigness of him seemed, when it turned, to aid that direction. He fell into a stupor. When the sun rose and poured light about him, it was seen what ravage the one night had made. When Colley came again he said, " He'll go, David, and it won't be long."

It was not. At sunset Bartram died.

At dawn we buried him — and the *Janet* seemed dead with him, the *Janet* and the sea.

McNaughton was captain. We had no time for grief or for memory, — time for nothing but a dull, eternal struggle with the pestilence.

Then McNaughton was taken, and in twenty-four hours followed Bartram into the sea.

Olafson came to me, with him Wheeler and Michaelson and others.

" We're come, Mr. Scott, to say that I do not wish to be captain of the *Janet,* sir. I'll do my duty as your first mate, but you be captain. All of us who are alive, and we think those who are dead, say the same."

So I was captain — Captain David Scott of the *Janet.*

The next day Colley was taken. For a little while he was very clear-headed. " I'm dead tired, David — too tired really to suffer. I'll go quick. — They never should have been! "

" You've done the work of a dozen, Colley. And always you've doctored and helped us ——"

" Yes, maybe. But they never should have been — the errands of the *Janet.* Leave her now, David — I'd leave her if I were you."

"Oh, Colley!" I cried. "Little fear but I shall be leaving her! Look around soon and you'll see me — and Olafson and Michaelson and all!"

He turned his head and turned it again. "And I'll be seeing, too, don't you think, David, the black folk?"

I was summoned for something, and when I returned he did not know me. As he said, it was quick and he suffered little. Colley died, and we dropped him into the sea.

We were a month from Africa, but because of the calm not a third of the way over. Of five hundred slaves the *Janet* held now a hundred and forty; of fifty white men there were now twenty to man her. And I was captain and Olafson was my mate.

CHAPTER XXIV

I STOOD by the man at the wheel and looked at the glassy sea. Then afar there seemed upon it a little darkening. It spread. I felt an elfin stroke upon my brow, my hand; a rope hanging near swung, though ever so slightly. It came again, more strongly. I looked at the man — he was a New Englander whom we called Dandy — and he looked at me. "That's wind, Dandy!"

"Praise God!" he said, and the water stood in his eyes.

The *Janet* started from her dream, shook herself and began to hum and move. Life! It was life again!

That day we had but five deaths and four new cases, three among the Negroes, one in the forecastle. The next day saw further lessening; the next it dwindled still. There came a day when was no death and no one struck down. The plague departed. It left alive upon the *Janet* one hundred and two Negroes and fifteen white men.

That day when with a great and weary breath we saw that it was gone, there came up with us the *Sharon* that had left Daga twenty-four hours after us. She was built for speed, and she packed close, carrying between six and seven hundred Negroes, though I know not how she did it. Now as she neared, there poured down the wind upon us her stench. We lay to; she came on and hailed us.

" *Janet*, ahoy! "

" Ahoy, *Sharon!* "

" The plague! Have you the plague? "

" We have had it. It is over."

" How do you stand? "

" One hundred and two Negroes living. Fifteen white men. Captain Bartram is dead, McNaughton and our surgeon."

" Who is that? "

" David Scott, Captain of the *Janet*. How is it with you? "

" Dying. We are dying! Do you know anything to do? "

" Nothing. We could do nothing. You've got your surgeon? "

" Yes, but we've never seen this thing before."

" It has gone from us. It will from you."

" If it isn't too late —— We've thrown overboard half our Negroes. — Good-by, the *Janet!* "

" Good-by, *Sharon!* "

She sailed swiftly. In an hour she had left us quite behind. The sea ran dark blue and in hills and vales; the warm wind behind us pushed us on, straight into west. But we were hardly half through the Middle Passage, and we had fifteen to handle the ship and our freight. David Scott regarded the latter, knowing by now every face, and seeing in them, when all is said, only Universal and Eternal Man. By now he had enough of their tongue roughly to understand and be understood. They had endured the plague and in some sort tended one another and had buried in the sea their host that was gone. Of those able or compassionate or higher men of their own who had at last stood out to serve, three or four remained alive. Over all rested as it rested upon us fifteen the shadow of something gigantic behind and over-topping life that was small. I went among them and talked, and it was to me as if I were at Old Mill Quarter, discoursing in the dusk after work with Old Hannibal and Eboe Sam and Pickaninny and Joe and the others.

I offered, the weather resting fair, to let them sleep upon deck — they having a great horror of below, where in the blackness companies of them had died. They would have had space enough down there now for some sort of comfort, but they had that horror. They might stay upon their deck — they should be unshackled — they should have abundant food and all the water we could safely give. What we could do for them we would. In return would they undertake obedience to orders? We had the guns, the cutlasses, the great guns, and always we could sink the *Janet*. And lastly, I wanted six to help clean the ship and carry the food.

A great black man — one of the helpers from
the first — stood forth. I will put his words into
plain English.

" Where are you taking us? "

" To an island named Jamaica."

" Are you going to kill us there to please your
god? Some of us think that."

" No. If a man has bad luck in Africa he
becomes a slave. You know all about being
slaves to head men and chiefs and kings. You
know about going into far countries to be slaves.
In Jamaica you will just be slaves to white
chiefs."

" Are there other black men there? "

" A great many. You will find folk who have
been your neighbors."

" What will happen to us? How shall we be
treated? "

" You will work to make sugar and rum and
tobacco, or to cut down trees. If you will not
work or if you run away, you will have hard
treatment. If you work and stay where you are
and make no trouble you will be treated differently. Some of you will be treated very kindly.
— You know a great deal about it, though you
have never been out of Africa."

His face seemed to work. He looked at every
man of us armed, and at the ship and the piled
sails and all the matters that were foreign and
marvellous to them, and at his people. Something solemn, something of rest awhile after that

Death Cloud, was upon them as upon us. Something of resignation, something of muteness before Destiny. After a time there might manifest among them, even here, that cheerfulness that was theirs by nature — but to-day was other coloring. The speaker for them, and he was tall and big and black as night, but his head was well-formed and his countenance showed homely strength, looked at sky and sea, the *Janet* and us.

"We cannot help ourselves. If we fight we just die and gain nothing. We do not know for what evil we are here and are going into a far land to work for others. Maybe it is for evil, and maybe it is for some good at last. We do not know. Maybe somebody bigger than you is taking us. We won't make trouble."

The good weather held, we cleaned the ship, the plague made no return, though we had a degree of other sicknesses, due chiefly to exhaustion and desolation. Our Negroes as a whole remained tractable, and helpful. God knows, by this time David Scott knew the good qualities and those not so good of Negro folk! On the *Janet* this disastrous voyage, the good rose, the bad sank away. There is in this people a Philosopher who is over and over again slain by Passion and who over and over again rises from the dead. He had, in this voyage, an exemplar in the big, black man, and the rest were guided.

We fifteen white men, divided into two shifts,

under captain and first mate, had our work, being so short-handed.

There was scant time for musing grief. I *saw* Bartram and Colley and McNaughton and others.

A week — ten days — went by of steady westward going. Then befell another calm. I heard Wheeler the boatswain say to Michaelson, " Somebody's gone to war against this ship."

" Aye, I'm thinking myself somebody has a scunner against us."

The third day of it Olafson and I went secretly and examined the water casks. We were only in mid-passage who should have been nearly to port. A hundred and twenty now drank water as against an expected five hundred and fifty. But for very need and mercy we had been free with it during the pestilence, giving the sick and dying what they cried for. That first dead calm had lasted long, and this, for all we knew, might equal or outgo it. Our faces were grave when we saw what we had — and the lift of any land so far away. Said Olafson, " Something less than the old allowance? " and I nodded.

David Scott and the black man together made the hundred understand and acquiesce. For the most part our fifteen and Tom and Don in the cook's galley met the stress with courage. We shared equally, black and white, captive and free. As captain, I said it should be so. At first there threatened mutiny, but Olafson and Michaelson and others stood by me, and it was so. Each soul upon the *Janet* had each day enough water just to do with and no more.

Again the *Janet* was pinned to the moveless sea.

The calm lasted — so hot, so still — with little to do for the ship. Dead distaste, dead weariness, bodings, and at last with us all nerve and temper a frayed and giving thing.

The fifth night of it I entered the captain's cabin — it was Olafson's watch — and lay down. There were the arms, there the books, stars glimmered in the window. There formed in me the words, "It's time!" I smelled rum. In one moment lust for it had me by the throat. It was more than that; it clutched in every member of the will as well as the body. I sat up. Already the delusion flowed about me — the delusion that everything and all was best served by my taking the key of the spirit room, going there softly, and returning with a great jug of rum. I arose and took it, and went barefoot and returned unseen with my store. I put it down, a cup stood by me. I sat upon the bed. A voice spoke in me — another voice, I thought then, than my own. "If you taste that cup you are damned."

At the same moment I was pervaded by a light that was not starlight, moonlight or sunlight. In it I saw the *Janet* with a drunken, mad captain, and saw disaster to her and to six-score human beings. I saw widely, intensely, with minuteness, many-formed disaster. The light went, the voice was silent, but a rod was lifted over my soul.

My fingers unclasped from the cup. I pushed it a little from me on the shelf by the bed, then motionless in the dark I began to wrestle.

All the rest of the night. — Toward dawn I got up and took the jug and restored it to the spirit room. But I kept the key. I could get it again.

The cold, the forlorn dawn streaked the sky. The demon and I still were locked. The bell struck. I must go on deck and send Olafson to rest. I went, and he exclaimed, " Are you ill, sir? "

" No. I could not sleep."

He and his men went to eat, to have a small measure of water and to sleep. Mine came wearily out of forecastle. On the deck the Negroes were still sleeping. A deathlike purple hung in the east.

I moved about the ship as was needed, or sat in my place upon the poop deck and I fought until I was spent. " I will not take it to-day, but as soon as it is night ——" When noon was passed Olafson relieved me, but I would not go to Bartram's cabin. I lay solitary upon the deck in the shadow with the dead mirror of the sea around and fought. Once I fell asleep but I

met a terrible dream and woke trembling, with
sweat upon me. The sun sank and I must take
charge while the others rested and sweetly
slept. Somehow the hours passed till midnight.
Olafson took the ship. I left the deck and sat
upon my bed in the cabin, waiting just for a
little when I should go barefoot, unlock the door
of the spirit room and bring the jug back.
Again said the voice, "If you do it you are
damned."

Oh, what lion, what tiger, what army, is like
this to fight? Oh, help — help to break a slave's
chain!

Once I went outside the door and halfway to
that place of storage that was to me Heaven.
But I saw in mid-air before me a mournful face,
and I turned back and sat again, shivering, upon
my bed.

And again dawn ——

All day — all day ——

It was sunset. The sun went down a ball of
fire, and there were no clouds. The west flared
carnation then ebbed to purple and the sea likewise turned to clear purple glass. I stood by the
side with the moveless sails in mountains above
me. The ship had its sounds enough but there
fell to my senses a silence like a night in space.
I seemed to stand alone in a quiet place. It was
like a battlefield a year after the battle. I stood
as one foredone, and yet I knew there was a victory. But who won it I hardly knew, whether

it was I or another. That raging desire in me died or fell asleep. I came quietly, stilly back to David Scott before or after his two weeks. And yet not to that David Scott either — seeing that on my part or on Another's part there had been a victory.

CHAPTER XXV

THE next day upsprang the wind and did not again fail us. Three days thereafter we met the *Edina* of Baltimore bound for Whidah. We hailed her; she lay to and the *Janet* near her. I went to her in our boat and spoke from it to her Captain, Weymarch, whom Bartram knew. Could they give us water? We would thankfully take no matter how little. They had had a quick and prosperous voyage, with but forty aboard. Weymarch knew the *Janet,* was sorry for Bartram's death. He offered three casks and when we had these shipped cried that he thought he could give another and did. It was our saving, and we blessed the *Edina* for kindness.

She dwindled toward Africa while we ran into the west. We were careful indeed with water, but thirst no longer tormented us, neither the white nor the black. We would stop at the first of the Bahamas and fill our casks before we took the Windward Passage downward to Jamaica.

Olafson, Wheeler, Michaelson and the rest of our seamen did well. I was used to them and they to me. I knew the *Janet,* the *Janet* knew me. The Africans, with that big black man their teacher, made no trouble that might not be argued or soothed away.

Michaelson said to me, " You'll be a Captain, sir, after the heart of Captain Bartram, rest his soul! "

And Olafson said, " The Company will confirm you Captain, doubtless, sir. I'd like to keep on the *Janet* with you."

But I was unhappy.

There broke a day that showed us the Blue Mountains. The anchor rattled down in Kingston Harbor. North the agent came alongside in a boat. " What's wrong? "

I delivered to him the hundred and two Negroes. The next day I saw them in the barracoon, and the big, black man still led and comforted them.

David Scott came and went, Kingston waterside and Kingston Harbor, keeping Bartram's cabin and watch upon the *Janet* that was being holystoned and painted and made all clean again. There was sympathy among the world of ships and men of the sea and dealers in black men. " Holy Bartram " had been much liked despite his queernesses. North sincerely missed him. " If there were more like him the trade wouldn't get the name it has! "

" Has it a name? "

" The world is getting finicky," he answered. " It wasn't always so! "

He had been long with the Company, was es-

teemed and had power to give a captain to a
ship lacking one.   Like a good agent he pon-
dered it, he talked with Olafson and the *Janet's*
men, and he weighed the claims of two or three
in Kingston who had had ships, had them not
now, and wished them again.   Then he offered
the *Janet* to me — Bartram's pay and all.

I thanked him and said I must think of it.

" There's just one thing that made me hesi-
tate," he said.   We were alone in his quiet house
behind the vines.   " But I assert that Bartram
never told me you had a cloud over you in Virginia.   If it ever comes out — and with common prudence, now after ten years, it never
need — why, I simply knew and know nothing
about it! "

" I understand."

" Lord! " he said.   " The high seas and the
land are different things, and Scotland and
Africa are different things!   Six out of ten men
bound for Guinea have strange stories."

" Mr. North," I asked, " when is the trade
going to stop? "

He stared.   " Why, when slavery stops, I pre-
sume.   There's no particular sign of that! "

" The factories and the slave ships might cease
and leave all the Negroes in America slaves —
till the world grows finicky again."

" There's finickiness and finickiness," he said.
" The Royal African Company don't see it to
that extent."   He laughed.   " Bartram used at

first to have those fits. But we've got to live —
and he came round to his bread and butter.
What's the use in being better than your time and
your work? But it made him a humane captain
and that's a good thing in any trade! Follow
him, and you'll do all right."

"I'll have to think."

He pursed his lips, then spoke, "There's just
this other thing, Scott, that I'm not supposed to
know about and yet *do* know about — except
when somebody asks that's got no proper or con-
venient right to know. God knows there's
drinking enough in the African trade — as there
is for that matter everywhere — but I understand that just at times you are as far as may be
from Bartram's way there. Now if you have
the right mates it's possible ——"

"It's my belief that I've quit drinking."

"For good?"

"If I take the *Janet* I won't drink while I am
upon her."

After a moment he said, "I'll take your word,
David. — Well, then, the Company offers you
the *Janet,* Captain Scott."

I said again, "I'll have to think."

Returning to the *Janet,* I tried to think — but
I loved the *Janet.*

Next day I got a horse and rode out to the
Blue Mountains. But from every height I saw
the passionate blue sea and the *Janet* and I loved
them both.

It was to my advantage to go with her. I could not now find new things. Bartram and Colley and McNaughton were in some sense there, there upon her still. — Bartram's cabin and the books and the long, clean voyages out. — Daga — I would turn the new leaf at Daga. David Scott, world flotsam with an easy job, and the Captain of the *Janet* were two things. If I took the *Janet* I would be true to her.

The voyages out — but the voyages back?

Cargoes of slaves. Distaste, heat, stench, fatigue, close watch and ward, barbarity and danger — all the deterrents that made men of the sea draw back at the word "Guineaman," that gave to the trade mostly hardened and reckless men. Well, was I not hardened and reckless?

I was used to it all. There was even a crude excitement in seeing each time if it could be done. Captains of slavers rarely at last left the slavers, died in the trade unless it threw them out, broken and useless hulls, decaying forever in some little port town.

I saw it, but I had known no human trade without distaste. Distaste in soldiering, distaste on Virginia plantations, distaste at My Fancy. I was used to the *Janet* — I was the slaver — there were reliefs.

Slavery. The hunting and trapping of black men and sailing with them, against their will, over the seas and selling them for life, them and their unborn children, the generations to come.

I got down from my horse and sat upon a stone, but between bough and branch I saw the extreme blue sea and the ships in harbor and the *Janet*.

Once, for five years, I had been almost as much a slave as if I were born in Africa. I knew the taste of the cup. In much it tasted the same, if you were white or if you were black.

Captain of the *Janet*. David Scott, Captain of the *Janet*.

If planters and merchants and others the world over did wrong in enslaving — and according to that Quaker they did — *what of me?*

Captain of the *Janet* — Captain of the *Janet*.

As I sat there the *Janet* seemed to come near. I saw her stem to stern, every mast and boom and spar and rope, her sails, her decks and her cabins. She seemed as she was when I climbed out of Christian Todd's boat upon her, but seemed more, with a thousand memories as of home and things endured and enjoyed. I saw the great cabin and the lanterns and the table and stacked in fairy columns the gold that would be my pay; and Bartram and Colley and McNaughton seemed with me there and approving. The sea flowed midnight purple, and the *Janet* had every sail spread, and the Trade Wing sang.

Somebody must do it — somebody must run the slave ships. Better the decent, the humane-as-might-be, than Garth and McKenzie and their kind! Better Bartram's kind on the *Janet* than some one who sneered at "Holy Bartram," and was himself a terror to white seaman and black slave! Bartram seemed to stand beside me in his cabin.

"David, let us sail her still together! I wadna like another ——"

And I was idle and indolent and slow in the inner man, distasting change where I had taken the groove.

As well be unhappy on the *Janet* as away from her! As for the slave trade and slavery, they would persist while I lived and while I died. The earth was wound with a chain. My being Captain of the *Janet* wouldn't enslave and wouldn't free a Negro of them all. Another wouldn't be so merciful a captain, and that was the solitary difference.

I saw the chain around the earth and that it held white men as well as black. It held us all, though some it appeared to gall less than others. Degrees of harshness and various masters, but all, all, all, possessors and possessed, in slavery!

I was again at My Fancy, roaming the great rooms at night and unhappy almost to self-murder.

I rose from the stone and mounted my horse and rode back to Kingston, and happening to meet North in the street, "Captain of the *Janet*, is it?" he asked, and I answered, "Not yet."

But next day, being on the *Janet,* silently, swiftly, like a serpent raising his head, David Scott spoke to that Unnamed One in prison within him, " If I am lost anyhow, I will walk, dance, and run a little first! " And sat down at his table in his cabin and wrote to North that he would take the ship.

CHAPTER XXVI

"SO the rum's not for you?" said Rathbone Lace.

" No."

" Then let us row without it up to Oil Palm village."

" I'm not going up the river."

He stared, peeled the fruit beside him and ate it, then spoke. " Does that mean that my room is better than my company? "

" No. But I have settled it that as I am Captain, I will be Captain."

" You mean captain like Holy Bartram? There are others you might copy. They live — he's dead."

" Yes."

" Your ambition is to be called Saintly Scott? "

" Perhaps —— "

He and I were at table on his veranda and it was dusk. He pushed back his native-wrought chair, I mine. A Negro woman with a large soft tread cleaned away food and dishes. Lace and I sat upon the steps where the night wind might find us. It was hot and there sounded a dull moaning and roaring from the bar.

" Daga —— " he said, and stopped to light his pipe.

"I saw this place," I said, "before I came to
it. There was a wild night in Edinburgh and
I was in danger. I stood against a wall, listening and looking into darkness. It opened before me, this African ocean and that castle, that
beach, those palms. Had my ear been as keen
as my eye, I would have heard those drums."

They were beating below us, below Factor's
Hill, in Daga village. They had, likewise, a
bonfire down there and some celebration. Beat,
beat, beat, beat ——

"I've heard tell of visions," he said. "I
don't have them."

"I can have them," I answered, "but the
trouble with me is action."

"You are beautifully clear. — An uninformed man would say that your life was sufficiently active."

"So he would — the uninformed."

He laughed. "The same old David —
plunging always from your stake and being
brought up short! Now I — I am free!"

The bowl of his pipe glowed. "Daga suits
me. I don't even want to be Captain of the
Janet. There's danger there — and no danger
here."

"I suppose not. At times life seems to me a
very big thing — but the next hour a most puny
and wretched one!"

He made a smoke cloud. Below us the
drums were beating and beating. "Then I say

again, Let's go in the old boat to-morrow up to
Oil Palm village."

" No."

Something appeared on the step beside us —
rum in a decanter with glasses.   The African
woman with no noise had put it there, then vanished.   Lace poured himself out a dram.
" None for you? "

" No."

He drank — the odor of the thing that made
you forget, that made you seem to yourself
powerful and gigantic, was in the air — the
drums were beating, beating.

" Man   is   a   preying   animal," he   said.
" White, black, red or yellow, what does it matter?   The successful is he who recognizes the
fact and preys and joys in it. — You'll be hap-
pier, Scott, when you bow to Nature! "

Through the dusk the sea still gleamed and
the *Janet* was riding there.   Nearer at hand a
last glow struck Daga castle and its barracoon
that was filling for the *Janet*.   The palms were
drawn against a copper sky.   " I do bow, Lace,"
I said and got to my feet.

" Aren't you going to sleep ashore? "

" No."

" Bartram again! " he said.   " When you fell
heir to his ship did you *become* him? "

In a certain sense it seemed to me that I had.
Going out to the *Janet,* while the men rowed,
hearing the waves upon the bar, marking the

stars lighted above Africa, it was Bartram that
I assumed. Assumed him in the sheer feeling
older — first manhood all passed, maturity here
and here for some time; assumed him in the
watchful, plodding care for the ship and her
great worth to me, her great and yet melancholy
worth; assumed him in a concentration on getting the thing done in the best way possible;
assumed him in his eye upon the stars. The
Janet encreased before me. I heard Olafson's
deep slow voice and a fiddle in the forecastle.

Within a week we began lading — Negroes
from Dahomey, from the Camaroons, the Niger
and the Zaire. At last all was done and we
would depart in the night. The elder and the
younger Lace and the captains of ships in harbor came aboard to drink farewell and good
voyage. Again in the cabin I was Bartram.
— Garth was here and he noticed it. " By God,
you've but to let your beard grow, Scott, to be
Bartram! And let me tell you, you might do
worse. 'Damn me, he trod too soft with his
niggers and his sailors, but he was a big man!"

They drank and talked and departed, and I
was glad to see them go, and that, too, was
Bartram. It was night. We made sail and
slipped the land while our slaves were below in
thick darkness. It never did to let them see at
any close range the receding shores. But up
through the gratings, as I walked the deck, came
the familiar crying and the familiar odor from

miserably crowded bodies in a tropic night.
We sailed, and I looked out and upward at
Bartram's stars.

Olafson rested first mate, and a good one, almost as good as McNaughton. He and I had
our own sympathy, the big Norseman, with
some story, I knew, behind and around and before him. For second mate I had taken on a
Scot, Alexander Nicol, who had been the same
on the *John Land,* lost by fire. And for surgeon, in Colley's place, there was Lisle from the
same ship — a good man, but not Colley.
Wheeler the boatswain, Michaelson, and the
seamen who had outlived the plague remained,
and Tom and Don who would stay with the
Janet till she sank. And in Kingston and in
Bridgetown we gathered twoscore and five seamen. As far as I could I picked them out; they
were not a bad lot.

Now and again, for mysterious reasons, the
Company operating there in England produced
changes in routes and markets afar. For a long
space of time a ship might be for the Islands,
steady as a ferry between the Slave Coast and
the British Indies. Then a notification, and for
a string of voyages ports of North America.
We had gone to Charlestown in South Carolina
the voyage before the disastrous voyage. It was
my port now. The Company agent there was
one Trevannion.

Using Bartram's cabin, taking his place at

table, sailing his ship, more and more I felt
Bartram and his stars. Yet was I also David
Scott. And around David Scott and Bartram
and all came at times like a flicker that strange
sense of being another and a larger, a Some One
that held and understood the others, but was not
they.

This first voyage from Daga proved a straight,
quiet, successful one. I delivered my cargo,
smaller by a very little than when it was taken
on. Trevannion I had met before. Charlestown harbor and waterside, Charlestown inns
and their frequenters, some of the houses, the
low, sandy, flowery country round about, the
rice fields and the great pine timber became
familiar. With a number of differences it yet
reminded me of Virginia.

Beginning now to use the continent and not
the islands, I reasoned one night, standing before the minute mirror in Bartram's cabin, as
to whether, after all these years, David Scott
should strive to provide for himself a different
physical aspect. As Garth had suggested, I
might become bearded like Bartram. It was
possible perhaps slightly to change my voice and
manner of speaking. — As for my story, that had
long been provided. Africa, Indies and the sea
between, it was known and forgotten that I was
some kin of Bartram, a Scot whose youth had
been passed in France but who had joined the
Janet on some one of her returns to Bristol.

And long ago Bartram and I had discussed it, whether or no I should change my name. But in us both was something that clung to the given name — especially if it was good Scots — and that hated for their own sakes disguises.

It was not far from seven years since I had run away from Daniel Askew. Standing before the mirror, I put side by side my man then and my man now, noted the difference and thought that the Captain of the *Janet* was safe enough, even though some fate should drive him into Chesapeake. And even if that were so, how un-likely any meeting with any who had known Daniel Askew's or Amory Hall while he was there! On my forehead I carried a jagged line of white, scar of a wound received at Amory Hall in a wood we were felling. A great storm came up suddenly with wind that tore branches from the trees and sent them flying. Such a one was borne endwise against me like a spear and gave the hurt. But who would ever meet me who knew that? I dismissed all thought of it.

Trevannion was a different man from North and other agents that I knew. I could tell tales of him, and of Charlestown that was both fair and unfair, courteous and uncourteous, right and wrong like the rest of the world. But now I am back upon the *Janet,* and we go to Africa for more Negroes.

So, coming and going, with various fortunes, David Scott spent two years.

CHAPTER XXVII

THROUGH that great block of space and time my mood was often and over the mood of My Fancy. Unhappy enough, I roamed an inner world that was a dark world, with here and there a tarnished gold. But then again I came to the outside and stayed there with the day's work and at night hard, dead sleep. Or if I could not ignore the inner world, I busily packed it with false shapes. And again there were other moods. In some sort I loved the ship and the sea and, strange to say, the human race, and in some sort I hardened to my trade. I became Bartram.

In Charlestown once I met travellers, a learned German with a book in mind, a gentleman from New England and another from New York. I forget what was the relationship between the three, but the two Americans, having leisure and liking adventure, were engaged in piloting the European down the continent, from snow in June to flowers in January. Massachusetts to Georgia, the colonies had passed or were passing before them. The German had a library of notebooks.

Charlestown is a town of a very polite society. When it read the travellers' introductory letters they did not lack entertainment. I met them at a supper party in a genteel inn, and I was there because I was in port and Trevannion took me. Trevannion was asked because the German had mentioned that he would like to meet the servant of the Royal African Company, one of his notebooks having a page devoted to that concern. The party was not a large one but was devised to furnish the learned man with the various information for which he hungered and thirsted. Three or four planters, a couple of considerable merchants, a lawyer, a divine, the travellers, Trevannion and myself were all. The lawyer who was host had caught, it seems, at Trevannion's suggestion that I be included. The traveller to be honored and fed knowledge might obtain something of value from the captain of a big slave ship who was also a decent person, not a bear at table, nor one to disgust with oaths and horrors of the Middle Passage — which last were largely mythical anyway.

I did not err in these respects, but erred, I afterwards found, in keeping silence. I never now discussed the slave trade save in precise and immediate business talk, and Trevannion might have known it. I never philosophized over it in company now, or speculated as to its course and end, or questioned it, or praised, or blamed, or extenuated. Something true in me held me back from that while I sailed the *Janet*. So I sat a listener, or when I answered a direct question answered it shortly, with the bald fact.

Rice, wheat, maize, tobacco and indigo cul-
ture, markets and prices — and the German
evidently making notes in his brain; the story
of South Carolina or of Charlestown, past, present and future; soil, forest, remnant of Indians,
back country where the red men still were
plentiful; the sea, trade with home, trade with
the other colonies, trade with the Indies; buc-
caneers and pirates, and it is certain we would
have a chapter on these; the Government, the
Church, the Law; Planting; the gentry and
others, plantations and plantation labor — and
here we are at slavery and the river through the
sea that feeds it from Africa.

And here it was that Trevannion was eloquent
and Captain David Scott was not.

They were all eloquent, the planters, the merchants, the lawyer, the clergyman, the agent, the
traveller from New York who spoke of the
Negro house boy and coachman whom he
owned, and the traveller from Massachusetts
who had shares in the *Amelia,* Captain Jonathan
Bolt of Salem, trading to Old Calabar. I knew
the *Amelia.* — Self-interest made them eloquent.

Self-interest!

Seated there, half listening to all that I had
heard a hundred times over, the word took hold
of me. Self-interest. The King's in his palace,
the Pope's in Saint Peter, the richest man's, the
poorest man's. Bartram's and mine and Col-

ley's; McNaughton, Olafson, Mr. Godfrey
North, Colonel Amory, Williams, Barget, Lace
the factor and Rathbone Lace. Black traders,
black chiefs, black kings in Africa, black men
and women in the villages who betrayed and
sold, and who when their turn came around were
themselves betrayed and sold. White men who
in thousands of ways did the same to white men.
Over all the world, black, white, red and yellow
— self-interest. It rose from its throne in me,
that word, and went up and down in a darkened,
vast hall, its face in its hands, as I had wandered
at My Fancy. What was interest? What was
self?

It was strange. I had been sitting there
stolidly, wearily, and they were all as so many
wooden figures with parrot tongues. — Something turned, slid, mounted. It was like a dewy
morning in the glen at home, in Scotland. Dew
and the dawn, hush and tenderness. It was like
that, but in the world of the soul or spirit, not
of the senses. I felt compassion.

For a breathless second it flooded me — compassion and understanding. Then it went,
but it left its echo and its mark, its sign and
seal.

I saw Earth a slave ship and the wake it made.
I saw that the yoke was of self, but not forever.
I felt the god bound in the human self who
would one day be free — bound in me, bound in
these, bound in those who served the table.

The room melted into sea and land, the rolling ball; the minute, like a streamlet, crossed the beach and was in the ocean. I sat there, and they did not notice increase of silence.

The party broke up with the Charlestown debonairness. Every one was courteous to me, even though I had not aided them with an already prepared and rosy light. The German said in parting, "You have a store, I think, sir, but you will not open the door."

Out under the stars with Trevannion he said, "You're a big, picturesque figure, Captain Scott, but you didn't help out with much more than that."

I said, "Look at the stars!" And indeed the whole sky had to me a strange, new aspect — strange, but not formidable; no, something to be understood.

The next day, waking at dawn, the sense of the moment at the inn breathed more faintly. But it was not gone; it was sunken in me. The business of the day covered it over; by eve I thought that I had forgotten it. That night I had ill dreams and woke in the morning in a bitter mood. That I had ever understood, that I had ever been truly and thoroughly compassionate, was unlikely indeed. Yet — yet — I *had* been!

In four days the *Janet* sailed. Charlestown harbor, the pleasant town, the live oaks and the pines, the tower of Saint Michael's church, we left them all behind. The ship was clean, the ship was fair; we experienced good weather. I could pace, pace, pace my deck in the day or the night; I could take a book that sometimes I opened and sometimes did not; I could talk with Olafson or Lisle or others. Olafson pleased me. Once I asked him what he thought of the stars and he told me of a vision he had had one night in the northern seas. He saw all the stars tied together with moving cords, the color of lightning. "All tied together, sir, and we with them."

Walk, walk, walk the deck, as though it were the great upper hall at My Fancy. Sit and brood and brood, as though poop deck or cabin were the reef out to which I used to swim. I was unhappy — life frustrated, bitter and weary, and that moment in Charlestown a dream.

When the Bahamas were half a day astern a sail upon the horizon drew our eye. She increased, coming down upon us with power, having the advantage of the wind and being built to sail. She was strange to me, and, " I do not know her," said Michaelson, who had been to and fro in the Trades for thirty years. We knew well enough the particular danger of these waters and we got the *Janet* ready and stood to arms. Twice before in my memory we had been chased, but more feebly than this pirate promised. He came nearer and nearer, but I looked at the sky which had been darkening for an hour. It was toward day close also. Up and out went his flag.

" Black, sir! "

" That's no news. Ready, gunners! "

She was on us now, a fast-sailing bark with pirate written over her as slaver was written over us. She cut across our bows, swung to port and gave us a broadside. We answered. A sea fight began. But the heavens meant their own way this time. There burst with fierceness wind and rain, lightning and thunder. We were driven apart, the pirate's foremast snapped; we left him with his wild wreckage and were gone, running before a tempest. Night came on; in the middle of it the storm vanished, leaving a heavy sea; in a dawn of piled clouds and purple waters we saw no other ship than ourselves. The *Janet* had some damage that could be removed. One man was killed; two or three had their hurts. The sea subsided, the wind came back to its steady, sweet blowing.

But that very dawning, looking up to masthead, I had a vision — being a Scot, being liable at times to *see* things that were symbolic or that were real in another order. What I saw this dawn was that we were flying a black flag. The dawn sent a beaker of light and spilled it against the outflowing web. It was black, it had upon it skull and crossbones. It was there as plain as my hand — the *Janet's* flag. I turned cold, I shivered. It streamed there, fastened to our mast, and behind it towered a purple cloud. I saw, it — it was gone. And then — the great strangeness — even as I grasped that it was gone and that I had put it there, opened within me so quietly again that clear depth of understanding — of understanding and compassion.

Seemingly it lasted no longer than a lightning flash, as it had done in Charlestown. When it was gone, again I was unhappy, torn. The black flag was not only upon the Guinea slaver — it was everywhere in life.

Days and nights, sun and stars, wind and warmth and the great sea, and we came to Daga.

How many times had I come to Daga? I hardly knew. It seemed of me now, of my flesh. This day that it rose before us was my thirty-seventh birthday.

The *Janet* hung in harbor a month. I did not drink with Rathbone Lace, or go with him up to Oil Palm village. In the place of that he and I quarrelled.

It was Markham the surgeon of whom I saw most. " Have you had any more visions? " he asked.

" Yes."

" There are a folk called mystics who have at times — or some of them have — visions. It's a well-known medical fact — which may or may not mean a fact of Nature. I've now and then seen just a flash of that race in you. It was in Bartram too."

" Yes, it was. Both of us put a stone upon it."

" For me," he said, " I've a weary vision of Daga going on forever. A world of Dagas. At any moment we see what we are and nothing else, and if all our moments prove the same color ——"

" If," I said.

" There you go!" he answered. " Well, have you got your full number of Negroes? "

In the month I had them and had them aboard — coast folk, hill folk, mountain folk, river valley folk. I sailed from Daga.

That evening there was a great sunset. It flared and flamed, and it cast light across upon Daga, all her whitened masonry. I saw her so, then over all flowed the tropic night, and these eyes saw her no more.

I had aboard docile Negroes and no pest or particular sickness. It was November, the best season for all our affairs. Day after day, day after day, the old routine — week after week.

I woke in the middle of the night, or maybe past the middle. It was as though a hand had been laid upon me, but when I sat up there was no figure, but only Bartram's cabin, star lighted. But I was awake as I had never been before. I left my bed and sat upon the bench beneath the window. The night was luminous, with a rushing, strong, warm wind, but only my outer man noted that. I sat upon the bench and I was a boy at school.

I will say as shortly as may be what I knew at last. I knew that God is the Whole of us. I found myself and my neighbor there and we were One. I found a greater Self — oh, a greater! — a SELF that left none out.

CHAPTER XXVIII

"SO you quit the Trade!" said Trevannion. "Well, so long as I stay in it, I'll maintain it's not so bad!"

"Yes, Trevannion. But one day you also will quit."

"Perhaps, and perhaps not," said Trevannion. "When you've fetched your bread and butter so long this way it's not easy to face getting it another way. I've a family."

"I know. It's hard to know what to do.— Well, I'm giving the *Janet* back again."

"I'm sorry! Men like you and Bartram who is dead keep us going. — Hoggard is the most probable man."

"There are better! If it were possible— Bartram loved the *Janet.*"

"I've heard you say you love her."

"I do."

"Then why leave her?"

"Ah, that, Trevannion, opens up so many things! But——"

"We *could* give her to Carraway."

"I'd prefer it — seeing that Olafson won't budge from being mate."

"Very good then," he said. "I'll do it.— And now may I ask what *you* are going to do?"

"I haven't quite decided," I said, and thanking him for his kindness rose to take my leave.

"You've got, I'm glad to know, a good deal of money with us here."

"Yes. Bartram's will left me his savings, and I've saved a little myself."

"Then," said Trevannion, "I sha'n't worry about you. Money's a great lifeboat."

"I should like," I said, "to make the *Janet* my home until Carraway's notified and comes aboard."

"Why, of course!" he answered. "You're Captain until then. It'll be about three days, I imagine. He's eager."

"He's as good a man as you've got. It wasn't his fault, the losing of the *Thistle*."

He went with me to the door. "Have you come into a fortune or been made a lord, or what? I've known you for more than three years, but you've hardly looked as you do now ——"

David Scott stood for a moment, looking out upon the town and the sea and the morning sun. "Trevannion, there's a lass named Happiness. She hasn't a penny, yet the world's her dower!"

"Oh, well, if you're happy ——!" said Trevannion, and we parted.

That money! I·drew it out in those days, leaving just enough to keep David Scott from want until he knew what course he would shape. It was not so much after all — Bartram's and mine together — about six hundred pounds. There was a merchant I knew in Charlestown, not in the trade, or gaining by it more than another, where all were touched. He managed matters for me. Out of the sum now in his hands I drew as I needed it for the purpose I had in mind. It had first occurred to me to buy and free as many Negroes as I might out of the *Janet's* lading this last voyage. But then I saw that I could not. I was by no means powerful enough to see them shipped back to Africa, sent there to their own people and released. How could I get that done, who would become outcast by the very mention of it to owners of ships and factories? And if I bought and freed them here in America? They were barbarians, free to fall into, and to cause, all manner of trouble in a world not theirs. At once they would meet the Law of the Land, and it would break them. Nothing could be done by me here and now. I saw that last lading that I had brought herded into the barracoons, and during a week sold, slave by slave, at the slave block.

What I could do I did. There was a mulatto shoemaker who sat in a hutch of a shop upon a half-road, half-street, and worked at cobbling and making. I used to pass him, coming and going from Trevannion's, and several times I had stopped for a cast of his trade. At first I thought he was a free Negro. But no, he said, Mr. So-and-so was his master and owned this hut. One half of what he earned he took each week to Mr. So-and-so; on the other he lived. Later, stopping again to speak to him, in a burst of confidence he let it out that from this half he was slowly putting by. "To buy myself." There was pride in his voice.

"Will Mr. So-and-so sell you? You must be profitable."

"Yes. He's a good man. When I have the money he'll free me."

"How long will it take you?"

He mentioned a term of years. His plans after that included freeing in succession his wife who was owned by another family, though in Charlestown, and his son and daughter owned by the mother's owners. He would be an elderly man before, barring accidents, it was all done.

Through the merchant and a lawyer I bought these four and freed them, and bought for them the cobbler's shop and tools. I found other men and women whom I bought and freed, working quietly. It hardly took a month to bring David Scott, so far as money was concerned, within a few pounds of where he was when on an autumn eve in Virginia he first cried, "Janet, ahoy!"

All this went on quietly, very few knowing anything about it. Carraway, it proved, had some arrangements and a short journey to make before he took over the Janet. For ten days still I was Captain and dwelled on my ship. When

at last Carraway appeared I removed to a small
inn by the shore.

Those ten days were strange, meditative days
to me, whose life had changed its road. I was
not unhappy; I was happy with some ache and
bewilderment at the new taste of the happiness.
And I think that it is the sense of growth, saying
forever, "Listen! Here is again something
new under the Great Newness," that makes one
feel one's self a child.

The *Janet* rode quietly in harbor, and I was
aboard her much of those ten days. There was
regret, I know, that I was departing, and yet
the seaman's nature is like the sea, and a new
Captain, said to be a not unkindly man, was
coming, and they would weigh anchor, and new
days would cover the old, and novelty is novelty.
But Michaelson and Wheeler and two or three
others and Tom and Don did grieve. As for
Olafson, I could not make him out in those days.

I felt Bartram, I felt Colley and McNaughton, and when I left the *Janet* I took them with
me.

I left her. I went one eve when the sunset
burned around her.

Carraway slept in the Captain's cabin and
walked the poop deck. If he in no wise equalled
Bartram yet he was honest and strove to be just
and had the name of a good captain. The *Janet*
would shake out her sails and be gone in a week.

The dawn in which she was to leave harbor I

rose while it was yet night and stole from my inn and walked the shore road till I came to a point whence I could see her sail. I sat down under a pine tree, and a pale light being now in the east, watched them making sail. The *Janet!* I watched her forth, the *Janet.* She went in the glory of the dawn, in the slant, golden light of the sun. I never saw her again with these bodily eyes, but ah! often and often by the inner light.

I returned to the inn. My affairs were nearly done. The money I had kept for David Scott would allow him short time before he must begin earning. Going by the waterside I looked at the ships in harbor, and when I reached the inn, there was Olafson sitting, waiting for me.

" Olafson! "

" I've left it too, sir."

We sat down. He spoke of the *Bright Nancy,* Captain Cobb, carrying sugar to Philadelphia. She had put in here for some need or other, and, he had heard, wanted seamen. Olafson knew her, a decent ship, with a decent captain and mates. He proposed now to sign with her as far as Philadelphia. He knew folk in that city who would help him to a mate's berth again — on some ship that was not for Africa. When I told him of my own lack of money and the ideas bred by it, he proposed that I also become seaman for this voyage upon the *Bright Nancy.* Philadelphia was a prosperous town, full of trade; there must be there many chances.

I sat and regarded Olafson whom I greatly liked, and the *Bright Nancy,* and Philadelphia of which I knew a little, and chiefly that it held many Quakers. Then I thanked Olafson, and took my hat, and together we found and hired a boat and went out to the *Bright Nancy.*

CHAPTER XXIX

THE forecastle of the *Bright Nancy* became for a time David Scott's sea home — his and Olafson's. The seamen there were just Dory and Dannet and others again. I was content to work so and journey so to Philadelphia. A stormy voyage gave the less time for thinking how much finer was poop than forecastle.

It did not trouble me. The light held for me, though with an unequal strength. Sometimes it sank and there was almost darkness, but never the darkness that had been. The pain was the yearning for more and more light.

We passed Cape Fear and passed Hatteras of rough seas, and saw on a morning the coasts of Virginia. I turned and turned again my eyes that way. We passed Virginia and passed Maryland and entered the great bay and river of Delaware, and sailing up the latter came to the Colony, great as a kingdom — they are all great as kingdoms — named for William Penn, and so anchored at last before the city of Philadelphia that held twenty thousand souls.

Olafson and I talked it over together. The *Bright Nancy* was a ship considerably to our liking. A great number of things about her might have been worse than they were. But that aside, I had determined, before she anchored, before I trod a Philadelphia quay, to renew with her Captain for one voyage more. To Olafson I said that I liked the ship and that I wanted the sea for just a little longer — but I did not say what I felt and that was that I must stay upon the *Bright Nancy*. Each time my mind turned to leaving her here and now I felt an arresting touch. I did not tell him, or perhaps I did tell him.

But when I said that my going just this one other voyage with the *Bright Nancy* must not affect him, who could surely with time get his mate's berth somewhere, Olafson shook his head and smiled through his golden beard. " I've never been what you call an ambitious man. She's a tidy ship and I like her name. I'll stay by her as long as you do."

So it was settled. One more voyage; we'd go one more voyage. She bought her sugar at Havana and brought it only to Philadelphia.

We anchored. When we had unladed her and made her more tidy than before, we seamen went ashore. Olafson and I kept together. The *Bright Nancy* would be ten days here, in the stately river, before the quay below High Street. Olafson knew a sailors' tavern, The Good Merchant Seaman.

Here we settled ourselves, and he went off to find the man of his own country who dwelled and prospered in this city. In two hours he returned. " He is dead, and his family have gone into the country. The warehouse is sold and the business wound up. — So, you see, it is the *Bright Nancy* for us both!"

"Just for a little while then, Jan," I said.

He sat and drank ale and then we went out to see the town. It was a pleasant, leafy place — the season was high summer — with good docks and warehouses and much shipping in the river, with wide straight streets and churches and brick dwellings in ample gardens. There seemed a civility plain and real. I thought, "I could clerk it here — studying and thinking when work was over. Long walks, studying and thinking——" I thought. "Later on I might teach——"

For two days Olafson and I sauntered and gazed together, but then old shipmates found him, and he must go with them, and I wandered alone.

The streets so busy, the many people, pleased me. I saw rich and poor, high and low, city folk and country folk coming into town, hunters and rangers and Indians from farther away than the planted fields, coming to William Penn's town on errands of their own. It pleased me to make out in the stream men and women whom I was sure were Quakers — though for some reason I never went to their meeting house.

Upon the streets, coming and going, I met or passed Negro men and women — slaves. They seemed chiefly house servants or grooms or

porters, for this was town, not farms or plantations.　Nor were they anything like so numerous
as they would have been in a like-sized town in
any one of the great southern, planting Colonies.
Those that I saw had evidently been born in this
country, or at least been brought very young
from Africa.　They were fairly clad and cheerful enough; and in Charlestown and Kingston
and Williamsburg one saw the same.

But the white man had enslaved them all and
kept them enslaved.　I saw beyond the Delaware, out upon the great sea, and there were the
ships that crossed and crossed, the *Sherwood
Oak,* the *Fancy,* the *Sharon,* the *Amelia,* the
Wreath, the *Janet* and so many more there was
no counting them.　I saw Daga, and the factories at Whidah, and Bonny, and Calabar and
where not.　I saw the Sugar Islands, and the
rice and cotton and tobacco lands, and these
northern towns as well.

Wandering and questioning as I did, I found
that in this city there were well-to-do Quakers
or Friends who owned slaves.　It came to me
with a kind of shock, remembering my Quaker
and the paper he had read me.　The man that
I questioned about this said that as a whole their
Society condemned the practise, and that many
would not touch it, but that the current was not
yet strong enough to check and turn Old Custom.

I went up and down and my week was wearing away. Between the High Street and the river stood a certain substantial place of business, a merchant house of warm, red brick with trees spaced before it. This place drew me; I would go out of my way to go by it. Through open windows I saw decent, quiet clerks; responsible looking persons went in and out of its broad door. One of these told me that it was an old house and furnished goods to villages and yet smaller settlements afar in the wilderness.

At last, when I had been by this house half a dozen times, when I had but three days and nights before the *Bright Nancy* should sail, I came on a golden, late afternoon even with the door at the moment when there issued a clerk, a man something younger than myself, slender of frame, with a pale, lined face. He asked, " Do you want anything, sir? "

" No," I said; then, " You have a pleasant place here in which to work."

" Aye," he answered. " These are forest trees still, and straight as masts."

I wondered. " Perhaps that is why I come and come this way." Aloud I said, " I am a seaman. This fine city comes freshly upon me."

" Aye, aye," he said. " What is your ship? "

" The *Bright Nancy.*"

We were moving together under the trees. The house was a corner one, the street we now moved upon quite quiet, with a great summer sky above. "The *Bright Nancy?* That's sugar from Havana."

"I have made but one voyage with her. She sails the end of the week."

He said, "I was upon a ship once — as clerk. It's been long ago, but the sea comes round me at times."

"Why did you give it up?"

"That," he said, "is a long story. It was the slave ship *Janet.*"

"Then I know your name," I answered. "It is Philip Smith, and I took your place and slept in your cabin."

David Scott went home with Philip Smith. He lived with a sister much his elder — just the two of them — in a small house by one of the creeks that fed the river, a mile from the house where he was clerk. By the time we had reached it he knew the fortunes of the *Janet,* and of Bartram, McNaughton, Colley and many another, and I knew why he had left the ship. It was as I thought — not the *Janet* in herself but the trade.

It came up in my mind again. I was talking to McNaughton.

"Why did he leave?"

"Ah, he was a brittle child! He developed scruples."

"You call that being brittle?"

"If you have your wark and your living, Mr.

Scott, I do! Aweel, he's doubtless howked himself to death in an almshouse. He wasna fit for much when he left us."

I looked at him walking beside me. He had not howked himself to death in an almshouse, but bodily frailty did mark him. He spoke as if he answered my thought, "I've never been strong enough to do much."

His house was neat as a pin, with flowers and a great walnut tree in the dooryard; his sister a quiet, strong person, like him in many ways. We had a frugal, well-cooked supper in a room with a sanded floor, and afterwards sat together in a great sunset glow upon the bench built around the walnut tree. When I said at last that I must go back to The Good Merchant Seaman, they would have me spend the night. I slept in a small room under the steeply sloping roof, all clean and fragrant of lavender. In the morning, breakfast eaten, I walked with Philip Smith into the heart of town, parting with him at the red brick house behind the forest trees, straight as masts.

That day I found Olafson and told him where I should be until Friday when we must go aboard the *Bright Nancy,* then paid my score at The Good Merchant Seaman and took my small chest of belongings to the small house under the walnut tree. In the afternoon, when the sun's rays were all slanting, I again met Philip Smith and we walked out together.

Upon the *Janet* he had never been completely out of my mind. It seemed that although he made no outward move to learn her fortunes, within himself he had always followed her. He knew Bartram, McNaughton, Colley, Llewellyn, Michaelson, Geordie, Tom and Don and most of the others whom I had found at the mouth of the River James, twelve years ago. We had common ground.

But there was something more than this. In a way he was like that Quaker who had come to My Fancy. Like and not like. He was not so conscious and advanced a man; much younger, not so given hand and foot to what he saw, not so centered there that he must act, act definitely from that place. He had in him the making of a man even with that man. But again in another way, for the power of variation here is great. He was not a Quaker. After his day's work, which he performed conscientiously and well, he read and dreamed and worked his garden and sat in silent content with his elderly sister. From his boyhood his health had been slight. He was a listener and observer, a taker apart in the mind and a putter together again, still in the mind. But he had light, he said, that at times seemed to go beyond the mind, into a bigger life.

We talked, walking forth from the heart of town and into it again, or seated on the bench under the walnut tree, or after candle light in the room with the sanded floor, Mrs. Dorothy sitting with us, her strong hands never idle.

We talked of slavery. It was widespread, he said; we were slaves within and without, to one another and to our own old Adam. When you began to free yourself you began within. Think it out and use the imagination and cry for a stronger, cleaner, kinder heart!

"Little by little there will be result in the outer world."

"Aye, little by little."

We talked of Negro slavery. "They are slaves to themselves, you know, too. Just like us."

"Yes," I said. "I know that. I know it abundantly. They'll break that slavery, little by little. Just as we do. In all that, they and we are one."

"I like," he said, "to look at the future of this country and the world — just as far as I can, which of course isn't very far. There are certain things that are plain to me. They — or their descendants — won't be in slavery to us — or our descendants — forever. I see the slave trade with Africa stopping first, then long afterwards, it may be, the host that will be here by then freed and become as hired laborers anywhere. — Long after that perhaps we may be all Christians in a Christian world."

"As Christ sees it."

"Yes. I am very certain that he does not see it as the world sees it now."

Mrs. Dorothy folded her work. "May his Kingdom come!"

I had but these few days with them, and sweet was the taste of that small, true home! Friday dawned; I said good-by and went to The Good Merchant Seaman, where I found Olafson, and together we rowed to the *Bright Nancy*. But it was settled. Only this voyage to Havana and back, and then I should part with the sea. I should come to Philip Smith and his sister and stay with them while I looked about. I should find work, and when it was found I might still make my home with them. There was the room under the roof; there were plate and knife and fork at the table in the cool, sanded room where the walnut leaves made patterns on the floor and wall. Here, too, ran a shelf of books. I said good-by, expecting to see them again in three months' time.

I was going alone toward The Good Merchant Seaman. It was early morning — the water gleamed and glistened brightly before me — there was a tree and a bench. I sat down. I leaned forward and clasped my hands. Light came around me and a determination to do what I could.

When a man sees MAN then he becomes that ONE'S servant.

Moments passed. — The fledgling bird cannot

long hold aloft. — I came down to thought that uses words.

So I thought, " I will go to England and find that Quaker and set myself to work with him and his circle." I knew that it was Great Britain who fostered the Slave Trade. I would go to England. There were men there, Friends and others, whom I would find.

When would I go?

I stood pledged for this voyage to the *Bright Nancy*. But when I came again to Philadelphia, I should stay but the shortest while in the house under the walnut tree. Some ship would be going to England, and I would go in her forecastle.

So my brain planned, not truly, I suppose, knowing the Great Mind. The light had lessened, and though with the sense of it set like a star before him a man assuredly goes forward in the general direction, just the path that is meant may not be seen or foreseen.

CHAPTER XXX

IT was late September and a little north of Hatteras — the time of the year and the place for storm and rough seas. The *Bright Nancy* met it, met tempest. The sea ran to meet the clouds, the clouds descended to meet the sea. A shrieking wind drove us, bare-masted. When forty-eight hours had passed and the wind lulled and the sun shone, it was seen that we were in bitter case. The foremast was gone, the mainmast hurt, and we had sprung a leak that we could not stop and though we pumped day and night the water deepened in our hold. We flung into the ocean her lading, casks and casks of sugar. We mended our masts and piled on sail, the wind being now all in our favor.

So we hastened as best we might, but before we reached Chesapeake her end was come.

She sank, the *Bright Nancy*!

Captain and crew, we were but a dozen, having lost two in the tempest. We took to our boats — got off clear — watched her go down — and wild and mournful it is to see a ship die!

Land loomed faint against the western sky. We rowed toward it, the sea being yet heavy. After an hour of this and no great progress made, a sail appeared to larboard, increased, became a trading brig with men noting our signal. She lay to — the *Miranda* of Baltimore — and we rowed to her side. After some parley and showing that we were almost unarmed, she agreed to take us aboard, her present destination being Norfolk.

The sea calmed itself. Captain Cobb was a sturdy man who could bear up against the sinking of a ship. He talked with Captain Bart of the *Miranda*; our seamen foregathered with hers. Olafson and I watched the sea and the misty, misty shore.

I said to him, "I have seen Norfolk before. I have been up the James River."

"This New World has so great rivers! What was your ship?"

But I did not tell him that at the moment nor why I was upon it. I said, "Olafson, do you believe that there is something deep in us that knows where it is walking?"

"Perhaps ——"

"There are two men in each of us. One knows, but can very rarely tell the other. The other is a child."

The sea grew calm and blue. The *Miranda*, passing between the capes, stood into Chesapeake. Captain Cobb came and talked to the *Bright Nancy's* seamen. The *Miranda* would make the shortest tarrying at Norfolk. She was what we saw, small and overmanned. Captain Bart would take him, Captain Cobb, and the two mates as passengers to Baltimore, and five seamen who would work for their passage. From Baltimore to Philadelphia was no great way; by water or by land we'd get to our home port. We seamen might decide among ourselves, by lot or any other way, upon those five. What was now concerning him was the remainder. We must look out for a ship that would bring us to Philadelphia. He had saved money and papers from the *Bright Nancy*. He would pay us, the five remaining, and take our word that, barring accident, we would get back to Philadelphia and report. Her owners would want all accounted for. He — Cobb — would get another ship presently, and if we wanted her forecastle we must be at hand. So Captain Cobb, a bluff, short man.

We listened, agreed, and when he was gone drew lots to determine who should cling to the *Miranda* and who should be left at Norfolk to seek another ship. Olafson and I both drew Norfolk.

It was falling toward dusk when this was settled. That night I dreamed of Scotland and of Mysie Johnston.

Morning broke red with a kind of high, intense light striking the shore that was now close to us. — I was again upon the *Janet,* again upon the brig *King William.* Twelve years — what are twelve years?

And yet, a thousand years might hardly span

from where I stood then and where now — the dead fire and the kindled fire and the living fire!

The wind ran fresh; the light made the low shores beautiful; little boats and two or three statelier ones were upon the green water; the white gulls flew around and overhead. We came to Point Comfort that I well remembered. We stood across to Norfolk.

Here it sat, the same town, but a little enlarged. I marked it under the bright, blue, autumn sky. It was now October. The seamen of the *Miranda* began their chantey, the anchor slid down, cut the water, and grappling with the earth became a root to hold the ship.

It held her no great while. The second dawn from the red, entering one, we watched her forth from river mouth into the Bay, Olafson and I, standing upon a wharf. The three left with us were sleeping or waking at the Seaman's Hearth. It was so early the wharf had few upon it beside us two. The white mist clung to the great river and the low, Virginian land. I said, "Olafson, I've never told you, but Bartram took me upon the *Janet* here. I was in trouble — I was fleeing."

He answered in his Viking voice, "That may happen easily to a man who follows the sea."

"Aye, but I was not following it then. I'll tell you some day about it all. It's enough now that though it's many a year, Virginia is not utterly without danger to me."

" Then," he said, " let's take the first ship we may, big or little. And I'll make the inquiry while you lie close at the Seaman's Hearth."

But it seemed to me slight danger. Years and years, and I was never known at Norfolk. And seamen looking for a ship are just that — few men inquire further. Still I did not, in the days that followed, seek crowded places.

No ship for Philadelphia presented herself. We heard however of the *Indian King* that would presently come in, receive her tobacco, and go on to the Delaware. She at last seemed our best chance. Olafson and I, after trials elsewhere, agreed to await her, seeing that we had little choice but to do so. But all suddenly those that were with us at the Seaman's Hearth — Bush and Allgood and Reddy — announced that they had signed with the *Marigold* of London, sailing with tobacco a week after the departure of the *Miranda,* and wanting men.

They went — a fickle lot — but Olafson and David Scott must stay for Philadelphia.

The *Indian King* came leisurely. We had sufficient money, and none seeing aught in me but Jack awaiting a ship, I at last threw away fear. It was October and gorgeous weather. Olafson and I lounged by the water side, talking a little and watching all the craft, great and

small. He too had a power of silence. We
might be together for hours, and content with
each other's company, yet our words would
never sail a boat. The Seaman's Hearth, just
by the water, with a bit of a yard and a broken
landing, had so much custom and no more.
Seamen came and went, making, the most of
them, short tarrying. The man and his wife
who kept the Hearth got used to two big men,
quiet and giving no trouble, waiting for the
Indian King.

The town was small enough. It took no long
time to view it over. It was a place of trade
and shipping as against Williamsburg that was
of Government, a College, and Polite Society.
Not that Norfolk, either, lacked a small polite
world of merchants and retired sea captains and
lawyers and others. It had inns other and
better than the Seaman's Hearth. Officers from
British and foreign ships were seen in these, and
planters on business, arriving in wherries or
their own sloops, or if of the neighborhood, on
horseback. What with the coming and going
of many seamen, of nations more than one —
for often one heard Spanish, French or Dutch
— and with frontiersmen appearing from the
forests west and south with their wares and on
their own business and quick, after their kind,
to take offense, the town had the name of a
quarrelsome one. To meet that condition the
officers of the law were numerous and arbitrary;

there were a prison, a stout mayor, a court and lawyers.

Olafson and I examined this borough, and then we sat by harbor side or walked afield — long walks, through October, into the land south of the James. Pine trees and other trees and rich and tangled brakes, and tobacco and tobacco. Now and then a good house, with Negro quarters near, oftener small houses built of logs; oftenest no house at all, but autumn forest, marshes, ancient, abandoned Indian fields, streams, autumn forest coloring like a sunset.

Olafson was not of an impatient kind and David Scott had learned to curb it. We walked dreamily, soberly, content to await the *Indian King's* good time. Meanwhile there was beauty of a low, forested land and sighing reeds by still, winding water, of magnificent single trees, and of a clear, pure, high heaven. I felt it as I had never done — it gave my heart a contented ache. Years ago I should have said that I hated Virginia, but now I had passed that bewilderment. These old, old forests, these still flowing waters, these fields, these horses, dogs, and others of four feet, these flying folk, these hasty roads and houses of log and now and then of frame and brick, the infrequent humans passing, white and black and colored and now and then a red man, the old and young, the child, the woman, the man, the mounted and afoot — all were now to me as they had not been. In this kingdom, when one enters it, long progressions happen in short times. I was not as I had been when I was in Virginia before and grew less so all the while. Now the momentary feeling of that evening at the inn in Charlestown had come to keep house with me. Compassion, hope, admiration. All things — David Scott with them — had become soul rather than body, with spirit our ultimate.

Olafson and I talked at times. I told him one day, walking under pine trees, having just passed a great, ragged, tobacco field, of why and how I had been in Virginia. He said at the end, "We'd better be more careful! The *Inez* that's going to Baltimore this week is a poor thing, but I think that her master will take us. Or one of us. You go. We'll find each other at Philadelphia. The *Indian King's* too much delayed."

But that finger with some meaning in it was laid again upon my shoulder. I did not take, or move to take, the *Inez*.

The days went by. It became evident that weather or some need had delayed the *Indian King*. But Olafson and David Scott were happy enough. There is something beyond happiness. Each morn when I waked I touched that. It held for a longer or shorter while, then faded through the day. But with each succeeding morn it renewed itself, though with an infinite variety. It was not dependent upon place or outward history.

October was flying, and still I waited. Perhaps I was waiting for the *Indian King,* perhaps not.

There came a splendid, frosty morning. The frost vanished, the windless, sunny day grew warm. Olafson and I debated whether we should walk afar or go down to our favorite landing and watch the water and its life. We went to the landing, out to the end, and sat upon the gray boards, our feet above the green water lapping the piles, our shoulders against unsawn logs brought down by some raft. Usually this was a quiet place, a lesser wharf and landing with no great business, but from it we could watch well the movement of the water world. So we sat there, and the sun warmed our backs, and the half hours passed, and we did not trouble to talk, being so much at one.

I was in Philadelphia, telling Philip Smith that I would go to England. Olafson's voice entered my ear.

"That sloop is making in here."

We watched her; she was from the river, not the sea. That and the look of her brought back something — the tang of up country, of the forests, of the gray landings like long forefingers, of the brick great houses and the fields. The wind was light, she came slowly.

I heard Olafson's voice again, "There are

more and more folk upon this wharf. We
had better go walking."

"Not yet," I said, and now I was upon the
Janet, and Bartram seemed to be saying something, saying it solemnly. I answered Bartram,
"God knows we all have sinned and sin! But
there is Something that has ways and means of
its own to draw us forth."   And then I was not
on the *Janet* or in Philadelphia or England, but
somewhere where the Something spoke.   And
it was not Something, it was All, it was One.
From that I came stilly, quietly down to the gray
wharf and the gleaming water under the October sky.

The sun shone warm. A small crowd — not
a great one, fifteen or twenty perhaps — was
gathering upon the wharf. The sloop might be
expected. A great, laughing black man with a
pole came by me and I thought, "You're like
Pickaninny."

The sloop grew in size. I saw her kind —
that she belonged to some planter — was bringing tobacco and other matters downstream and
would take back goods, and likely enough had
on board her owner. She came on, a fair creature; she was close and they prepared to bring
her alongside the wharf. Behind us two seamen some one shouted a welcome and voices
answered from the sloop. Then strangely,
strangely, to David Scott, there began to play a
flute. A shaggy man in a squirrel-skin cap,

seated cross-legged on the deck by a heap of
pelts, breathed into the instrument, and the soar-
ing, dropping notes relimned for me the River
James from a sycamore south of Daniel Askew's
to the side of the *Janet*.

Without thought, of its own accord, my hand
went up to that scar across my forehead.
Neither swiftly nor slowly I got to my feet and
turned my back upon the sloop. There were
folk upon the wharf, but not enough to impede
movement. I walked away, Olafson following
me. They saw but two seamen, so fulfilled with
ships that a mere river craft was no magnet.
When we were quit of the wharf I spoke. " I
know that flute player. He would not say
my name if he thought, but he might not
think."

We returned to the Seaman's Hearth and ate
our dinner. Afterwards the question was if
we should stay by the Hearth or should take a
long walk into the country. We went, and the
smell and feel of it come back to me to-day, and
the goodness of Olafson. We returned under a
tremendous sunset, red and purple ships of the
gods on a golden sea. That night I slept sound
and deep, and when I waked at dawn it was with
the sense of having been in a far country, far and
great and dear.

Olafson and I ate breakfast. That over, I
said that we would not mew ourselves up because
that old Indian trader and flute player was in

town, or more probably somewhere upon the edge of it. The chance of meeting was very slight, and he was not an enemy; he was a friend. If I could meet him where none other was by I should like it.

Olafson still demurred. He said that he did not know how it came to him but he had a sense of danger. But I was restless. I could not stay within — I was drawn forth — and when he proposed the country again I said no. At last we went to the water side to watch for the *Indian King,* but to another wharf than that by which lay the sloop from up river.

The *Indian King* did not appear to-day, either. Toward noon we began our return to the Seaman's Hearth. We might have taken obscure ways but we did not. When Olafson proposed it I shook my head. So we came into the principal street.

Before us rose the chief tavern of the place — we made to pass it; there were loungers about, and a knot of men emerging from the house, two or three important persons, it seemed, with satellites. Together they were enough to halt us; we made to go around in the dusty street and a voice said, "Those are seamen. Ask them, Colonel!"

We were stopped. Another voice spoke. "Are you men from the *Indian King?* Is she in?"

Olafson answered No. As for me, I said

nothing. The questioner was Colonel Giles
Amory. There he stood, now a quite elderly
man, but still firm and fine. Two or three
neighbor planters were with him, come down
upon his sloop, a new one that I had not recognized. I knew his old one, the *Daphne*. Moreover, he had with him one who still served as his
clerk, though now with pay — Gervase Morrison, to wit — and also the overseer Barget. All
were older, but there came around me a glamor
of Amory Hall and Old Mill quarter. The
Negro there behind Barget — it was Pickaninny.

I could not tell Olafson; Colonel Amory held
him in talk of ships. I made to go away myself, but a man, a planter whom I did not know,
put himself in front of me. " Are you of the
Inez then? " To this day I do not know what
was their insistence about these ships. They
had some business with them, but I do not know
what.

But I was held. And in a moment, glancing
toward him, I saw that Gervase Morrison
recognized me. He recognized, but he would
not tell; he turned his gaze away. It had
scarcely happened before I knew that Pickaninny —— He became ashy, his eyes bulged;
I saw him quiver all over, and I thought, " Now
he will tell," for I knew how often excitement
and drama force the Negro past reticence. But
he did not tell. I saw him stand, gather and

control his big, excited body, and turn his face away.

It was Barget. I felt him looking at me — it was idle now to go — I might burst through the crowd, take to my heels, and that would be but to shout, "After me! I have reason to run away!"

He moved a little nearer — the overseer whom I knew so well — older, all weather-seamed and bitten, with graying hair, but the same. Years rarely alter a man beyond recognition — and if he have a great, known scar upon his forehead.

His eyes were upon me first — the all of me — then upon that scar. His lips parted; he cried, "David Scott! Yon's David Scott!"

Colonel Amory swung around from Olafson, "David Scott!"

Barget seized me. I said, "I'm not your man, Barget. Don't you remember that Daniel Askew bought me?"

"He's dead!" he answered. "And a runaway's to be apprehended, no matter whose he is, nor how long gone!"

And well enough David Scott knew that! There was commotion — another man was helping Barget, though I made no resistance. Olafson would have fought but I did not wish that and cried to him that naught could be done and not to try it. It was Colonel Amory who interrogated me.

"Well, Scott! And where have *you* been?"

I smiled. "A good many places, Colonel! Out of these parts and into them again. Olafson here and I were upon the *Bright Nancy* that sank a while ago, this side Hatteras. We were seeking to get back to Philadelphia. Except for being seamen together, he has naught to do with me — a free, Danish sailor."

He still stared. "It's been years! — How old are you?"

"Something over thirty-nine."

"Well, by Gad! you know the law. You were sold for a servant when you might have been hanged. You ran away — and here you are again! In the King's name I apprehend you and commit you to the gaol here. Daniel Askew is dead, but we'll notify his son Geoffrey." He continued to stare. "Well, you're big, and somehow you've grown in bearing. You seem calm enough. Maybe you've learned wisdom. We all have to learn it one day!"

I answered him, "Yes, we all have to — one and all. I don't propose to give you any trouble, Colonel Amory. I'd like to speak if I may to Gervase Morrison and Pickaninny. And if you'll be so good as to give me two or three minutes with my friend here I shall thank you."

He gave them, being in much a kindly man and kinder now that he was old than when he was young. Olafson and I spoke together, Barget watching.

Olafson's face worked. "What can be done?
Something must be done!"

"What should it be?" I asked. "Nothing
now that comes to me is useless, Olafson. Do I
look unhappy?"

"No!"

"It was at Daga that I was unhappy — and
at My Fancy — and on the *Janet*. And of old
here in Virginia also. But I shall not be so
again. — I'll give you a letter for Philip Smith."

We spoke together a little longer, and then I
must go to gaol with Barget and a helper or two
and a constable who had appeared. Olafson
kept with us. Barget, walking beside me, was
willing to answer questions. Williams? Williams had retired — he, Barget, was full overseer. Old Mill quarter? Well, a different
crowd was there now. As for him he lived in
Williams' house. Did I remember Dick
Merry? Well, Merry's seven years was long
out, and then he had worked for the Colonel for
wages, and now for three years had been under
overseer. "You might have done something
like that yourself! The world moves and there's
been a lot of changes. The Colonel's daughters
are all married and there are grandchildren
now. And my daughter Nelly is dead — she
was a rare and good one!"

So we came to Norfolk gaol, Olafson moving
near me, walking as in a dream, his blue northern eyes upon ships and seas. As for me, I can-

not say that I did not feel captivity. I did. But it was not heavy upon my soul as once it had been. . . .

It was not heavy when, in two or three days, the son of Daniel Askew came and claimed me. I remembered him as a frightened boy, shuddering always away from his father. Now he was not demon like the other, but a timid, blustering man.

It was not heavy when Barget came and told me that Colonel Amory had bought me from Geoffrey Askew, bought me back to Amory Hall and the woodcutting and the tobacco. "Aye, and I hope you'll determine to bide with us now!"

I laughed. "Aye, for a while anyhow, Mr. Barget, seeing there's some reason, I think, why I should and must. But you know none of us is going to bide forever in our common slavery. Not you, not me, not Pickaninny, not the Colonel."

"You must not talk that way," he said. "It makes against contentment."

"There is high contentment and there is low contentment," I said, and left it at that.

Olafson came to tell me good-by. He and I were well enough used to danger and what is called disaster — well enough used to partings. But the tears stood in our eyes when we said good-by, tasting the sea, the wind and the ships. I had the means to write a long letter to Philip

Smith and I had done so. I said that I had a
conviction that I would be held some years in
Virginia, how many I did not know, though I
guessed at seven. That I did not intend to run
away again. That I felt in my soul that there
was some reason on the part of Life that is
Higher for things being as they were. It might
be that my knowledge was to encrease, here,
withdrawn again from liberty of the body.
Outer knowledge, inner knowledge. I felt that
a time would surely come when I should be used
in other ways. Then perchance I might see him
again, then perchance I might go to England.
It was all in the future's keeping. But now I
was not astounded, cast down, or wretched. I
begged him to believe that, and that I should
remember him, having in effect remembered
him ever since I came first upon the *Janet*.

I gave the letter to Olafson. We said good-
by; he went, he sailed away from Virginia upon
the *Indian King*.

Another day and another in Norfolk gaol —
and Colonel Amory had ended his business in
this borough. His sloop, the *Amaranth*, waited.
I trod again the gray boards of the wharf, and
went down into the little ship. Barget said,
"I'm responsible, so I'll just tie a rope around
you and to the mast," and did so. In an hour
the Colonel came aboard and the sails were
made.

Toward noon Gervase Morrison found or

made an opportunity to speak to me. "Well, David Scott——"

"Well, Gervase Morrison——"

"Are you witheringly unhappy?"

"No, not in the least!"

"Well, that's a gain!" he said. "You used to be unhappy. I need not lie awake of nights for you then?"

I smiled. "No, you need not. And how are you and how have you fared?"

"Oh, on the dead level road and so-so! I am my own man, as it is counted, but I do not know that it counts very far."

"Not so far but that there is a further."

He answered with a dry disconsolateness. "There always is — only how to set foot upon that road! Well, I'm rather glad to see you, though sorry you come back so. And what has been your life?"

"In part a blind and ill one," I said. "Then my own Self struck me, Morrison, and I see!"

He stared, then he said, "Well, sight is a blessed thing!" and was called away.

We sailed up the River James. I watched the shore and thought of the *King William,* of Scotland and the Indies and Africa, of the *Janet,* of Bartram and Colley and McNaughton and others. The air breathed fine, the banks were golden and crimson. I thought of the forest and the woodcutter's task — one of the oldest in the world. The ax and the hoe — old, old. . . .

The Slave Ship

I thought of Old Mill quarter and the servants and slaves there. I thought of the fields. I heard Old Hannibal singing,

> "When have I done with the trouble of the world?
> Ooh! when have I done?"

A time would come — a time would come — when Earth should put on Heaven. I thought, I felt, I lived. I knew my work. I was upheld.

THE END